FROM

BRUGE

WITH

LOVE

FROM BRUGES WITH LOVE

A PIETER VAN IN MYSTERY

PIETER ASPE

TRANSLATED BY BRIAN DOYLE

OPEN ROAD
INTEGRATED MEDIA
NEW YORK

Translated from *De kinderen van Chronos*, copyright © 1997 by Pieter Aspe

Translation copyright © 2015 by Brian Doyle

Cover design by Mauricio Díaz

978-1-4976-7889-7

Published in 2015 by Open Road Integrated Media, Inc.
345 Hudson Street
New York, NY 10014
www.openroadmedia.com

FOR MY PARENTS

FROM
BRUGES
WITH
LOVE

Qui craint de souffrir,
il souffre déjà
de ce qu'il craint.
—Montaigne

1

"Mommy, Mommy!"

The elongated shriek was sharp and piercing. It easily drowned out the screech of the electric drill. Hugo Vermast turned, annoyed. His daughter, Tine, was on the other side of the meadow waving a twig. She looked for all the world like a dazzling ghost in a sea of gold-green grass.

"Mommy, Mommy!"

Even Joris looked up for a second. His sister was dancing about as if she'd just been stung by a hornet. She did that a lot when Mommy didn't come running right away, so Joris paid no attention and continued counting screws. The box said there should be a hundred.

When Tine didn't stop screaming, Hugo unplugged the drill. He rubbed the layer of dust from his eyes with both hands, leaving stripes of grime on his cheeks. They made him look like an American marine in a low-budget war movie.

Now he could see her better. There didn't seem to be anything out of the ordinary. He knew his daughter was a hyperactive child. It wasn't the first time she'd screamed blue murder because she hadn't gotten her way.

Hugo's wife, Leen, was on a lounger soaking up the sun and listening to Bart Kaëll on her CD player. Bart was her favorite crooner. Tine's third shriek reached her between songs. She yanked the headphones from her head and raced to the scene of the calamity.

Hugo shook his head at the sight of his wife running barefoot through the stiff grass. *Next thing, she'll stand on something sharp and I'll get the blame as usual,* he thought. Whenever she hurt herself, he would first curse under his breath and then fetch the disinfectant and a bandage. Fifteen years of marriage had made him docile. She liked that sort of subservience. An armed truce was always easier to live with than a grueling war.

He had no real reason to complain. There were plenty of men worse off than him. Leen was thirty-eight and still darned attractive for her age. She looked a picture in her tight swimsuit. A couple of pregnancies had barely left a mark on her figure, and her colleagues weren't above a twinge of jealousy.

"Mommy, look what I found."

Tine wielded the bone as if it were a drumstick. She had seen people do the same at the fair. She was proud of her trophy. Leen peered in horror at the shinbone and the pit beyond. She grabbed Tine and tried to worm the bone from her hand.

"It's dirty, Tine. Come, give it to Mommy."

"No, it's mine."

Like so many other modern mothers, Leen didn't insist. She took hold of Tine and dragged her back to the house. "Daddy isn't going to be happy."

The girl started to cry. She knew that meant Daddy wouldn't speak to her for the rest of the day.

Hugo recognized the hullabaloo. *Leen'll take care of her,* he thought, *give the little piglet a good scrubbing.* He plugged the drill back in as Joris handed him a screw. Hugo winked at his son. All that commotion over a twig! They had better things to do with their time.

Guido Versavel found Van In lunching in the police station's brand-new kitchen. The building dated back to the 1970s, and the policy makers called it modern. After four reluctant petitions from the rank and file, the powers that be finally decided to install a kitchen. That was six months ago. It didn't amount to much, just a cheap microwave and a secondhand refrigerator, but that was all they were prepared to offer to keep up the police force's morale.

Van In spooned the remaining chunks of his fruit salad into his mouth. He didn't look very happy.

"Enjoy," Versavel said with a grin.

Van In pushed the empty Tupperware box to one side. "And there's cod on the menu for tonight. Boiled fish. Jeez . . . doesn't bear thinking about."

"You should be happy Hannelore's looking after you. If you ask me, you've lost at least ten pounds."

Van In pulled his baggy shirt tight. The last three months had been hell: cornflakes, fish, vegetables, fruit, water, and every now and then a glass of wine. She had even rationed his cigarettes. And *she* was the pregnant one! Van In ferreted a precious cigarette from his breast pocket.

"Save that for the car," said Versavel, feigning sympathy. "They just called in a Code One."

Van In waved his words aside and carefully returned the cigarette to its place of safety as if it were made of solid gold. "Why didn't you tell me that five minutes ago and spare me from having to eat that miserable crap?"

"I could have," said Versavel with a cynical grin. "But you know I don't like disturbing you at mealtimes."

They headed downstairs. For once, Van In wasn't out of breath when they arrived at the lobby.

It may be bursting at the seams, but even a city like Bruges can boast the odd patch or two of unspoiled nature. There are places between Sint-Andries and Varsenare, for example, that the project developers seem to have missed. The Vermast family's restored farmhouse was one of those oases. To reach it, Van In and Versavel had to turn down a dirt track with a sign reading

PRIVATE ROAD. The rusty-brown tiled roof was barely visible above the lush hawthorn hedge that bordered the domain with a square of green.

The gate was open, so Van In drove onto the property and parked. The setting was rustic-romantic, to say the least: sandblasted brick, antique tiles, whitewashed walls, and the smell of a thousand pigs drifting over from the farm next door. There's hardly an overworked mortal these days who isn't dreaming of his or her own little plot in the country. Tastes change. In the 1960s, when everyone was into concrete and aluminum, goat sheds like this usually fell foul to merciless demolition contractors. Nowadays, there were smooth operators all over the place ready to help you cocoon. It was even trendy. Modern folks needed isolation, a place to be themselves, to let their hair down. A hovel with a puddle in the basement was advertised as a unique country property with spring water. Leaking roofs and rotting woodwork were styled authentic. Versavel and Van In approached the man standing outside the house.

"Mr. Vermast. You made the call I presume."

Hugo nodded. The contrast between his pale skin and the black stripes on his face made him appear angry, forbidding. "I did, Detective. My wife's too upset."

"Did you find the skeleton?" Van In inquired offhandedly.

Versavel sized up the gaunt figure. Vermast was wiry enough, shame about the hollow back and collapsed chest.

"My daughter dug up the bones," he explained, and pointed to the other side of the meadow. A pile of earth marked the spot. "We've been renovating the house, and she always wants to help Daddy out. You know what kids are like. They mimic everything."

Vermast laughed nervously, or perhaps neighed would be a better description of the gurgling sound that came out of his mouth. Van In didn't react. The idea that he was soon to be saddled with a little smartass of his own didn't bear thinking about.

"And you're sure they're not just sheep bones?" Van In asked.

It wouldn't have been the first time one or another townie had sounded the alarm after digging up a pile of animal bones in the garden.

Vermast gasped for an answer like a fish out of water. "Don't think so . . ."

Van In and Versavel exchanged a knowing glance. "So you're not sure?" Van In pressed the point.

"My wife's a nurse. She was pretty certain . . ."

"That answers my question, Mr. Vermast. I imagine your wife knows the difference between human bones and sheep bones." Van In tried to sound sure of himself, but he wasn't. He'd heard the craziest things of late from the medical ranks.

Vermast heaved a sigh of relief. Imagine getting the police out because your daughter dug up a dead sheep.

"Personally I'd have preferred sheep bones," said Van In. "The paperwork is a lot less complicated."

Vermast concurred with a stoic smile. You had to be careful with the police at your door.

"So let's just confirm what we're dealing with, Mr. Vermast. I suggest we take a closer look at the corpus delicti."

Vermast hesitated. "Corpus delicti, Detective?"

"The skeleton, Mr. Vermast," Versavel affably explained.

Hannelore Martens tore onto the property like a rally driver run riot. But her delicate Renault Twingo was on its best behavior. The souped-up soapbox screeched to a halt less than two yards from Hugo Vermast and her colleagues. Hannelore pulled on the hand brake and jumped out of the car in a single fluid movement. She was wearing a white sleeveless summer dress and flat running shoes without socks. Van In still found it hard to believe that she was already more than five months pregnant.

"Afternoon, gentlemen."

Hannelore embraced Van In. Her kiss made him tingle. Jesus, she felt glorious, sparkling. She then kissed Versavel on the check. The sergeant accepted her kiss with a smile. There were times he wished he was straight.

"Is he behaving himself?" she asked Versavel.

Vermast stared at the threesome, a little perplexed.

"The fruit salad was delicious, and he can't wait for tonight, right, Pieter?"

Van In grunted. Versavel was worse than his mother-in-law. The sergeant didn't waste a chance to help Hannelore realize her satanic plan. *Love is eating what she eats*, Van In thought. At that moment he would have sold his soul for a burger and fries.

When Hannelore realized that Vermast was staring at them wide-eyed, she introduced herself.

"Hannelore Martens, deputy public prosecutor. I'm in charge of the case."

Vermast wiped his sweaty hand dry on his grimy shorts. "Pleased to meet you, ma'am."

"We were just about to take a look at the remains," said Van In. "Mrs. Vermast is sure they're human."

"OK," said Hannelore.

The prospect of a confrontation with a skeleton filled her with disgust, but she was determined not to let it show.

Leen Vermast was sitting on a bench in front of the farmhouse with the children, a glazed expression on her face. After a series of threats and pleas, she had managed to pry the shinbone from Tine's hands. The scrawny bone was lying on the ground in front of her. Tine was sulking, her eyes red from crying. Joris was still counting screws. The shinbone didn't interest him. The box was two short of a hundred and that was enough to absorb his complete attention.

Hannelore smiled at Leen. Vermast's wife was clearly in a state. The thought of a body buried in her garden must have horrified her. Hannelore was certain she was close to collapse.

"I'll be right there," she shouted as the men crossed the meadow toward the sandpit and the dug-up bones.

Van In noticed that Hannelore was concerned about Vermast's wife. *Not a bad thing,* he thought.

"Clearly not a sheep." Versavel pointed at the skull half-buried under the sand. Vermast nodded eagerly. The older policeman seemed quite friendly. Van In said nothing and jumped into the pit. *Amazing what a child with a spade can do,* he thought. The hole was at least four feet deep.

"Did your daughter do this all by herself?"

Vermast neighed a second time, apparently the way he laughed when he was nervous. "Of course not, Commissioner. I needed sand to make mortar, and it's all over the place around here. I dug the hole myself, but as you'll have figured by now, kids like to play with sand."

The improvised sandpit had been a gift from God. Tine spent hours playing in it, and it kept her out of mischief.

Van In got to his knees and brushed the dry sand from the skull like an expert archaeologist.

Versavel frowned. "Leo's on his way," he said, unable to disguise his concern. "We should wait for him to take his photographs."

Van In halted his excavations. Versavel was right. This was a job for the experts from the judicial police. He hoisted himself carefully out of the pit. The onion-yellow skull glowed in the blazing sunlight. Van In wondered if anyone would ever be likely to look at *his* skull from that angle.

"Shall I have the grave taped off?" Versavel asked. He used

the word *grave* deliberately. It might have been old-fashioned, but he thought the dead deserved respect.

"Do that, Guido. Otherwise we'll have the public prosecutor's cronies on our back."

Versavel made his way to the police car. Like Hannelore, he seemed to be immune to the blistering summer temperatures. There was barely a trace of perspiration on his crease-resistant shirt. Van In, on the other hand, could feel his boxers clinging to his balls, and he didn't like it one little bit.

Now that they were alone, Vermast seemed slightly ill at ease, unsure if he should say something or keep his mouth shut. Van In wasn't exactly reveling in the silence either.

"A remarkable discovery, don't you think?" said Van In. "I hope for you it's not your mother-in-law. If that's the case, we won't have far to look for the killer."

This time Vermast didn't neigh. Killing his mother-in-law would be plain stupid. The bitch was paying half his mortgage.

They all arrived at once: Leo Vanmaele, the police photographer; Rudy Degrande from forensics; the police physician, Alexander De Jaegher; and four police officers from the station in Bruges. Vermast's front yard suddenly looked like the parking lot of a busy supermarket.

After exchanging the obligatory politenesses, Leo got down to business. His Nikon buzzed like a bee in a field of jasmine. The short and chubby police photographer took forty shots in less than ten minutes, then the police physician clambered down into the grave.

De Jaegher was more than just a familiar face in Bruges, or at least that's what he thought. The man had a busy social life in and around the city. He was chair of several cultural organizations and promoter of the local carnival association. De Jaegher was thin and bony, a profile that didn't square with the image of exuberant bon vivant he was determined to assume, whatever the price. He sought recognition in a world that wasn't his own. His reputation as a doctor was nothing to write home about. The College of Physicians had almost dropped him fifteen years earlier after a serious professional error. A career with the prosecutor's office seemed like a meaningful alternative at the time. There was much less chance of making a second mistake on a diet of dead bodies.

Van In focused his gaze on De Jaegher's bald head. *One skeleton examining another,* he thought, amused.

"Human remains, irrefutable . . ." De Jaegher declaimed, his tone professorial.

He lifted the skull in both hands and held it up to his audience as if it were a cheap trophy. Versavel looked the other way. In spite of his years in the trade, the police physician still didn't have a clue about forensics. Such lack of professionalism had rendered important evidence unusable more than once. Small wonder the public had little faith in the courts and the judiciary. Rudy Degrande appeared to share Versavel's thoughts. He comforted the sergeant with a wink.

Van In reacted to Hannelore's poke in the ribs with a suppressed squawk. De Jaegher was clearly annoyed by the interruption, but when he caught sight of Hannelore, a broad smile glided across his lips.

"Aha, Deputy Martens. I had no idea you were already here."

Hannelore maintained a safe distance from the pit. Corpses weren't her forte. "Can you say anything about the cause of death, Doctor?"

De Jaegher wasn't much more than five foot three, and with his lower half in the pit he looked like a moving plaster bust. "No, ma'am."

De Jaegher placed the skull on the edge of the pit. Hannelore had the creeping feeling that its hollow sockets were staring at her. Or was it De Jaegher peeking under her skirt?

"I'm afraid there are no *de visu* indicators that would allow me to formulate a proper conclusion. Further analysis will have to determine whether the victim died a natural death or not."

Van In made a crooked face. Versavel concealed the beginnings of a smile behind his hand.

"You mean I'm going to have to wait for the autopsy report."

"Precisely, ma'am."

"And when can I expect it, Doctor?"

This was probably the first time anyone had asked De Jaegher such a question. The poor man gasped for breath. *How dare she,* he thought. "I'm going to need a few days, ma'am. What about early next week?"

"But today's Monday," said Hannelore, clearly disappointed.

De Jaegher looked around and said resignedly and with a wilted grin: "I'll do my best to complete the postmortem by the end of the week."

Hannelore rewarded him with a radiant smile. "That'll do nicely, Doctor." She turned abruptly and headed back to the farmhouse. Even Van In was a little taken aback.

"What time is it?"

Versavel looked at his watch. "Four twenty."

Van In sipped at his mineral water and made a face. To add to his woes, it was flat. The glass had been standing for more than fifteen minutes in the blazing sun. Hannelore and her diet can fuck off. He raised his hand and the sharp-eyed waiter responded immediately. Van In and Versavel were his only customers.

"Another two Perriers?" the outdoor café waiter asked eagerly.

"No, my friend. I'll have a Duvel. As cold as possible."

Van In leaned back contentedly in his rickety cane chair. He knew exactly what Alexander the Great must have felt like when he split the Gordian knot.

"Lucky Hannelore had to rush off to the courts," said Versavel.

Van In had been expecting one or another prickly remark. "Do you have a problem, Versavel?"

"Not me, Pieter. But when she makes you get on the scales later . . ."

Van In shrugged his shoulders and tossed the lukewarm mineral water onto the thirsty grass. "Skeletons remind me of the desert, Guido. And the last time I sinned was a good two weeks ago. I'm dying of thirst."

It didn't sound coherent, but Versavel was used to it. Every association Van In made led, in the final analysis, to a Duvel. "Most people in the desert are happy with water. You must be the only man in Flanders who drinks Duvel to quench his thirst."

"There's an exception to every rule, Guido. You're gay; you should know that."

"You don't have to tell me," said Versavel, faking a high-pitched voice. "But if I were you, I'd start practicing for the day we're in the majority."

The service was perfect. The waiter appeared within the minute with an ice-cold Duvel and a sparkling Perrier. Van In bored his nose unashamedly into the thick froth and guzzled. Versavel let him get on with it.

"Vermast can forget about that meadow of his," said Van In cheerfully. "In a couple of days, it'll be unrecognizable."

"Do you think there might be more bodies?"

"Who knows, Guido. The Europeans are getting the hang of this serial killer business. The Americans don't have the monopoly anymore. I pity the public prosecutor's boys having to dig up all that ground."

"I don't," said Versavel dryly.

They both burst out laughing.

• • •

The telephone rang just as Yves Provoost was locking the door to his office. He sighed, turned the key, and went back inside.

Provoost was only a mediocre criminal lawyer, but he was still able to boast a colossal villa in exclusive Knokke, an apartment in Cap d'Agde, and a chalet in Austria. His legal practice was located in an imposing town house along the Groene Rei, the most picturesque part of Bruges.

Provoost made his way down the long corridor, his footsteps sounding hollow in the lofty narrow space. Unlike the rest of the house, his office was a virtual exhibition of contemporary Italian design: shiny tables in polished cherry, futuristic cabinets without visible doors, black lacquered chairs in which no one could relax for more than fifteen minutes, and whimsical lamps that offered little light.

"Provoost," he barked into the receiver of an exceptionally flat olive-green telephone.

"Yves, Lodewijk," was the gruff response, matching if not exceeding Provoost's curtness.

Provoost stiffened. When Lodewijk Vandaele barked, it usually meant bad news.

"We have a problem, Yves."

"I'm listening."

"Not on the phone, Yves. Crank up your computer, and wait for my email."

Before Provoost had the chance to ask for an explanation, Vandaele hung up and marched to his desk. In contrast to Provoost's office, Vandaele's was the epitome of old-fashioned quality: oak furniture, brass fittings, velvet and nineteenth-century paintings by long forgotten masters, and a pearl-gray IBM computer on a Louis XVI–style table. The machine was as out of place as a Big Mac in a three-star restaurant.

Vandaele was old school, but that didn't mean he shunned modern technology. As a disciple of Machiavelli, he made use of whatever means he had at his disposal to serve his goal. And as a good Catholic, he would have married his daughter to a Muslim without blinking if he figured the relationship might bring him some degree of advantage. Fortunately, Vandaele didn't have a daughter. He had stayed single for a reason: women meant trouble.

Vandaele switched on his computer and posted his message in Provoost's electronic mailbox. He used what he called a "robust" code, to which only Provoost had the key.

Chief Inspector Dirk Baert of the Bruges police heard Vandaele shuffle along the corridor leading to the front door of his house. He had known the man for a long time. As a young cop, he once caught him with a half-naked boy on the backseat of a parked car. After a brief exchange, they had settled the matter as adults would. Vandaele had paid him ten thousand francs, and that was the end of it. Baert knew the ropes. If he had started proceedings instead of taking the bribe, he knew that Vandaele would simply have bribed someone else farther up the line. It made no difference for the pedophile either way. But for Baert the difference was ten thousand francs, and that was money he could use at the time. When he met Melissa a couple of weeks later, a woman who was to cost him a small fortune, he got cheeky and decided to give Vandaele another call and negotiate a final payment. The old fox refused to give in to the blackmail attempt, but he didn't send Baert home empty-handed.

He suggested the young officer work as his contact person on the force. In exchange, he would receive a fixed sum per month. Substantial bonuses were assured if he had to take risks or provide important information.

"I apologize for keeping you waiting. I was on the phone with my niece . . . you know how women are." Vandaele laughed. "Please, take a seat."

"Thank you, Mr. Vandaele."

Baert hoped that Vandaele would cough up some cash. Melissa had been dreaming out loud about a wide-screen TV for months.

"You know how much I appreciate your loyalty, Mr. Baert." Vandaele was six three, radiated authority, and his stentorian voice had left many an opponent quivering.

"So my information was useful?"

Vandaele pursed his thin lips. His pink little mouth gave Baert goose bumps. Deep down, Dirk Baert hated pedophiles.

"*Useful* would be a slight exaggeration, dear Mr. Baert. Let's just say it was *interesting*. I bought the farm a long time ago. A skeleton on the property is back-page news. Surely you don't think . . ."

"Of course not, Mr. Vandaele."

Baert gulped. The skeleton had also been under the ground for quite some time. News of its discovery had clearly startled Vandaele. Why had he rushed to his study in a panic when Baert informed him about it? The old bugger was clearly in a flap, and that story about the phone call to his niece only confirmed it. It was as transparent as Melissa's negligee.

"Your concern deserves an appropriate reward nonetheless."

Baert's face brightened up. Money was all that could silence him. Vandaele fished four ten-thousand-franc notes from his wallet. Baert beamed unashamedly. Tomorrow Melissa would have her wide-screen TV. When he got home and told her the good news, she'd be naked in a heartbeat, or perhaps she'd slip on that little lace number he gave her for Christmas. "That's very generous of you, Mr. Vandaele."

Vandaele patted him warmly on the shoulder. "You'll keep me posted on further developments, I hope?"

"Goes without saying, Mr. Vandaele. If there's news, you'll be the first to hear it."

Hannelore installed herself in the garden, with her legs up and a glass of ice-cold V8 within easy reach. The sun's last rays skimmed the edges of an ominous cloud, their scattered light coloring the whitewashed walls of their private earthly paradise corn yellow as if someone had slipped a Polaroid lens in front of it. If they were to believe the weather forecast, this was the end of the summer.

Van In placed three cigarettes on the table, his movements exaggerated, and sipped at his pinot noir. He was allowed two glasses.

"Taste good?" she asked.

"Heaven."

The muffled sound of church bells could be heard in the distance. The wind blew in from the southwest. There was rain in the cards, as predicted.

"The diet's doing its job." Hannelore reveled in her new man. Van In was in his boxers. The car tire around his middle had shrunk in three months to the size of a flabby bicycle tire.

"Versavel said something similar this morning. So what's the next step? A dog?"

Hannelore raised her eyebrows. "A dog?" she asked, not quite sure what he was talking about.

"Then you can make me take it for a walk every evening. Think of all the calories I would burn."

A sudden gust of wind rustled the leaves. It sounded like a rattlesnake.

"You might be happy you have a dog to walk when the baby's here."

"What d'you mean?"

Van In lit a cigarette and relished the heady rush of nicotine. Hannelore lifted her skirt, took his hand, and placed it on her belly.

The bulge was more prominent when she was sitting.

"I'm having trouble picturing Commissioner Van In changing diapers." She grinned. "You'll thank me for sending you out with Fido."

Associating her shiny belly with a pile of soiled diapers tempered his nascent lust.

"We can start the countdown, Pieter. I felt it move for the first time this morning."

Van In pressed his hand firmly against her belly but felt nothing. "I wonder if all those emotions are good for you," he said, his tone unexpectedly serious.

Menacing clouds colored the grass dark green, and the setting sun gave way to dusk as Hannelore sipped on her V8.

"We're not living in the Middle Ages, Pieter. I'm not going to give birth to a monster because I looked at a skull."

"I wouldn't laugh in your condition. My mother always said—"

"Nonsense! Don't tell me you believe in that old wives' crap." *Why do men behave like infants when their wives are pregnant?* Hannelore thought to herself. The women had to do all the work, didn't they? For the men, it was wham, bam, thank you, ma'am.

Van In peered longingly at the two remaining cigarettes, like pieces of chalk on the dark wood table. He grabbed one and lit it double-quick.

"Everything used to be so much simpler." Van In sighed, sucking the smoke deep into his lungs and swigging at his glass.

"Don't tell me you're worried about changing your baby's diapers."

"I wish we were on a desert island," said Van In. He could picture it in his mind's eye. "No more fuss. Slurping juicy cocktails, grilling fish, and lying around on the beach all day long."

"No beach, Pieter, just diapers. This is the Vette Vispoort, there's no more wine, and there's rain on the way."

Storm clouds were accumulating above the scarlet red rooftops.

"D'you know what?" she said with a cryptic smile. "If you solve the skeleton case within the month, I'll treat you to a week in Portugal."

"You're not serious."

"Don't you believe me?"

"Of course I do. But when was the last time you checked our bank balance?"

"I've got a little nest egg put aside for a rainy day."

"That's money for the baby," Van In protested. "And what makes you so sure I'll be given the case?"

"I can take care of that, sweetie."

"Out of the question."

"Case or no case, I want a trip to Portugal soon. In a few months we can forget it," she said, digging in her heels.

"You know that pregnant women aren't advised to travel by plane, Hanne."

"Is that right?"

Hannelore got to her feet and slipped slowly out of her

dress. She looked like a Botticelli model: sensual, fertile, and primitively feminine. Nothing is more beautiful than a mother to be. "So flying is out of the question. What about some in-house flying then?"

"Come on, Hanne," Van In groaned.

"Don't tell me the commissioner's got a headache."

He ground his half-smoked cigarette into the grass and threw himself at her. High above their heads, layers of warm and cold air collided to produce a first peal of thunder that rolled across the city like a bowling ball. Van In floated on a cushion of air that whispered sweet words in his ear. He barely noticed the heavy drops of rain spatter on his back like painless projectiles.

2

Van In filled the corridors of the police station with the pungent smell of musk. He was wearing faded jeans and a beige cotton shirt. Hannelore had banished his old camouflage sweaters to the rag bin for eternity. Holding in his belly was a thing of the past. *Life can be generous at times,* Van In thought, *very generous.* When he opened the door to Room 204, Versavel was whistling like a cheerful construction worker.

"Good morning, *girlfriend*," he said grinning.

Van In ignored the sexist remark and lit his first cigarette with a smile. "Life does indeed start at forty, Guido. You were right all along. I'm ready for it. Bring it on."

"What . . . now?" asked Versavel, milking the double entendre.

"No, not 'now,' and certainly not with you. What's the news on our skeleton friend?"

Versavel took a deep breath. Skeletons made him think of maggots writhing in hollow eye sockets. "Our John Doe, you mean."

He preferred the American euphemism. In the U.S., corpses were stiffs, someone who didn't survive the ride to the hospital was dead-on-arrival or DOA, and an unidentified stiff was either a John or a Jane Doe.

"You know I'm allergic to that transatlantic crap, Guido. Let's just call the skeleton Herbert. A little originality can make all the difference, don't you think?"

Versavel folded his arms like a chief proudly accepting the unconditional surrender of his tribe. "Your wish is my command, Commissioner."

Van In puffed a belligerent cloud of smoke in his subordinate's direction. "That's how it works, eh, Versavel?"

The sergeant plucked pensively at his mustache. At least he knew how to deal with Van In when the man was depressed. But when he was in one of his bouts of euphoria, his boss was as hard to handle as a teenager without pocket money. He had only one option: cut the crap and get on with it.

"A fax just came in . . . fifteen minutes ago," said Versavel, straightening his face. "I didn't know we were in charge of the case."

Van In took the fax.

"I did," he snorted.

"Aha, so it's like that, is it?"

"Don't get me started, Guido. She's pregnant. What can I say?"

Van In reluctantly stubbed out his first cigarette. There wasn't much left of it to smoke.

"'Probable cause of death: a broken neck,'" he read aloud. "'Age: between twenty-five and thirty. Height: five ten. Gender: male. Date of death: between 1985 and 1986. Distinguishing marks: old shin fracture, extensive jaw surgery, plus twenty-four porcelain teeth.' Jesus, that must have cost a fortune."

"De Jaegher was on the ball for once. Didn't Hannelore set Friday as the deadline for his report?"

"She called him yesterday afternoon." Van In sighed. "Someone at the public prosecutor's office whispered in her ear that examining a skeleton took no time at all. And it doesn't take a genius to spot a broken neck. De Jaegher should have seen it already when he was down in the pit."

Van In lit a second cigarette. Versavel said nothing. He knew from experience that Van In's resolutions weren't destined to last long, especially if they had something to do with booze and cigarettes.

"Still a bit of an achievement if you ask me," Versavel said. "On Hannelore's part, I mean. De Jaegher's a stubborn old bugger. Even the public prosecutor treats him with kid gloves."

"She wants to go on vacation next month."

Versavel was taken aback. The commissioner's brain functioned in the strangest of ways. He could normally follow his boss's train of thought, but this morning was an exception.

"Hannelore wants me to tie up the case as quickly as possible," Van In explained. "She's already got the prosecutor around her little finger, and De Jaegher would happily have sliced up his own liver to get into her good graces. She's also hoping I'll make chief commissioner one of these days, preferably sooner than later."

"Then you should transfer to the federal police. Not much chance of making chief with the local boys these days," said Versavel. He had a problem with the federal police, and he never wasted an opportunity to vent his frustration.

"Go on, Guido, laugh at me. Women are complicated creatures. When I think of it, you should thank God you're gay."

The second cigarette wasn't as good as Van In had expected. Those things started to stink when you cut back.

"Thanks for the compliment, boss."

Van In shrugged his shoulders, sat down at his desk, and read the fax a second time. They had to identify Herbert first before moving on to his killer.

"You can start by checking if any males around thirty were reported missing between 1985 and 1986."

"In Bruges?"

"We have to start somewhere, don't we, my dear Watson?"

"Is that all?"

"Of course not. Put a couple of officers on the phones. Have them call all the dentists and orthodontists in the region. All that porcelain in Herbert's mouth has to be traceable."

Versavel took note. "Shall I get Dirk Baert involved?" he asked with a faked grin.

He knew that the very sound of the man's name would send shivers down Van In's spine. Baert was a slippery bastard, a climber who had maneuvered himself to chief inspector using whatever back doors he could find. He had followed a class in "crime analysis" the year before at the NIC—the National Institute for Criminalities. The class had a fancy name and the fact that such courses were being organized gave the public the idea that the judiciary was finally dragging itself into the twentieth century. In reality, Baert could barely operate his PC, in spite of the diploma above his desk that claimed the contrary.

"Do we have an alternative?"

Versavel shook his head. "Afraid not, Pieter. Don't you ever read official orders?"

They say rats can sense disaster before it happens. Some people have the same gift. Van In wasn't one of them, but Versavel's sneering tone made him suspicious.

"What official orders?" he asked guardedly.

Versavel took a deep breath. "So you haven't heard that De Kee appointed Chief Inspector Baert to our department."

Chief Commissioner Carton had succumbed to a brain hemorrhage the month before, so his predecessor, De Kee, had returned to his old job while they looked for a suitable successor.

"Jerk. When's he due?"

"Tomorrow," said Versavel hesitantly.

Bad news has its advantages. If it's really devastating, it can stun a person into silence. Van In was no exception to the rule.

He tried to formulate a curse, and when he didn't succeed he left the room in a sulk.

William Aerts read the news about Herbert at the breakfast table in the kitchen. His craggy jaws tensed. After so many years of relative calm, the acid in his belly now started to hammer hard. He tried to extinguish the pain with a swig of lukewarm tea. Linda offered him a slice of buttered toast. A couple of eggs spattered in a greasy frying pan. She shuffled to the stove, removed the pan from the heat, and slapped the eggs onto a plate.

"Something wrong?" she asked.

Linda Aerts was once a good-looking woman. Now she was thirty-five, plump, and scarred by excessive alcohol use. Ten years earlier she had reigned supreme as the uncrowned queen of Bruges' nightlife. There wasn't a man who hadn't wanted her, but Linda didn't want to tie herself down. She danced through life like a nimble nymph and drove her admirers crazy. She flirted, let them fondle her, and laughed as her victims skulked off unsatisfied to the men's room.

One day William Aerts appeared in Bruges. Everyone admired him. He drove a Jaguar, wore Armani, and always had an entourage of girls in heat—big boobs, nipples erect. He ignored the reigning queen, and she found it hard to swallow. Linda had bedded him within a couple of weeks. They got married in a hurry, and the party lasted until William's money ran out. That was the last day of her youth.

Former friends now looked at her with contempt. "Fat Linda," they called her. Mirrors were enemy number one. Every reflected glance exposed her sagging breasts, pouchy belly, and fast-growing birthmarks with bristly black hair in the middle. Her fate seemed crueler than that of Dorian Gray's and might even have moved Oscar Wilde to a level of pity.

"What could be wrong?" William asked, lining up for a fight.

Linda rubbed the sleep from her eyes and lit a cigarette, the sixth in forty-five minutes. "You look as if you saw a ghost, that's what." She dumped the plate with the runny eggs on the table in front of him.

"Who asked you? Mind your own fucking business." William shook open the paper.

She drove a lungful of smoke through her nose, unable to disguise her contempt. "It wouldn't *kill* you to be kind now and again," she snorted.

The word *kill* didn't miss its mark. Linda knew he was about to explode, so she withdrew strategically toward the door . . . and not a second too soon. She was still standing in the doorway when he grabbed the plate of eggs, and just as he tossed it at her, she pulled the door closed. The plate sailed through the air like a Frisbee and smacked against the wall. The eggs slipped off in midflight, splattering on the floor like yellow-white slime.

Linda heard him curse and shift his chair. She raced to the liquor cabinet and grabbed a half-full bottle of Elixir d'Anvers. William threw open the kitchen door and screamed that he was going to kill her. That's what William always did when he lost his cool. Linda rummaged through the cigarette supply, stuffed two packs of Marlboros into her dressing-gown pocket, and ran upstairs. She knew the storm would die down in an hour and she could return to the kitchen. Linda locked the bedroom door and listened. This time he didn't smash any furniture. He didn't even come banging on the door. She uncorked the bottle of Elixir and tossed it back. William returned to the kitchen table, a photo of his mother in front of him in a frame. The mourning ribbon in the top left-hand corner reminded him of the tragedy that had visited him sixteen days earlier.

Van In parked his VW Golf in front of the closed gate. There was no sign of a bell. Hugo Vermast was standing in the roof gully of his farmhouse sledgehammering a soot-covered chimney. His blaring transistor radio drowned out the rustle of the autumn leaves and the song of a plucky thrush.

Van In wasn't in the mood to hang around, so he cupped his hands to his mouth, took a deep breath, and roared at the top of his lungs. After a couple of spine-tingling hellos, the radio fell silent. Van In waved his hand in the air, the first time in an age.

Vermast responded to the commissioner's salute with an enthusiastic arm gesture. *Next thing he'll fall*, thought Van In with a hint of malicious delight.

Suddenly the gate opened automatically. Vermast climbed down his ladder and came toward him.

"Handy, eh?" Van In pointed to the remote Vermast had used to open the gate.

"There's no stopping technology, Commissioner. What can I do for you?"

"I wouldn't mind a cup of coffee."

The two men crossed the property, weaving their way through piles of building material.

"Such romantic surroundings," said Van In as they made their way into the kitchen through a rickety back door.

"My wife's childhood dream. She's wanted to move to the country for years. It's a unique opportunity for the kids too. They were prepared to pay whatever it cost to get out of the city. Just like their mother."

Van In couldn't bear the thought of one of his own little pains in the ass driving him out of his home. *Children should follow their parents,* he thought. All that liberal parenting crap was an illusion devised by a handful of crazy doctors. A couple of decades after publication of Spock's first book, the man was forced to acknowledge the fact that he had maybe ruined the lives of millions of young families. His theory had spawned legions of pains in the ass. Doctor Spock. Jesus. For Van In there was only one Spock. And with him at least he could hope—beam them up, Scotty.

The interior of the kitchen consisted of a colorful collection of floral pottery, dried flowers, and poorly varnished furniture. The table was covered in jam. Circular burn marks left behind by red-hot pots and pans direct from the stove gave it an authentic character.

"Hi, Joris."

Van In tried to sound friendly. The boy was still in his pajamas. He barely reacted to the stranger's greeting, preferring to concentrate on a grid he had made by carefully arranging sugar cubes.

"Don't we say good morning, young man?"

Joris ignored his father's request. He lowered his eyes and rearranged the cubes in a different pattern.

"Joris has problems with people he doesn't know," said Vermast. *He probably tried to sell that to anyone crossing the threshold of his house for the first time,* thought Van In.

"No problem, Mr. Vermast. As long as they're amusing themselves," he said. He did his best to sound convincing.

Vermast put the kettle on the stove and grabbed a couple of cracked and chipped mugs from the kitchen cupboard. Van In could see that something wasn't right from the way the man rummaged nervously in the cupboard.

"Is tea OK?" Vermast asked, a little embarrassed. He produced an empty canister with a crusty layer of coffee grounds on the bottom.

"Whatever you have is fine," Van In lied. The supply of sugar on the table reassured him. Three cubes were enough to make even dishwater drinkable.

"Have you lived here long, Mr. Vermast?"

"Three months, Commissioner. There's still a ton of work to be done, as you can see. But you know how it goes." Van In had no idea whatsoever how it went but decided wisely not to pursue it.

•   •   •

The growl of the diesel engine made the recently replaced windows (still labeled) buzz and vibrate. Van In looked outside. He saw the gate swing open and Leen driving carefully onto the property. She parked the dilapidated Volvo between two piles of sand. With the kind of force only an old Swedish car could handle, Tine threw open the passenger door.

"Lively girl," said Van In. "Is she always so full of energy?"

He hadn't meant it as a compliment, but it visibly cheered Vermast nonetheless.

"My wife thinks she should go to a school for gifted children, but there isn't one in the neighborhood. Her IQ is way above one hundred thirty, so that can be problematic, especially when you have to deal with teachers who don't understand."

Van In raised his eyes to heaven. *Kids. Jesus H. Christ.* The boy was half-autistic, and to compensate, they'd bumped up the neurotic girl to prodigy status.

Vermast grabbed a third cup and filled all three with tea. The stuff smelled of dirty laundry. Van In should have known better, but now it was too late.

Leen pushed open the kitchen door with her foot, bulging brown paper bags from the local supermarket under each arm. She dumped them on the kitchen counter.

"Hi, honey. Good day, Commissioner."

Leen was wearing a sleeveless minidress. She collapsed on

a chair with a sigh, involuntarily hitching up the short skirt. Most women cross their legs out of modesty, but Leen didn't make the least effort to conceal her snow-white panties from the commissioner's gaze. Van In was convinced she knew what she was doing. He looked up. The tops of her breasts were quite visible in the V-neck of her dress, and that sight was much more interesting.

"Mommy, I want carrot juice," Tine whined. Vermast smiled sheepishly. Van In, by contrast, would quite happily have treated the little monster to a clip on the ear.

"Mom, I want carrot juice. You promised." The girl pounded her head stubbornly against Leen's shoulder.

"Later, sweetheart. Mommy's having some tea first."

"Mooom. You prooooomised," she said, stamping her feet. The girl's screeching cut to the bone. Van In gritted his teeth as he used to when someone ran fingernails across the blackboard at school. Leen let her daughter have her tantrum, sipped at her tea, and smiled every now and then at Van In. The girl turned to her father in a rage.

"Renovating a place like this must take a serious toll on your energy."

Van In hadn't been planning to raise the subject, but the circumstances forced him to. Tine pestered her father relentlessly, constantly trying to grab his attention. Going on about the house seemed to be the only way to restore communication between him and Vermast.

"And the rest, Commissioner. I worked on the place day and

night for eight months before we could move in. It was more like a cowshed than a farmhouse back then."

Vermast pushed his daughter aside and joined Van In at the table. Leen finished her tea and fetched the juicer from the cupboard with clear reluctance. She ripped open one of the brown bags on the kitchen counter and grabbed a bunch of carrots. Tine clung to her mother like a black widow on her partner.

"I can show you some photos of what it used to look like if you're interested."

Van In nodded, trying to hide his lack of enthusiasm. Things were going from bad to worse.

"Let's go to the living room. It's quieter there," Vermast suggested, hoping fervently that the girl would stay with her mother.

They had just arrived in the living room when the juicer started to whine at an earsplitting pitch. Vermast was wise enough to close the door, reducing the volume by a good forty decibels. He invited Van In to take a seat on a rustic sofa, the upholstery of which was in a lamentable state, much like the rest of the furniture.

While his host searched for the promised photographs in a quasi-antique linen closet, Van In sized up the Vermast family habitat. They had probably paid a fortune to some canny antique dealer for the rickety furniture. The cupboards were full of bursts and cracks and were covered with caustic soda stains. A clumsy endeavor to camouflage the stains with thick layers of furniture polish had clearly failed. An orange crate would have fetched more at auction. The rest of the woodwork was worse than the furniture, if that were possible. In an eager attempt at giving it the authentic farmhouse look, Vermast had tried to clean the grime from the beams supporting the roof. Without the protective layer of paint, the wood now looked like dried gingerbread. It was nothing short of a miracle that the place was still standing. The state of the wooden floor defied description. Capricious tunnels testified to the unflagging zeal of a wood-worm colony.

Their things had clearly been put together from rummage sales and flea markets—artificial pewter plates, a rusty set of fire irons, a chandelier in the form of a wagon wheel, and a selection of agricultural implements on the walls, all intended to create a country feel. What irritated Van In the most, however, were the unrecognizably mutilated toys scattered all over the room. *Anything goes,* he thought.

"Finally," Vermast groaned. He had emptied half the linen closet by this time. "Here they are."

Vermast turned to reveal a torn cardboard box. He placed it between them on the sofa and removed the lid. It was overflowing with photos, most of them simple family snapshots.

"These are from last year." Vermast handed him a pile of underexposed Polaroids. Van In examined them carefully. The piece of land was only recognizable from the hawthorn hedge and the leafless elms against the ominous fall sky. Vermast hadn't been kidding. The original building was little more than a hovel.

"Incredible, Mr. Vermast. You've worked wonders with the place. It's close to a miracle." Vermast smiled like an amateur cyclist winning his first race. The compliment had tickled his vanity. He walked over to the old-fashioned dresser, where he kept a bottle of cognac behind a pile of magazines and newspapers.

"Leen's brother-in-law has a buddy in the real estate business who pointed us in the right direction. It was a bargain, let me tell you. He also took care of the necessary building permissions."

Van In raised his eyebrows.

"The new house will be three times the size of the old place," said Vermast, grinning conspiratorially. "The property is designated for agricultural purposes, if you get my drift?"

Van In didn't understand. Vermast took a surreptitious look at the kitchen door, filled a couple of glasses with cognac, and hid the bottle where he had found it.

"According to the letter of the law, we aren't allowed to extend the building more than thirty percent," said Vermast eagerly, tossing back his cognac in a single gulp. "But I don't have to explain the law to you, do I, Commissioner?"

Van In sipped carefully at his glass. He had to admit that the cognac tasted pretty good.

"With the money we saved on the purchase of the house, we can now afford a luxury or two. I managed to pick up a batch of Burgundian antique floor tiles last week. Not cheap but perfect for the living room. Another cognac?"

Van In emptied his glass, a bad move after three months of enforced abstinence. The stuff burned in his stomach, but that wasn't reason enough to refuse another glass. "Just a small one." He couldn't say no.

Vermast tiptoed back to the dresser like a naughty schoolboy and refilled the glasses.

"The remote-controlled gate must come in handy too," Van In observed in passing. The noise of the juicer in the kitchen finally stopped. Leen must have made a gallon of carrot juice.

"Not really my thing, Commissioner. I'm not into gadgets. The remote was installed by the previous owner."

"A modern farmer, no doubt?"

Vermast shook his head, tossed back his glass, and looked at Van In with imploring eyes. Van In was forced to follow his host's example. Vermast snatched his guest's glass and returned both to the dresser unwashed.

"The place used to be owned by a nonprofit organization." Now that the glasses were safely back in the cupboard, Vermast seemed more at ease with himself. "Leen knows more about it than I do. Some kind of charity, I think."

At that moment Tine stormed into the living room with a huge glass of carrot juice in her hand. "Look what Mommy made for me," she yelled in triumph. The girl threw herself onto the sofa whooping with delight and managed to spill a third of the juice on Van In's freshly washed jeans.

"Tine, for goodness' sake," said Vermast, his tone mildly reproving. He jumped to his feet and gave her a symbolic little smack. The wretch burst into an uncontrollable fit of tears, attracting her mother's immediate attention.

"What's going on?" she asked.

Vermast explained what had happened. He knew exactly what his wife would do. First comfort Tine, then fetch a towel.

"Don't worry, Commissioner. Carrot juice doesn't stain."

Leen got to her knees and dried Van In's jeans without the least embarrassment. Not an unpleasant experience. He noticed from his new vantage point that she wasn't wearing a bra. Good thing Hannelore wasn't around.

"Helping Our Own, it was called, for people in need. I think Benedict was on the board."

"Benedict?"

"Benedict Vervoort, the real estate agent who arranged the sale of the house. If I'm not mistaken, they used to organize weekend camps here for scouts and the like."

Leen was so thorough that Van In had a hard time controlling himself.

"Any idea why the charity wanted to get rid of the place?"

"According to Benedict, they found something bigger. They had grown over the years and urgently needed more space."

Growing was the last thing Van In wanted to think about. "I guess that's dry enough, Mrs. Vermast." He did his best not to groan.

"Are you sure?" she asked, still concerned.

3

Benedict Vervoort ruled the roost at a modest real estate agency in the center of Waardamme. A neon sign above the door and display window covered the entire breadth of the facade. Van In read the sign: VERVOORT SERVICES. The capital *V* in the middle of the name already spoke volumes about the branch manager.

The street was empty, but Van In chose to park his VW Golf in the agency's parking lot, which, as another sign read, was reserved for clients only.

The office was located in Benedict Vervoort's modest parental home. The living room had been transformed into a counter area, little more than a glorified closet, and with no clerk in attendance behind the glass barrier. But Vervoort's business was multifunctional, and real estate was only one of the many services he had to offer. The average farmer could use it to deposit cash and bonds, as Van In observed from the various handwritten posters that graced the office walls.

A middle-aged woman—the front office junior clerk—welcomed him. She was the image of Audrey Hepburn but without the makeup.

"Mr. Benedict is expecting you," she said in a formal tone when Van In introduced himself. "Please take a seat."

A cock crowed in the distance. Van In wasn't dreaming. This was the West Flemish countryside, where fortunes were being made behind the walls of banal houses and where a mud-covered Mercedes by the front door was the only visible sign of luxury. Benedict Vervoort hadn't even considered it necessary to replace the floral wallpaper.

"Good morning, Commissioner." Benedict Vervoort approached Van In with open arms. He was wearing a loud suit, a canary-yellow shirt, and a grass-green tie. The majority of the Mafiosi in Sicily were less ostentatious.

Van In shook his hand. The young businessman's chubby, ring-adorned fingers felt sticky. The aftershave with which he had lavishly sprinkled himself smelled of toilet cleaner, a stench Van In could barely stand.

"How are you, Commissioner?" asked Benedict in polite West Flemish. "And what can I do for you?"

Benedict eased back into his fake leather office chair. His head seemed to consist of pink lips, puffy cheeks, and little more. Van In had a hard time concealing his opinion of the man opposite him. .

"Am I talking to Mr. Vervoort?" he asked with more than a hint of condescension.

"The man himself," said the grinning yellow-green harlequin.

"Do you mind if I smoke?" Van In fished a cigarette from his breast pocket. Benedict raised his hand. *Shit*, Van In thought.

"Allow me to offer you a cigar, Commissioner," said Vervoort with a gesture of hospitality. He opened one of the drawers in his desk and produced a flat box of Havanas. "They belonged to my late father."

Van In was obliged to accept the offer. The cigar crackled like a freshly unrolled sheet of papyrus.

"Any relation to Aloïs Vervoort?" Van In inquired.

The question seemed to please Benedict.

"Aloïs was my father," he said with undisguised pride.

"Really?"

Aloïs Vervoort was Flanders' cycling idol in the 1950s. The plucky Waardammer had managed third place in the Paris-Roubaix race on a couple of occasions and even won a stage during the 1956 Tour de France.

"Woe betide anyone who dared make a noise on Sunday afternoon, when the race was broadcast on TV," said Van In.

Benedict laughed like an American presidential candidate in the middle of a campaign.

"Laugh, go on. But I remember getting more than one pasting because of your father."

"Happy to know it, Commissioner." His father's status radiated from Benedict's face like the sun setting on Mount Fuji.

There was also a hint of the Orient in Vervoort junior, the spitting image of a sitting Buddha.

"The real reason for my visit is the Vermast family and their property in the Bremwegel."

Benedict unfolded his hands, placed the tips of his fingers on either side of his nose, and pretended to be deep in thought.

"Is there a problem?" he asked, anxious and curious at once.

"I presume you read the papers."

"You don't mean . . . surely—"

"I do mean, Mr. Vervoort."

"Nothing to do with me," said Vervoort resolutely.

"What has nothing to do with you?" Van In's curt tone drove Vervoort to abandon his defensiveness.

"The murder, of course."

"Murder?"

"Well . . . I mean . . . they found a body, didn't they?"

"A skeleton," Van In corrected.

"A skeleton. Of course, Commissioner. That's what I read in the paper."

Van In looked Vervoort in the eye. The countryside realtor clasped his hands behind his head and leaned back in his gaudy chair. He clearly wasn't going to be pressured.

"Happenstance."

Now it was Van In's turn to be caught off guard, an opportunity Vervoort deftly deployed to regain control of the conversation.

"Life is a succession of unexpected events, Commissioner. If you had found the skeleton before the sale, I would have been stuck with a worthless property. Who wants a house with a grave in the garden?"

Van In puffed on the dry cigar and did his best not to cringe. The thing smelled of rotten wood and dog shit.

"Mr. Vermast informed me that the farm was owned by a charity called Helping Our Own," said Van In as he placed the cigar in an ashtray, hoping it would go out by itself.

"Not exactly, Commissioner. The farm was owned by one of our benefactors. The charity was given free use of it."

"Can you tell me a little more?"

"Don't you know the charity?"

Van In shook his head. "Should I?"

Vervoort inspected Van In with the air of a student who had just left his first psychoanalysis class. "It was founded in 1986 by a number of idealists determined to improve the quality of life of the country's less well-off."

Van In would have bet his bottom dollar that Vervoort had just quoted from the charity's brochure, word for word, and all pretty hollow.

"So if I understand correctly, the charity is about helping people, helping Flemish people . . . hence the name."

Helping Our Own was already beginning to sound a bit paternalistic, with shades of the far right.

Vervoort didn't let Van In's moderate sarcasm throw him off balance.

"Helping Our Own has been collecting funds for years to

fight poverty here at home," he continued unperturbed. "The charity offers financial assistance to people struggling to make ends meet with the crumbs this welfare society of ours throws at them."

Vervoort's words became increasingly emphatic. His fleshy chin quivered like blancmange on a Power Plate.

"We offer study grants, housing, holidays, cheap loans, legal support—"

"We?" Van In cut in.

"Yes, we," Vervoort responded enthusiastically. "I'm the charity's treasurer. Does that surprise you?"

Van In wasn't sure what to say—that he'd rather see Mother Teresa strip for *Playboy* than Vervoort giving twenty francs to a beggar on the street?

"Far from it, Mr. Vervoort. If I haven't forgotten what they taught us in religion class at school, Jesus also had a soft spot for both whores and Pharisees," said Van In, slightly taken aback by the impulsiveness of his own reaction. But such statements could also yield remarkable responses at times. He noticed Vervoort's eyes narrow in a flash.

"'Love thy neighbor' is very close to our Christian hearts, Commissioner. It may not seem obvious in a world governed by egoism and self-interest, but perhaps you'd like to get to know our work a little better? You would be more than welcome to visit Care House whenever you have the time."

Vervoort paused with the panache of an African president addressing the plenary assembly of the United Nations. "Care

House is our most prestigious realization," he continued with renewed vigor. "The farm offers a home to twenty single people and ten families. The entire project is self-financing. We produce our own food and cover the rest of our needs by selling fruit and vegetables."

"So you sold the Vermast place to finance the new project," said Van In guardedly. He stubbed out the half-smoked cigar. This was the biggest pile of crap he'd heard in a long time. Benedict seemed to read his mind.

"When the big service clubs brag about their charitable achievements, Joe Public thinks it's fantastic. They organize a tasteless banquet a couple of times a year, have their members pay a fortune to attend, and hand over ten percent of the takings to one or another good cause. The press loves it. But Helping Our Own doesn't need publicity. Our funds are used directly to help the poor improve their lives, to give them a better future."

"A very noble goal," said Van In dryly. The puffed-up rhetoric of this Samaritan from West Flanders was beginning to get on his nerves. "I'll be sure to visit Care House when the investigation is over, but in the meantime, I have to be moving. I have a busy afternoon ahead."

Vervoort walked Van In to the door. They shook hands.

"By the way, Mr. Vervoort, Vermast's farm had a gate with a remote control. Did the charity install it?"

"It was already there, Commissioner. The former owner probably knows more about it."

"Of course," said Van In. "And do you happen to have the name of the former owner?"

"Is that important?"

"In a murder investigation, everything is important, Mr. Vervoort."

The realtor may have felt cornered at that moment, but he didn't let it show.

"I'm afraid my hands are tied, Commissioner. The farm was made available to us by a benefactor who wishes to remain anonymous."

In polite conversation, such a response would have been enough to prevent further inquiry, but Van In didn't consider it polite conversation, not in the least. "Listen very carefully, Mr. Vervoort. As a realtor, you know as well as I do that such transactions are always registered. For me it's only a question of time before I identify your anonymous benefactor. The choice is yours."

Vervoort swallowed his indignation and switched back to the good little boy approach. He had made a mistake, and he had to correct it.

"My apologies, Commissioner. I didn't realize such information might be important to the investigation. I hope you understand our need for discretion when it comes to our financial backers. The majority prefer to remain anonymous. That's why I—"

"The name please, Mr. Vervoort."

"Are you familiar with Lodewijk Vandaele?"

Van In nodded. Lodewijk Vandaele owned one of the largest contractor companies in West Flanders.

"So we're talking about Lodewijk Vandaele," said Van In.

"Indeed, Commissioner. But I beg you to use this information only if it's absolutely necessary for the investigation. Mr. Vandaele detests publicity, and Helping Our Own is deep in his debt."

"I'll do my best," said Van In. He glanced at his watch. "But now I really have to go. Good-bye, Mr. Vervoort."

Van In made his way to the parking lot. His VW Golf was alone as he had left it. Only then did Van In realize that Vervoort's multifunctional real estate agency had been client-free throughout his visit.

Linda Aerts was snoring, flat out on a narrow single bed, an empty bottle of Elixir d'Anvers on the nightstand, and a Marlboro still smoldering in the ashtray beside it. A two-inch ash clung to the filter like grim death. The room stank of sour sweat, cheap deodorant, and dirty laundry, and the chaos was enough to turn the average teenager green with jealousy. Fortunately the curtains were closed. The piles of dirty underwear appeared in the half-light like fluffy flowerbeds and the plates with rotting food like a Tracey Emin installation.

Linda was wearing a satin nightgown. The shiny cloth mercilessly accentuated every band of fat around her loins. Her sagging breasts heaved up and down with the rhythm of her breathing.

The telephone had been ringing every ten minutes for more than an hour. Linda dreamed that she was part of a funeral procession. The hearse, a black Chevrolet with chrome bumpers, sliced through the unruly crowd like a prehistoric batmobile. Linda was on the back of a white stallion. Everyone was trying to catch a glimpse of her. People chanted. Linda recognized dozens of them from her childhood. She reveled in their adulation, her head held high, parading in the wake of the Chevrolet.

The hearse was carrying a glass casket, its lid buried under bouquets of lilacs. William had been laid out on a velvet mattress, his head resting on an embroidered pillow with tassels on each corner. He was breathing, but the public didn't seem to notice. No one could see the silver shackles that bound him to the casket, nor the linen tethers around his neck, chest, and pelvis that pressed him firmly to its base. His eyes reeled. Beads of mortal terror covered his forehead.

"What a babe," Linda heard someone shout.

"Need a bed for the night, darlin'?" another lusty admirer intoned.

The funeral procession approached the center of the city. The square in front of the bank was full to bursting. Linda slackened the reins as the deferential crowd gave way. She turned as she passed the bank. The building, a cage of steel and mirrored glass, reflected her image. She was naked. The onlookers broke into a song, its words vile and disgusting. Suddenly a jester appeared in front of the horse, grabbing the reins and groping greedily at Linda's thighs. The bells on his cap drowned out the uproar. Linda tried to fend him off. She kicked the white stallion into action. It shivered, reared, and bolted, leaving Linda behind on the cobblestones. The last thing she remembered before opening her eyes was staring at William's smirking face. He was about to tie her up. She screamed.

Linda woke up on the floor next to the bed. The telephone was ringing, and this time it didn't stop.

"Hello," she said with a quavering voice.

"Is William there?"

"William isn't home. Who's calling?" she asked, still dazed from her dream.

Provoost cursed under his breath and hung up.

Chief Inspector Dirk Baert put down the receiver.

"Any luck?" he asked Versavel.

Sergeant Versavel had just notched up his thirty-seventh call to a dentist.

"The same story every time. Either they can't remember and ask you to call back tomorrow or you get their answering service telling you they're on vacation. No wonder it costs a month's salary to have a crown fixed. In the old days, that used to pay for a nugget of gold in your gob. They need us like a hole in the head . . . so to speak."

The word *gob* wasn't part of Versavel's usual vocabulary. It was a sign that he was pissed, and not only because of the dentists. Baert's endless whining was driving him up a wall.

"I managed to get an orthodontist on the line. The man's

name was Joyeux," said Baert. He waited patiently for a reaction. Versavel knew that Baert would repeat himself if he said nothing. "I managed to get an orthodontist on the line. The man's name was Joyeux."

"And?" asked Versavel wearily.

"Not even remotely *joyeux*. The man was furious. He insisted he was still a student back in 1985 and couldn't have been involved. He said we should have checked first before we interrupted him."

Versavel glanced at his watch. "I suggest we stop for coffee. This is getting us nowhere."

Versavel popped a filter into the machine, switched it on, and returned to his desk. Baert rolled his chair a little closer. This wasn't the kind of detective work he had expected.

"I wonder if Van In's made any progress."

The first drops of boiling water exploded in the coffee filter.

"Is he as good as they say?"

The tone of Baert's question was halfway between hesitation and admiration.

"Van In is the best," Versavel answered, sure of his words. He wasn't in the mood to pick a fight with the chief inspector. The man had a bad reputation. He tried to sow dissension wherever he went. A few colleagues were even convinced he had a couple of bats in his belfry. For a moment, the *drip-drip* of the coffee machine was all that broke the silence.

"I've heard," Baert whispered with a feigned smile, "that—"

"I don't give a shit what you've heard, Chief Inspector."

55

Baert was taken aback by Versavel's reaction. His nostrils started to quiver as he readied himself to read him the riot act.

"Speak of the devil," said Versavel, relieved at the sight of Van In in the doorway. "Any luck?"

Van In popped a chocolate toffee into his mouth hoping no one would notice. He was starving. Versavel served coffee as Van In delivered his report, ending with the name of the benefactor who'd previously owned the property. Baert listened eagerly.

"I think I need to have a word with our friend Vandaele. It may be sheer coincidence, of course, but according to the coroner, Herbert was killed between 1985 and 1986 . . ."

"And Vandaele donated the farm to the charity in 1986," Versavel finished his sentence. They could read each other's thoughts after so many years of intensive teamwork.

"Something like that, Guido. And it bugs me for some reason."

Versavel stirred his coffee. The name *Vandaele* brought him back in time to a period full of good memories. "Perhaps Jonathan can help us."

Who the fuck is Jonathan? Van In wanted to ask.

"If I'm not mistaken, Jonathan worked for Vandaele back then. He was his accountant for years."

"One of your 'buddies'?"

"Long ago," said Versavel with a twinkle in his eye. "Shall I give him a call?"

"Poor Guido. You'd do just about anything for king and country."

Dirk Baert stared at the two like a pygmy looking up at the Eiffel Tower for the first time.

"It's a deal." Versavel beamed. "I'll call him right away."

Every Tuesday evening, Van In and Hannelore headed to their favorite restaurant, the Heer Halewijn, on Wal Square. Diet or no diet, Tuesdays were sacrosanct. Hannelore was nuts about their grilled sirloin, and it gave Van In a valid excuse to down a bottle of Medoc with impunity.

The small idyllic square, one of the most romantic locations in Bruges according to those in the know, was a hive of activity. Waiters in long aprons did their professional thing with flair, and the tourists nodded approvingly. Strangers are inclined to feel at home in Bruges. They're served hand and foot, and even when they're difficult, tireless waiters are ready to engage them in their native language. And if the occasional expletive slips out in the local dialect, the tourists just laugh along good-humoredly. A little local color is vital if you want to cultivate that sense of being abroad.

The terrace in front of the Heer Halewijn was packed. In contrast to the other bars and restaurants on the square, most of the customers had a Bruges accent and spoke the local dialect—no beer-swilling Germans, cackling French, English Chunnel trippers, loud Americans, or equally loud Hollanders hunting the smell of food. There was actually something Dantesque about the place. You could ascend from hell into heaven in a heartbeat.

The owner, Suzanne, came to welcome them personally. Van In had known the boss at the Heer Halewijn for years. She kissed him fleetingly on the cheek. There had been a time when she would have lingered. A card on their favorite table read RESERVED.

"I'm guessing an extra portion of pickles?" said Suzanne with a wink.

Hannelore nodded eagerly. Van In gallantly pulled back her chair. She sat and fixed her dress.

"You look like a girl of eighteen," said Suzanne.

"Don't overdo it, Sue."

"I'm not overdoing it." She meant it. Hannelore was truly breathtaking. Her dress concealed a body that Pythias would have killed for. Although Hannelore appeared to dismiss the compliment, she clearly wasn't indifferent to it.

"Come. Put your hand here. He's been kicking all day long."

Hannelore smoothed her dress as Suzanne leaned over and rested her hand on the elegant bulge.

"Unbelievable," said Suzanne.

Van In sat upright and pushed out his belly.

"And what about mine?"

Suzanne turned. You could see from the wrinkles in the corners of her eyes that she had a snappy remark at the ready.

"Eight months. Or am I mistaken?"

"But the poor soul is really doing his best," said Hannelore. "Before long he'll weigh less than me." It was impossible to tell from her tone whether she was jesting or not.

"In your case the extra pounds are only temporary, thank God. He's stuck with them for a good twenty years." Suzanne grinned.

Everyone on the terrace who had been listening to the conversation burst into laughter. Van In looked like a naughty puppy. Hannelore leaned forward, caressed his neck, and gave him a resounding kiss. Plenty of the men present would happily have cut off their little finger to be in his place.

Served on a plate to share, the grilled sirloin, a good twelve ounces and more than an inch thick, was warm, juicy, and tender. Van In put a generous amount of butter on his baked potato. He then washed it all down with a glass of 1989 Château Corconnac. Hannelore gobbled the gherkins and the salad drenched in vinaigrette. Only a tiny morsel of beef remained on the plate.

"So, any news from the front?" She pushed the plate in Van In's direction, and he didn't hesitate to accept her generous offer.

"Not much. Without Herbert's identity we're groping in the dark. But it became clear to me this morning that this world of ours is being overrun by little brats, and one of them goes by the name of Tine." Van In told her about his visit with the Vermast family.

"OK, then we can scratch the name from our list. If it's a girl, we'll call her Godelieve. Happy?"

Van In poured himself another glass of wine.

"Don't the experts say that children turn into their parents when they grow up?" Hannelore teased.

"If that's the case, then I hope she turns into you. Perish the thought that—"

"Don't go there, Pieter Van In. I was winding you up. You're certainly not the worst of them. The same experts insist with the same vigor that the fathers of most geniuses were over thirty at conception. If you don't believe me, check it out in the encyclopedia."

"I'm one step ahead of you," said Van In sullenly. "Herr Hitler wasn't the youngest either when little Adolf was born."

"Here we go." She sighed. "Time for a cigarette. At least then I'll be spared your grousing for ten minutes."

Van In lit up without missing a beat.

"Back to the question, Pieter: Is there any news about our skeleton?"

The "our" part gave her the creeps.

"I thought the public prosecutor's office was in charge of the case," Van In stalled.

Hannelore smiled engagingly as her foot shot forward. Van In was too slow to react.

"Ouch. Jesus." His hand disappeared under the table to sooth the afflicted shin, his face twisted with pain.

"Did it hurt?" She grinned.

Suzanne, who had watched it all happen, figured it was the ideal moment to serve her chocolate mousse.

Van In attacked the dessert without responding, only returning to the conversation after he had licked the last trace of chocolate mousse from his spoon. He told Hannelore what he'd discovered about Vermast's farm. Van In was a talented investigator who had solved more than a few sensational crimes in his day, most of the time by steering clear of orthodox procedures. According to his philosophy, every capitalist was a potential killer. Van In was at his best when he got the chance to pillory one or another respected citizen, but he sometimes forgot that conclusive evidence was necessary to nail a suspect. In modern crime prevention, intuition was about as worthless as ten million deutsch marks after the Second World War.

"Only an imbecile would sell property knowing there was a corpse under the grass. And Vandaele is no imbecile."

Hannelore pushed her chocolate mousse to one side. Van In glared at it with hungry eyes.

"Nothing's stopping me from having a serious chat with Mr. Vandaele, even if he has nothing to do with Herbert. Why the generous do-gooder? That's what I want to know," said Hannelore, consciously setting aside Belgian judicial process. "It's still a free country, eh, Pieter?" She treated herself to another tantalizing spoonful of chocolate mousse.

"OK, I get your point. But explain to me why Vandaele would outfit his property with an expensive remote control gate. The damn thing's worth more than the pigsty Vermast's trying to salvage."

"I don't understand where you see the connection between a gate and a murder." Hannelore pushed her plate to Van In's side of the table. "Help me finish?"

Van In dug in. Tuesday evenings only came once a week.

"I don't believe in coincidence, Hanne. I want to know why Vandaele handed over his farm in 1986 to an obscure charity."

Lodewijk Vandaele welcomed Yves Provoost, the lawyer, with a thin smile. Provoost looked exhausted. He hadn't slept for the best part of twenty-four hours.

"I'm not happy, Lodewijk. We should never have taken William Aerts into our confidence."

Vandaele puffed at his expensive cigar, his face devoid of emotion. His tiny, lusterless eyes blinked at regular intervals, but that had more to do with the smoke from his Davidoff than anything else. "Relax, Yves. Every problem has its solution."

Vandaele accompanied Provoost to the drawing room. Both men installed themselves by the window. It was still reasonably warm outside, but the ochre-yellow rays of the setting sun bore the full promise of fall.

"Aerts has disappeared, Lodewijk, and I want to know why."

Vandaele poured Provoost a drink and himself a fruit juice. One of them had to keep his cool.

"You know Aerts. He read the news in the paper and panicked. He's probably scared we'll want to punish him. He should never have buried the body on the farm. That wasn't the deal, and Aerts knows damn well that we paid him plenty for his services. Let's wait and see what happens," said Vandaele in an effort to reassure Provoost. "We need to stay calm. He'll be back, mark my words, and with his tail between his legs."

"Did you talk to Brys?" Provoost asked abruptly.

"Johan is in Burundi for the moment. I'll call him as soon as he gets back."

Provoost gulped unashamedly at his whiskey.

Vandaele sat down beside him and rested a paternal arm on his shoulder. "Why would Aerts kill the goose that lays the golden eggs? I practically *gave* him the Cleopatra. William Aerts makes a healthy enough living. He has no reason to betray us, none whatsoever."

Provoost felt the weight of Vandaele's arm on his shoulder. He knew all about Vandaele's generosity. Aerts had coughed up a paltry five million francs for the Cleopatra. The dilapidated villa on the Maalsesteenweg was a third-rate bar in those days, where retired whores from Brussels could enjoy a well-earned rest. The occasional traveling salesman frequented the place, usually frustrated, always convinced that a bottle of lukewarm bubbly was a ticket to paradise.

Aerts had done a professional job. He turned the place around, importing young agile girls: mulattas, Filipinas, Polish blondes, Thai masseuses. In less than six months, he had the cream of Bruges and its immediate vicinity banging on his door.

"What if the police identify the skeleton and connect it with Aerts? It doesn't bear thinking about. The bastard will turn us in without a second thought, rest assured."

Vandaele stubbed out his expensive cigar. "You mean Aerts will turn *you* in," he said. "After all, you're responsible for—"

"Counselor, how dare you?" Provoost was clearly on the edge. His bulbous lips filled with blood.

"Easy does it, Yves. Trust me, it'll never get that far. We'll solve this problem together. Have I ever let you down?"

It was a bizarre conversation. Provoost was known for having the gift of gab. In court he was a superior orator, a man feared for his caustic rejoinders. At least that was what people said. Face-to-face with Vandaele he was like a schoolboy who didn't dare speak to his teacher.

Vandaele knew his pupil. He stroked Provoost's head. "My dearest Yves, the chances that the police will draw a link between Aerts and the murder are exceptionally small. It's all so long ago, remember. Aerts is nowhere to be found. And anyway, who's going to believe him if he starts shooting his mouth off? It would be your word against that of a pimp. This is Belgium, Yves. No one gets convicted in this country unless guilt is established beyond dispute. You should know that. And don't forget, you enjoy the protection of the minister of foreign affairs."

Vandaele's words appeared to do the trick. Provoost calmed down and emptied his glass in a single gulp. The alcohol dissolved the anxiety in his eyes. Vandaele poured him another glass and included himself this time around.

"You're probably right, Lodewijk," said Provoost. He sounded determined. Whiskey always made him overconfident. "I've cleared dozens of criminals in my time, most of them a lot more miserable than me."

Vandaele was happy that the whiskey was having the desired

effect. "That's the spirit, boy." He slipped another Davidoff from its silver sheath. Smoking wasn't allowed, not since the legion of black cancer cells had invaded his lungs and were now readying themselves to annex the rest of his body. His death was in clear sight, but his good name had to continue, and no stupid murder could be allowed to change that. They would name streets after him. Lodewijk Vandaele hoped that young people would remember him as the man who purified his country of foreign decadence.

"But Aerts still bothers me," said Provoost after a long silence. "Turning stool pigeon is fashionable these days. No one is likely to feel any sympathy for a lawyer on the witness stand. The plebs would have a field day, and the gutter press would call for my head on a plate. Aerts is a cunning little bastard—we both know that. He's always been unpredictable."

Vandaele suppressed the desire to clear his throat, lit his cigar instead, and took a puff. "Don't let that worry you, Yves. I promise you one thing: Aerts will be taken care of."

Provoost leered at the bottle of whiskey on the coffee table. *One more*, he thought. Then he could sleep.

4

Only a handful of passengers checked in for the scheduled flight to Rome, but that didn't mean Brussels National Airport was quiet. The charter flights to the Canary Islands attracted their usual stampede. Pretanned retirees dragged overfilled baggage to their assigned departure desks. These days, sun and sea was available on prescription. There was nothing more inspiring than the thought of succumbing to a heart attack on a subtropical beach.

William Aerts passed though passport control without a hitch. He looked like the average businessman: casual suit, lightweight Delsey carry-on, and a copy of the *Financial Times* under his arm.

Aerts had been looking forward to this moment for more than fifteen years. He had finally found the excuse he needed to flee the shit-heap country that sired him. No more Linda . . . whining fucking hippo. And the pedophile? No more humiliation . . . the fucker couldn't touch him anymore. Today he was a free man. The timing wasn't perfect, but what the fuck. Real men follow the path chosen for them by fate.

The thrust of four screaming jet engines pushed him back into the soft upholstery of his ample seat. A minute later he was in the clouds. Rain had been forecast, and the Belgians were welcome to it, every last one of them.

"Would you like something to drink, sir?" A freshly scented flight attendant leaned toward him. *This was the life,* he thought. He was flying first class and was sharing the compartment with no more than six other passengers.

"Campari, please."

Aerts stretched out his legs. He had dreamed of this sort of luxury all his life and had paid a pretty penny for the extra space. After three decades he had finally managed to defeat his adversaries. He was on his way south, and his erstwhile buddies were up to their ears in shit.

"Your Campari, sir."

The flight attendant smiled affably, or so it appeared. Or was she smiling because she thought he was stinking rich?

Aerts sipped at his aperitif and closed his eyes in contentment. The corpse had earned him more than he could ever have imagined.

"Mr. Vandaele can see you in a few moments, Commissioner Van In."

Vandaele had retired, officially, but he still spent the best part of his day at the office. The old bugger liked to keep a firm eye on things.

The secretary accompanied Van In to a small waiting room looking out onto an empty concrete courtyard, the company's trademark. Yellowing photos graced the walls, probably the work of an overzealous office clerk. The pictures portrayed bridges and roads, with men dressed in black in the foreground, one of them invariably cutting a ribbon.

Louis Vandaele, Lodewijk's father, had earned a fortune in his day from public contracts. In the 1960s, he had blacktopped half of Flanders' roads.

Van In thanked the bespectacled secretary with a smile.

"Coffee, Commissioner?" the gray-suited creature inquired.

"No, thank you."

She was the image of Audrey Hepburn, just like Benedict Vervoort's assistant.

"I demand to speak to the manager this instant," Linda Aerts snorted.

Marc, the counter clerk, tried to calm her down. There were three other clients behind her. One of them was Mr. Ostijn, and Mr. Ostijn wasn't fond of disturbances. Hilaire Ostijn was the chairman of the local businessman's association and one of the branch's best clients.

"No need to get upset, Mrs. Aerts. Mr. Albert will be here in five minutes. I'm sure he'll agree that there must have been some mistake."

"If you give me ten thousand francs, you can tell Mr. Albert to stay where he is," Linda roared.

The counter clerk looked back and forth between Mrs. Aerts's red face and Mr. Ostijn's tight lips. In the past he could have solved the problem without thinking. He would simply have handed over the ten thousand francs. But minor counter clerks didn't have that kind of authority anymore. No numbers, no cash. The new rules were set in stone.

"Are you going to get a move on, or do I have time to tell everyone how I came to know Mr. Albert in the first place?" asked Linda as she turned to the customers behind her ready for a fight. Ostijn pretended not to recognize her. The bank clerk, on the other hand, knew that both his boss and Ostijn frequented the Cleopatra. He grabbed the money from the drawer and typed the amount into his computer. At that moment the door flew open. The speed with which Albert Denolf responded to the situation was nothing short of astonishing. He knew why Linda was here, and he knew her temperament.

"Mrs. Aerts," he said, his voice dripping with sweetness. "What a delight to see you. No problems, I hope?"

Marc returned the money to his drawer and canceled the withdrawal, much relieved.

"No problems?" she jeered. "Where do I start?"

"Linda," Denolf interrupted. "If there are problems, we can talk about them in the quiet of my office."

His compliant approach worked. Linda suspended hostilities, turned with a flounce, and followed Denolf into his office.

• • •

Ostijn had come to redeem some bonds, collect his daily statements, and pay a pile of bills. The wealthy businessman was old school to the core. Internet banking wasn't at all his thing. Marc sighed inaudibly. Ostijn's transactions were likely to take at least fifteen minutes of his time. But their routine exchange was suddenly interrupted by a crash of glass. Ostijn reacted like every right-minded capitalist would: he first slipped his bonds across the counter and only then looked around to see what was happening.

"But, Linda, for goodness' sake," he heard Denolf lament with a suppressed roar. The door to Denolf's office flew open, and the shards of glass from the smashed ashtray crunched under Linda's heels.

"That was *our* money!" she screamed.

Denolf was rooted to the spot.

"And you gave him the whole thing without batting an eyelid."

"The money was in *his* name, Linda. I tried to make him change his mind, but this is a bank, and my hands were tied—"

"So your hands were tied," Linda screeched. "You fucking asshole. Do you know what would cheer me up right this minute?"

Everyone, including Ostijn, listened with bated breath.

"The sight of that Catholic wife of yours' face when I tell the bitch what her respected husband gets up to every month."

"Linda, please." Denolf hurled himself at the door, most

likely breaking the world indoor triple-jump record in the process. He slammed it shut and pulled out his wallet.

"Here . . . ten thousand. William will be back in a few days, I'm sure of it. Then we can look for a solution."

"Make it twenty," Linda ventured.

Denolf sucked in so much air in the following few seconds that he was on the verge of hyperventilating.

"William might have stolen our money, but the videos are still in our safe," she bragged. "Try to picture the malicious delight on the faces of the police as they watch them, Albert," she blurted out, adding insult to injury.

Denolf had fallen victim to a nightmare in broad daylight. He gestured that she should wait, grabbed the phone, and called Marc.

"Give Mrs. Aerts twenty thousand francs from my account on her way out."

"Tell him to bring it," Linda snarled.

Denolf nodded like the perfect slave. It always worked, with or without the leather outfit.

"Leave it, Marc. I'll collect it myself."

Lodewijk Vandaele welcomed Van In with a jovial handshake. He pointed to the cozy lounge suite close to the window. In contrast to the waiting area, Van In's new surroundings boasted a magnificent view and a carefully maintained rock garden with a splashing fountain in the middle. Every self-respecting human being had one.

"A drink, Commissioner?"

Van In was tempted but said no. It would be a sign of Roman Catholic hypocrisy if he were to turn a serious sin into a daily one.

"Be a sport, Commissioner. A wee dram never killed anyone."

Van In was still tempted but shook his head.

"Coffee then?"

"Please."

Vandaele rested his fat cigar in the ashtray and ordered coffee via the intercom.

"I should make it clear from the outset that my visit is off the record," said Van In in a formal tone.

"Take a seat, Commissioner."

Van In sat down in an imposing chair that almost swallowed him up completely. Vandaele sat opposite, the hefty old man towering over Van In like a golem.

"I presume your visit has to do with the discovery at the farm, Commissioner, at the Love?" He anticipated a potential question from Van In with the air of a modern-day Nostradamus.

Jesus H. Christ, Van In thought. Vandaele had even given the dilapidated hovel a name. He was reminded of his youth, playing on the beach at Blankenberge with his sister and the local grocer's daughter. The city's peeling villas also rejoiced in pompous names like Camelot, Beau Geste, and Manderley. A fancy name was cheaper than a lick of paint.

"Precisely, Mr. Vandaele. According to the police physician, the murder was committed around the time you owned it. The

72

Love . . ."—Van In had trouble even pronouncing the ridiculous name—"was still in your ownership back then, wasn't it?"

Vandaele stretched his left leg and massaged his knee.

"Rheumatism," he groaned. "My knees have been bothering me for years."

The old fox was clearly stalling for time by trying to change the subject, but Van In was onto him.

"Do you mind me asking if you visited the place on a regular basis?" Van In inquired casually.

"Aha, Commissioner. My father built the Love with his own hands. I spent most of my summers playing there. Later I liked to paint there from time to time. The house was something of a childhood memory."

"Did you ever rent out the place?"

Vandaele roared with laughter.

"My dear commissioner, I own a slew of houses, villas, and apartments, and I rent them out. The Love is nothing more than a bit of nostalgia. It was our first holiday home, but as far as I can remember, the shed has always been dilapidated. People expect comfort these days, Commissioner. No one would pay rent for such a dump."

Van In was happy that they at least agreed on one issue. It also explained why Vandaele had transferred the Love to the charity. Everyone knows that rich people only give away the things that have no value to them or the things they themselves can no longer use.

"So the Love has been empty all this time?"

Vandaele puffed vigorously on his cigar. A discreet pale-faced young man appeared with a tray.

"Leave it on the desk, Vincent. We'll serve ourselves."

Vandaele got to his feet, creaking and grousing. In profile he looked a little like President de Gaulle—commanding and unapproachable.

"I used to bring a couple of cousins now and then," he said cheerfully. "Children love old houses, especially when they can do whatever they want. We even stayed the night at times. Then we would light an enormous campfire. Not allowed these days, but back then no one cared. We drank gallons of cola, sang songs, pretended we were actors in a play. I can remember the summer of 1972 as if it were yesterday. It was so hot we all slept outside. I don't see myself doing that nowadays either," said Vandaele, pointing to his knees.

Van In also had some treasured memories of the same hot summer. August 20, 1972, was the first time he slept with a girl.

"Later, when one of my cousins was a leader with the Scouts, the Love served as a campsite for a number of youth associations."

Vandaele poured the coffees. "Sugar?"

Van In shook his head.

"So no one ever lived in the place," he insisted.

"Correct, Commissioner. Several years ago I handed it over to a charitable organization. The youth groups weren't interested anymore. They only set up camp if there are showers and microwaves nearby."

Vandaele laughed. "Young people these days are too demanding. Romance is dead, Commissioner. The only thing that still interests them is starting a career and making money, and preferably sooner than later."

Van In didn't think Vandaele was the man to be making such observations, but he nodded nonetheless and sipped his coffee.

"I know a thing or two about that myself, Mr. Vandaele," he said diplomatically. "It all has to be fast and automatic. Imagine the panic if we were to ban remote controls starting tomorrow."

Vandaele nodded his head to every word. He put his cup on a side table and said: "We would be totally helpless, Commissioner. Most people would be up in arms, call a technician, insist they come and fix what they presumed to be broken."

Van In played along, making a clumsy attempt to imitate the gloating building contractor. Was it too obvious, or did Vandaele realize that he had walked into Van In's trap like an inexperienced cub?

"Of course, we shouldn't blame the youth of today for all the sins of humanity," said Van In in an unexpectedly serious tone.

"Go on, Commissioner. Luxury can be an addiction, even for us grown-ups. Those gadgets can come in mighty handy at times," said Vandaele, ostentatiously massaging his stiff knees. "I'm not averse to a bit of modern technology now and again, Commissioner, and I'm not ashamed to admit it. The garage door at home is fitted with a remote. It saves me the hassle and pain of getting in and out of the car. It's easy to get used to such comforts, then—"

"Do you have remotes installed everywhere, Mr. Vandaele?"

The elderly contractor's signature jovial grin seemed to freeze for an instant. He sipped at his coffee, pretended it had gone down the wrong way, and feigned a coughing fit. The theatricals gave him a few seconds' respite.

"I presume you're referring to the gate at the Love, Commissioner."

Van In nodded.

"That wasn't a question of laziness *or* of stiff knees," said Vandaele. He tried to sound dramatic. "The installation of the electric gate was a direct consequence of the bend in the road."

Van In listened to his story. The entrance to the Love was immediately behind a sharp bend, and there had been an accident in 1979 in which someone had almost died. A motorcyclist had crashed into Vandaele's parked car while he was opening the gate. The road was narrow, and Vandaele's Mercedes took up most of it. The victim had survived the crash, but Vandaele had sworn it would never happen again.

"That's why I had a remote installed on the spot," Vandaele concluded his story. "Prevention is still better than a cure, eh, Commissioner?"

Vandaele's account was plausible, and Van In thought it a shame. He would have Baert check it out. Anything to keep the irritating chief inspector busy and out of his hair.

"It's probably a redundant question, Mr. Vandaele, but my job requires me to ask it."

The old man puffed long and hard at his half-smoked Davidoff. He was happy that Van In didn't want to press him on the gate story. "Please, Commissioner, feel free."

"Has anyone ever drawn your attention to digging going on at your property?"

Vandaele had been expecting a totally different question. "No, Commissioner, absolutely not."

"And you've never found traces of an attempted break-in?"

Vandaele shook his head. He didn't even have to lie. "As I said, Commissioner, I was only there on the rare occasion. I suspect whoever buried the body was aware of that."

"I think so too," said Van In. "There are plenty of similar cases in the police literature. Perpetrators usually pick remote places to dump their victims, but such places are pretty few and far between in Flanders. That allows us to conclude, give or take, that the killer was familiar with the area in general and with your property in particular."

"Sounds like a plausible hypothesis, Commissioner. I wish there was some other way that I could be of assistance."

Van In finished his coffee and got to his feet. Now he was looking down on Vandaele for once.

"Don't worry, Mr. Vandaele," he said with a smile. "You've helped me a great deal."

It was an old trick he had learned at the police academy. Always give the impression you know more than the person you're interrogating thinks you know. Doubt is a seed that can germinate in no time at all, urging suspects to be rash. "I'll keep you up-to-date on the evolution of the case," Van In promised.

"I'll be waiting with bated breath, Commissioner."

The old man struggled to his feet and accompanied Van In to the door. He seemed a lot less self-assured than he had an hour earlier. Or was Van In imagining things?

Most tourist guides advise unwary visitors not to wander around alone when they're in Naples. William Aerts heeded it and took a taxi to the port. The wallet in his trouser pocket was stuffed with fifty one-hundred-dollar bills and four million lire in large denominations. In spite of the unbearable heat, he had kept his hand in his pocket for the entire length of the train journey from Rome to Naples. This was Mafia territory, where throats were cut for a fraction of the amount he was carrying.

Once an exotic destination, the Bay of Naples now looked like the gray armpit of a dying organism called a city. A crazily honking taxi driver piloted Aerts through the chaos with genuine disregard for his own safety. He paid no attention to the traffic lights, carving his way through the congested streets with a curse for every obstacle. The fact that he managed to deliver his client safely to his destination was nothing short of a miracle.

Ports always stink, but the more acceptable smell of fuel and tar was nothing compared to the stench of rotting fish and urine Naples had to offer. Aerts took the inconvenience in stride. If everything went according to plan, he would be onboard within the hour.

The ferry to Palermo was packed. Aerts had to settle for a place on the forward deck out of the shade. He didn't give a damn. He'd have traveled in a coffin if he'd had to.

"Adieu, Linda; adieu, bastards," he said under his breath as the grinding engines churned the grimy water. Half an hour later, the wind massaged his sweating face. The distant horizon beckoned. A boyhood dream was about to be fulfilled.

Lodewijk Vandaele left his office five minutes after Van In's visit.

"I'll be away for the rest of the afternoon."

His secretary fetched his straw hat and cane.

"Fine, Mr. Vandaele. See you tomorrow."

"See you tomorrow, Liesbeth."

Liesbeth held open the door for him and then returned to her duties.

Vandaele was in the habit of lunching in an exclusive restaurant on the outskirts of the city, but today he drove straight to his villa on the Damme Canal. The conversation with Van In still bugged him—not so much the content but the subtle way the commissioner had introduced the question of the gate. The man was dangerous, and something had to be done about it.

Vandaele grabbed a bottle of Exshaw from the liquor cabinet in the lounge and poured himself a generous glass of the twenty-year-old cognac. He then consulted his diary and punched in the number of the ministry of foreign affairs.

Johan Brys was at his desk when the phone rang. The minister had landed at the airport in Zaventem only an hour earlier. His working visit to Rwanda had yielded precious little. The country was a mess, and the hundred million francs in emergency relief he had promised to his Rwandan colleague—a substantial sum in those days—wasn't likely to make much of a difference. If they wanted to bring those guilty of genocide to justice, the country's legal apparatus had to get back on its feet, and that was going to cost a great deal more than a hundred million. It was also by no means certain that Rwanda would ever see the promised support. Brys wasn't really interested. The TV news appearance later that evening, in which he was to announce that the Belgian government (i.e., himself) was intent on doing whatever it took to help the Rwandan judiciary trace and try those responsible for mass murder, was more important for his career. Parliamentary elections were only a couple of months away, and the more he appeared on TV the more likely he was to score.

"I have a Mr. Lodewijk Vandaele on line one, Minister. He says it's urgent," his secretary announced apologetically.

"No problem, Sonja. I know Mr. Vandaele," said Brys. "Put him through."

"Hello, Counselor Lodewijk."

"Hello, Johan. How was Burundi?"

"Rwanda," Brys corrected him gingerly.

"Rwanda, Burundi. What difference does it make?" Vandaele laughed.

He took a sip from his glass. The fact that he could get through to the minister of foreign affairs without the least resistance had a relaxing effect.

Van In arrived in Room 204 at two thirty to find Dirk Baert busy on the phone.

"Still no results?" he asked with more than a hint of condescension when Baert hung up.

"I've covered Bruges and the surrounding area. There isn't a single dentist who remembers a patient with twenty-four false teeth, so now I'm focusing on hospitals and orthodontists."

"Reasons to be cheerful?"

"Negative, Commissioner. What about you?"

Van In turned away, irked by the question. *Nosey bastard*, he thought.

"Is Versavel back?"

"No, Commissioner. He left around eleven. He should have been back by now."

"Let me be the judge of that, Chief Inspector."

Baert pressed his fingernails into the palm of his hand. Why did no one like him? He grabbed the telephone book and checked off the next number. When Van In realized he was about to continue his odyssey, he stopped him, sensing a handy opportunity to get the nuisance out of his hair for a while.

"I'd like you to check the records for me, Baert. Vandaele claims there was an accident back in the summer of 1978. He's not sure of the exact date, but he remembers a motorcyclist driving into his parked car. Find out if he's telling the truth."

Baert slammed the telephone book shut and left the room.

With the chief inspector gone, Van In planted himself in front of Versavel's old-fashioned Brother typewriter. There was paperwork to be done, and someone had to do it.

Sergeant Versavel arrived at three forty-five. "Now that's a sight for sore eyes," he said, chuckling at the sight of his boss sweating over the keyboard.

Van In stopped halfway through a sentence full of typos. "Finally," he jeered. "Looks like Mr. Versavel's been having a good time. Was Jonathan worth the visit?"

"Un-be-liev-able," said Versavel, parking himself on the edge of the typewriter desk and still clearly radiant from the encounter. "He treated me to lunch at the Karmeliet. Jonathan is a connoisseur, always has been. We started with roast breast of duck on a bed of raspberry preserve with lukewarm artichoke mousse, then moved on to monkfish tartlets with stuffed endive and trout roe, followed by rack of lamb with—"

"I got coffee," Van In interrupted with a glower.

"And Mouton Rothschild," Versavel continued unperturbed. "1984, no less. I'm a mere mortal. How could I refuse?"

"Good thing Frank isn't hearing this," said Van In.

Versavel shrugged his shoulders.

"Frank knows I had a relationship with Jonathan. That's

the difference with you straight guys. Men like us don't sweat past affairs. A friend is a friend. Frank and I aren't jealous types."

The Mouton Rothschild hadn't done Versavel any favors. The sergeant was acting like an aging hippy on his way down from an LSD trip.

"Did Jonathan have anything interesting to say?" Van In asked.

Versavel ignored his boss's sarcasm. In his head he was still in the Karmeliet, face-to-face with Jonathan.

Van In hadn't had a smoke for a full three hours. He rummaged for his cigarettes convinced that this was an emergency. What else do you do when you're forced to listen to a gay man on the wrong side of fifty waxing lyrical about an old flame?

"Surely you don't think I'm drunk, Commissioner?" Versavel inquired, looking his boss up and down with a boyish grin.

"Get to the point, Guido. You can siesta when you're done."

Versavel grabbed a chair, the smile frozen on his lips.

"According to Jonathan, the Love, which is what he called the place, functioned as a whorehouse for the wealthy and influential, although it still looked like a dump from the outside." Versavel pronounced the name of the place with an American accent, stretching the *o*.

"Names, Guido?"

"He couldn't help."

"How did he know they were influential?"

"He just figured."

"I see, he just figured."

Versavel twigged to his boss's cynicism. Visiting whores wasn't a crime.

"Jonathan accompanied Vandaele a couple of times to a brothel on the main road to Male, and the Love cropped up in the conversation. The guy operating the place, a certain William Aerts, confessed that he was expected to bring the better clients and the more exceptional girls to the farm, where they could do their thing without onlookers."

"So if I'm understanding this right, Vandaele placed the Love at the disposal of his business partners," said Van In, clearly disappointed. He hesitated at the long *o* and what came out sounded like *Loaf.*

"Try pronouncing it *Luuv*, with a double *u*," said Versavel.

"*Luuv*." Van In did his best. "Any better?"

"Not bad," said the slightly tipsy sergeant. "But *Loaf* isn't bad either. Plenty of bread changing hands. You know how it works, Pieter."

Van In shook his head in confusion. "Time for coffee if you ask me," he said, crossing to the window and filling a jug with water. A woozy sergeant was about as useful as a priest at a freemason's deathbed.

Van In was now up to more than half a pack a day after twelve weeks on a more restricted cigarette diet. Hannelore let him get on with it. She treated herself to an extra glass of Moselle and silently resisted the intense desire to light up and join him. They had both had a difficult day.

Van In stubbed out a half-smoked cigarette in the ashtray. The sight of the still smoldering butt almost drove Hannelore crazy.

"Something up?" he asked routinely.

"No. What about Herbert?"

Van In didn't have much of a grasp of the female psyche, but he wasn't an idiot. Her eyes moistened as if she was about to burst into tears. "Shall I heat up a can of sauerkraut?" he suggested obligingly. He could be sweet at times. "A portion of fries?"

Hannelore's hand glided across the table. "I want a cigarette," she said, clearly determined.

Van In tried to grab the pack, but she beat him to it.

"You can't be serious, Hanne."

Her eyes blazed as she filled her lungs with smoke. "Just one," she pleaded.

"I thought we'd agreed you'd stop," he erupted. "In exchange I agreed to follow a strict diet. I've been keeping my side of the bargain: ten cigarettes a day, salad, tasteless fish, and high-fiber bread full of sawdust."

Hannelore puffed at her cigarette like a woman possessed as the color bled from her face. "You've smoked half a pack since you got home," she protested. "I've been counting."

Van In tried to control himself. He asked himself if he would be capable of stopping altogether.

"OK, one cigarette. But for the love of God . . ."

"For the love of who? Does the commissioner think he's the only one dealing with stress? Try spending a day at court!"

"Hanne, tell me what's the matter, please."

Hannelore got to her feet, something she always did when her emotions got the better of her. "I'll tell you what's the matter. You grouch half the evening and puff away to your heart's content, and you dare accuse me of not keeping my part of the bargain!"

Van In hadn't been silenced like that for a very long time. He immediately recognized the old enemy. Irrationality left him powerless. He felt like he was being choked and the rage built up in his gullet as he was confronted with a past he thought was dead and buried. He jumped to his feet and stormed into the kitchen, his jaws locked tight. There was still half a bottle of scotch in the fridge.

Hannelore took a final puff. Her head was spinning. She looked up at the stars, heaved a sigh, and flicked the butt between the roses. The refrigerator door closed with a gentle thud.

"Go on, get soaked. I'm going to bed!" she yelled as she marched through the kitchen.

Van In took a swig at the bottle of J&B. The whiskey burned in his stomach. He listened as she climbed the stairs in tears, and felt lonelier at that moment than Robinson Crusoe.

The crossing by catamaran from Syracuse to Malta was uneventful. The sea was smooth as a baby's bottom and the futuristic boat glided across the water like a spaceship. The hundreds of tourists onboard had enjoyed their trip to Sicily. No one paid the least attention to the oddity on the afterdeck staring at the vessel's wake.

Aerts had paid the second officer five hundred dollars to allow him to travel incognito and not include his name on the passenger list. The foam-crested waves would soon erase his final traces forever, freeing him to start his new life. Amand had arranged everything to perfection. They could search the entire planet, but they would never find him.

"Sorry, sweetheart. Forgive me. I take the blame, all of it."

Van In placed the bottle of Moselle on the nightstand and offered Hannelore a cigarette.

"Take another. I had no idea that it was causing you so much pain."

She was lying on the bed and seemed fragile, vulnerable.

"Never mind, Pieter. I'm beginning to feel better."

Van In got to his knees and held her in his arms. The tears returned.

"I had an appointment with the gynecologist earlier."

Van In suddenly felt as if a hundred spiders were crawling up his back.

"I knew there was something," he said, sounding awkward. Men are often left speechless in such situations. "Does it hurt?" he asked after a few moments of silence.

She dabbed her eyes with a paper tissue. "I'm worried about the baby. I've asked for an amniocentesis."

"An amniocentesis! But why the worry? You're always so confident."

Hannelore ran her fingers through her hair. She wanted to be sure he didn't feel guilty, whatever the cost.

"I want to be sure, Pieter. I'm thirty-six, for Christ's sake."

Van In poured himself a glass of wine. He was forty-three. His lungs were full of tar, and his blood only kept flowing because he thinned it every day with alcohol.

"Another sip?" He held out his glass. "A drop of wine won't do him any harm."

She wasn't interested.

"The boy has alcohol in his genes," said Van In. "Believe me, on that score I'm the dominant one."

Van In could be incredibly illogical at times. Hannelore didn't understand why she followed his argument and accepted the glass. An unpleasant silence filled the air, leaving time enough for Van In's head to fill with apocalyptic images of hideously deformed babies.

"What do we do if . . . I mean . . . Suppose . . ." he stammered.

The mental specter with which Van In was now struggling had been chasing Hannelore for days. "I wasn't planning to tell you this evening. Maybe I should have waited . . . To tell you the truth, Pieter, I don't know what to think. Everyone's talking about heredity these days and genetic research. The papers are full of it. And you're right. I used to laugh about it in the past, but yesterday my sense of security collapsed like a house of cards. Now I need to know if everything's OK."

Was this a moment for a man to put on a brave face, or was he allowed to show his emotions? Van In had no idea. The answer was probably in a book somewhere, a book he hadn't read.

"This is your last warning," Leen Vermast roared. "It's eleven o'clock. Get to bed and go to sleep this instant, both of you."

Tine heard her mother thunder up the stairs a few moments later and quickly stuffed her discovery under her pillow. Joris was sitting on the bed cross-legged. He stared at his sister in desperation but didn't budge an inch when his mother barged into the room. Leen felt sorry for him. She tucked him in and gave him a kiss. Then she turned to her daughter.

"If I hear another sound, you're grounded."

Tine bowed her head, chastened. She was planning to go riding the next day with her friends. Mommy didn't have the right to steal her fun.

Leen switched off the light. She took off her dress on her way downstairs and appeared in the living room topless. Hugo had only forfeited two items of clothing. Jef was in his socks, and Annelies was fully dressed. How come she always lost when Jef and Annelies stopped by for a game of strip poker?

5

A couple of miles outside Victoria, the island of Gozo's largest city, Amand Dekeyzer ran the only three-star restaurant on the Maltese archipelago. Originally from Knokke on the Belgian coast, Amand had discovered a gap in the Maltese market and had exploited it for the best part of twenty years. While the local islanders bent over backward to give the tourists what they wanted, their culinary skills tended to fall short on a variety of levels. Was the lack of gastronomic inventiveness a result of British influence on their eating habits, or was the island's overwhelming dryness to blame? In ancient times they called the place "the land of honey," but that didn't square with present-day reality.

Whatever the explanation may have been, Amand realized that the customary combination of plum pudding, pizza, and couscous was open to improvement. He started small, importing produce from Flanders, and after five years he was proud to call himself the owner of a popular restaurant cum nightclub.

William Aerts arrived in the late afternoon. Amand was taking a breather on the blustery terrace in front of the restaurant. He recognized his old friend immediately.

"William!" he shouted enthusiastically. "I didn't expect you so early."

They shook hands long and heartily. Amand snapped his fingers and ordered pilsners—Belgian, of course—and snacks.

"Finally," said Aerts. "From this day forth, Belgium can go screw itself."

"Fantastic, William. Now that calls for a celebration."

Versavel sailed into Room 204 like a well-rigged packet boat— stately and majestic. He was wearing a trendy suit, a bronze-green shirt, a black tie, and a celestial smile.

"You're late," Van In grunted.

Versavel took off his jacket, tossed it with a flourish over the back of a chair, walked to the window, and took a deep breath.

"It's nine fifteen, Guido. Don't tell me your head's still full of Mouton Rothschild. I'm the one who gets to be late around here, remember."

Versavel stretched his neck and shoulders and swiveled on his axis like a Russian ballet dancer. *Mais où sont les neiges d'antan, mon ami?*

"Jesus H. Christ, Guido. Which do you prefer—a psychiatrist or a straitjacket?"

Versavel wasn't intimidated. He recited a couple of strophes from François Villon's ballad and then flopped into a chair. "Problems, Commissioner?"

"Spare me the funnies, Guido. I'm not in the mood. If you keep this up, half the office will be at the door trying to catch a front-row seat. What kind of demon's gotten into you? You look like an ageing crooner, and you're acting like a third-rate clown."

"Is that a pleonasm or a tautology, Commissioner?"

Van In got up from his chair, marched across the office, and stopped in front of Versavel's desk, legs apart. "Dearest Guido, would you mind telling me what the fuck is going on?"

"Good news, Pieter. Nothing but good news. Jonathan called me yesterday. He's coming over for dinner tonight, and Frank has promised to make my favorite guinea fowl recipe with gooseberries."

Van In rolled his eyes upward. He had plenty of experience when it came to relationships with the opposite sex, of course, but he had learned by trial and error over the last twenty-five years that there were some things a woman wasn't likely to accept—like inviting your mistress for dinner and asking your wife to cook.

"And Frank's happy to oblige?"

"Frank thinks the world of Jonathan."

Versavel leaned back in his chair, stretching and yawning at once. His eyes glistened like polished jet.

Dirk Baert knocked first before coming in, proof that he had been eavesdropping.

"Good morning, Commissioner."

"Good morning, Chief Inspector."

Baert greeted Versavel with an almost imperceptible nod of the head. The sergeant didn't bother responding.

Van In returned to his desk, grabbed some paper from the drawer, and started to scribble furiously, a trick he usually reserved for unexpected visits from the big boss. Most of the police reports Van In was working on were years old. Versavel frowned, not quite sure why Van In would put on such a performance for a subordinate like Dirk Baert.

"So what's the story, Baert?" said Van In.

Baert was still standing at attention.

"Jeez . . . take a seat, man."

Baert crumpled like a puppet cut free from its strings. "I'd like to report back on the accident outside the Bremwegel in 1979," said Baert in a formal tone.

"The Bremwegel, Baert?"

"Lodewijk Vandaele's country residence," the chief inspector obliged, nodding. "You asked me to check if a report had been filed in 1979 on an accident involving Lodewijk Vandaele and an unidentified motorcyclist." Dirk Baert spoke the same way he wrote his police reports: in serious officialese.

Versavel mimicked his boss by grabbing a sheet of paper and scribbling a few notes. Van In pretended he wasn't listening to Baert and concentrated on a yellowed police report from the impressive pile on his desk. Versavel's penny dropped. Any normal person would ask to be transferred to a different department after a week of Van In's games. He hoped Dirk Baert was a normal person.

"And the rest, Chief Inspector?" said Van In, irked.

Baert gulped, his bouncing Adam's apple clearly betraying his mood. "Mr. Vandaele reported the incident in person. The motorcyclist, a certain John Catrysse, suffered a concussion. The entire business was settled out of court. Vandaele took care of the costs."

"Address?" asked Van In dryly.

Baert was taken aback. "Bremwegel 38, Commissioner."

Van In made a face that would have been enough to make a bored MP jealous. "Catrysse's address, Chief Inspector."

Baert flushed hot and cold in rapid succession. "I'll have to check, Commissioner. I thought—"

"Leave the thinking to us, Baert."

Versavel coughed conspicuously. Baert swallowed his indignation and beat a wounded retreat.

"That's him sorted." Van In grinned as he returned the pile of reports to the drawer.

"So Vandaele was telling the truth," said Versavel. "What do we do now?"

"I trust Dirk Baert as far as I can spit," Van In grunted. "Ferret that address out for me, would you? Catrysse's address."

Versavel stared at his boss in surprise. Baert might have been incompetent, but he wasn't a fool.

"And I want to know how much Vandaele paid him. According to the letter of the law, he was in the right. Catrysse crashed into a parked vehicle. His insurance should have covered any damage to the Mercedes, in principle at least."

Versavel nodded. Van In's explanation added logic to his request.

Van In ran through the few details they had at their disposal. According to Jonathan, the Love functioned as a love nest for Vandaele's business associates. His contact was a certain William Aerts, proprietor of a renovated café on the road to Male. Herbert was buried on the grounds of the Love in the mid-1980s, and in 1986 Vandaele handed the farm over to an obscure charity. Van In scribbled a short note to himself: *Did Vandaele close down the brothel or relocate it?*

"I think we should have a word with Mr. Aerts. Perhaps he can tell us who used to hang out at the Love."

Bruges' courthouse has to be the most modern in Belgium—it's the only one to have its own bar. In contrast to the usual gravity that tends to prevail in such places, the atmosphere in Bruges is relaxed most of the time and even prone to merriment on occasion. Today happened to be one of those high-spirited days. More than fifty cheerful lawyers had assembled to celebrate the opening of the new judicial year. The beer flowed, and the anecdotes became more suggestive by the hour. Hannelore was welcomed with a resounding cheer and inundated with compliments. She shook them off like a pet rabbit scuttling into the living room after a rain shower. She ordered a cup of tea and installed herself on the outside terrace, another feature of the building, which offered a romantic view of the city's windmills. The warmth of the autumn sun felt good. She stretched out her legs and closed her eyes for a moment or two.

No one was paying attention to Leo Vanmaele, who joined her on the terrace a few minutes later. This was his first time in the holy of holies. Lesser staff members weren't normally allowed in the bar. With the exception of the odd court clerk, the place was restricted to lawyers and magistrates.

"Shall I get you a drink?" she asked when Leo took a seat beside her.

"No thanks, Hanne."

"It's no trouble."

Leo shook his head.

"You're probably wondering why I asked to meet you here of all places," she said.

Leo had indeed asked himself that question.

"Because it's safe. De Jaegher never sets foot in the place—"

"And you've been planning a clandestine meeting here with an unknown admirer for quite some time," Leo jested.

"How did you guess?"

"Don't the rumors scare you?" Leo inquired, gesturing toward the boisterous assembly of legal eagles in the bar.

"They think you're a young intern," Hannelore sniggered. "Every September the place is crawling with them."

"I'm forty-seven, Hanne."

"I know you are," she quipped. "But my colleagues aren't exactly sober enough to judge for the moment."

"Given the circumstances, a beer doesn't sound so bad after all," said Leo, disappearing toward the bar.

"And I'll have another tea," Hannelore shouted at his back.

"Pieter wasn't reachable," said Leo when he returned with a tray. "I figured Versnick's information was important, so I called you instead."

Hannelore sipped her tea and relaxed into her chair. She was even temped to kick off her shoes. This was bliss!

"Speak to me, Leo. I'm all ears."

"Koen Versnick is a solid guy, not your typical pathologist, but what's to expect? It can't be easy for young doctors to find work these days straight out of college."

"He can join the club." Hannelore sighed.

Leo was familiar with her assertiveness. A substitute with leftist sympathies was about as rare as a cactus in a rain forest.

"Koen Versnick examined De Jaegher's autopsy report, and he's pretty certain the man missed a crucial detail."

"Everybody knows De Jaegher is prone to the occasional mistake," said Hannelore resignedly. "And recent medical school graduates don't know everything."

"Versnick's father is a renowned plastic surgeon, Hanne. Koen took Herbert's X-rays home with him because he smelled a rat. And his father had no doubts. The victim's jaws weren't sawn through; they were split, which means he underwent some kind of aesthetic surgery."

Leo sketched a jawbone on the back of a beer coaster and tried to explain the difference between the two surgical procedures.

"According to Versnick senior, De Jaegher should have noticed," he said with a hint of pride.

"So why the operation?" asked Hannelore.

"If you split the jawbones, it pulls back the chin. The procedure softens and normalizes the contours of the face."

"Our Herbert was prone to vanity."

"Or he had a facial deformity that made the procedure necessary. According to Versnick's father, the technique is relatively new. It would have been pretty exceptional back then."

"You mean we should be able to identify Herbert pretty easily on the basis of this information?"

"That's what I mean, Hanne."

"Pieter will be happy to hear it."

"I guessed he would. Why else do you think I dared enter the forbidden zone?"

Hannelore got to her feet, unhurried. "I think you've earned a second beer," she said with a grin.

Van In was familiar with the Cleopatra's reputation, but he had never visited the place. He parked his VW Golf on the gravel in front of the villa, its windows framed with blue neon.

"Pretty dead if you ask me," he said to Versavel as they got out of the car.

The Golf was the only car in the improvised parking lot. Versavel shrugged his shoulders.

"It's only one forty-five, Pieter. What did you expect?"

Van In ignored Versavel's naïveté. When Belgium's roadside "cafés" were in their heyday, they were open 24/7 and had customers by the busload. Every traveling salesman with a grain of self-respect would stop by on a regular basis to celebrate his trade successes with a half bottle of sparkling wine and a girl on his lap.

Van In peered through the window into the unlit café before ringing the bell, noticing the traditional oak bar with a line of tall barstools and the obligatory rustic sofas with greasy, flattened cushions. A jukebox glowed in a corner. Pretty unique in this day and age.

Linda was in the kitchen when the bell rang, staring at an empty bottle of Elixir d'Anvers. She fidgeted a cigarette from an almost empty pack and lit it. When those assholes at the door were gone, she was planning to get dressed and drive to the supermarket to replenish her supplies.

"Maybe it's closing day," Versavel suggested when no one answered after five minutes.

"Nonsense. They probably spotted the Golf. The police aren't exactly welcome in places like this. Let's take a look around back. Who knows, maybe they're sunbathing in the yard."

Versavel kept his finger on the bell. Linda, distracted by the noise, didn't notice Van In staring at her through the kitchen window. She almost had a heart attack when he tapped the glass.

"We're closed," she roared.

"Police, ma'am. Is Mr. Aerts around? We'd like a word."

Cops, she thought. *This could be fun*. She shuffled toward the back door.

Versavel heard Van In shouting through the window. He stopped ringing and hurried to join him at the back of the building. Linda opened the door and let them in. The kitchen looked like a bomb had struck it. The smell of rotting leftover food almost turned Versavel's stomach.

"So you want a word with my husband," said Linda, the drink still in her voice.

"Correct, ma'am. We hoped to find him here. Is he on the premises?"

"Take a look for yourselves," she baited.

Van In wasn't planning to let a drunk brothel keeper rile him. He parked himself on a chair. Versavel followed his example, almost stepping into a dried egg yolk in the process.

"We can wait till he gets home," said Van In.

"Then you'll have a long wait. The bastard left me . . . yesterday."

And probably not for the first time, Van In wanted to say. "When do you expect him back?" he asked.

Linda was leaning against the kitchen counter, her dressing gown hanging open wide enough to reveal a pair of plump legs. She deliberately waited until both men looked away before covering up.

"I told you . . . the bastard isn't coming back," she blurted out.

"What makes you think that, Mrs. Aerts?" Van In asked,

rummaging a cigarette from his breast pocket and lighting it. The stench in the place was beyond belief.

"One for me too?"

Van In gave her a cigarette, leaving only one left in his pack. It seemed to calm her as she puffed it a couple of times in quick succession.

"He took his mother's photo with him," she said, pointing to an empty space on the mantelpiece. "He's never done that before."

Versavel was reminded of his own mother and the photo he wore of her around his neck since she passed three years earlier. It was precious to him, a sort of talisman. She and Frank were the only people who had shared his life through all its ups and downs, and he missed her at that moment. Van In followed Linda's eyes, which lingered most of the time on the empty bottle of Elixir d'Anvers. Her fingers trembled as she puffed her cigarette.

"So it's not the first time your husband has left the marital home?" Van In inquired, not entirely comfortable with the formality of the expression.

"The marital home," she brayed. "If I'd known at the start that the man was incapable of keeping his hands to himself, I'd never have married the pussy-chewing fucker."

Versavel looked at Van In. Both men were struggling to contain their laughter.

"So you think he's not coming back," Van In mumbled through his teeth.

Linda tossed her half-smoked cigarette on the floor and mooched another. Van In gave her his last. She still had at least six in her own pack.

"I don't give a fuck if the bastard's been cheating on me, but he should've kept his grubby paws off my money."

The truth was out. She didn't mind them knowing that her ass-worshipping husband had run off with her money. That made him a thief in the eyes of the law, and cops were paid to catch thieves, weren't they?

"Your money, ma'am?"

"Right, my money. That oversexed banana sucker is a common thief."

"Am I correct in assuming that you would like to file charges against your husband?"

"Is that too much to ask?" she snarled.

"How much money are we talking about, Mrs. Aerts?" Van In inquired.

"Sixteen million Belgian francs, and I earned at least half of it."

Neither Van In nor Versavel had known Linda in her younger days, and they were both having trouble imagining how she managed to earn so much money.

"Sixteen million is a pile of money, Mrs. Aerts," said Versavel incredulously. Xanthippe had once driven the wise Socrates to despair. He understood that when men were baited to the verge, they could do the weirdest things. A little money was always welcome, but sixteen million . . . With a nest egg like that, he'd have left her years ago.

"Was your husband a gambler?" Versavel inquired.

Linda jumped and turned toward him. Versavel tried to look innocent.

"Only when it came to women," she said. "Clearly not your cup of tea, eh?"

Versavel was taken aback and turned to Van In. His boss was having a hard time keeping a straight face.

"Do you have any idea where your husband might be? With friends? Family? A girlfriend?"

Linda's face hardened. She suddenly regretted having confided in the police on a whim. William might have been a slippery smooth talker, but when it came to the cops, he knew what he was talking about: *a bunch of brainless bunny fuckers.*

"Do you really think I'm that stupid? Of course I called his friends."

"And there was no sign of him," said Van In guardedly. In the meantime he tried to think of the best way to formulate the next question; next to a white shark, a woman aggrieved had to be the most dangerous creature on the planet. "Did Lodewijk Vandaele perhaps figure among the, eh . . . friends you contacted?"

"What kind of question is that?" she snorted. "What would William want with Vandaele?"

It was the first time she had used her husband's first name.

"Didn't William work for Vandaele?" Van In asked.

Both men thought she was at the point of exploding.

"Work, work. William's self-employed. He works for no one."

"I'm talking about sex-industry work, Mrs. Aerts—earning money from illicit sex," said Van In.

"Illicit sex, Jesus Christ. What's that all about?" Her hoarse voice flipped into a croaky screech. "Is this the Middle Ages? What planet are you on? Illicit sex? In this day and age you can grease your flagpole whenever you like."

She shrieked with laughter. Van In had to admit that her vocabulary was pretty original.

"According to the law, sex between adults is not forbidden as long as there's mutual consent. Without consent we're talking rape, Mrs. Aerts, and that's a felony." His argument was on the feeble side, but it was all he could think of.

"Rape, my ass," she roared. "I'm trying to report a theft, and mister police officer here rambles on about sex. D'you know what you are? A bunch of pervert baton fuckers."

"Hold it, ma'am. Tone it down or we'll have to charge you with disturbing the peace. You need to watch that mouth of yours."

Linda Aerts drew herself up to her full height. "You can go to hell!" she screamed. "Out of my house right now, or I'll call the feds."

She legged it indignantly to the other side of the kitchen, where a grimy telephone was hanging on the wall. "You've got thirty seconds," she snorted.

• • •

Van In jerked open the Golf's door in a rage. Versavel took his place in the passenger seat and fastened his seat belt.

"What do we do now, Pieter?"

Van In rummaged in vain in his breast pocket. "The bitch finished my cigarettes," he growled. No one had ever called him a baton fucker before. "Call the station. I want a surveillance vehicle here on the double with four cops in it. If the bitch sets a foot outside, I want her arrested and locked up in Hauwer Street Station."

"On what grounds?" Versavel asked.

"Drunk and disorderly. The bitch was drunk as a skunk and running out of cigs. My guess is she'll be heading out soon for supplies."

Versavel passed on his boss's orders via the radio.

"I thought the baton-fucker thing was pretty funny," he sniggered.

"She was talking to you," said Van In. "What the fuck would *I* want with a baton?"

"Dildo, Pieter. We call them dildos."

"Jesus, Versavel, give it a rest."

When the police vehicle arrived with backup, Van In gave them the necessary instructions, shifted the Golf into first, and sped off. Versavel was happy he was wearing a safety belt. Van In drove like a madman, and the sergeant counted at least ten infringements on the way to the station. He only missed ramming a twenty-ton truck by a hair's breadth when he hammered through a red light at the Kruispoort.

It took Van In three cigarettes to calm down. He called the police stationed outside the Cleopatra every five minutes for a report and paid little if any attention to the fax Hannelore had sent him. All he could think of was Linda Aerts. He was going to get the bitch, and sooner rather than later.

It took almost forty-five minutes. Officer Deschacht reported that Mrs. Aerts had finally been arrested.

"You should have warned them she was no easy game," said Versavel when Deschacht had finished his report.

Van In rubbed his hands with contentment. He didn't give a damn that they'd followed her all the way to Maldegem—a good ten miles—and had been forced to drive her off the road. The fact that she'd punched one of the officers to the ground was music to his ears and only fired his determination.

Officer Deschacht looked disconcerted when he walked into Room 204. "The suspect is safely behind bars," he said, his relief unconcealed.

"What about the wounded officer?" asked Versavel, concerned.

"Ronny was taken to emergency. The doctors are worried he might have broken his collarbone."

"Perfect," said Van In. "Call the public prosecutor's office. I want her held for at least twenty-four hours."

Deschacht nodded enthusiastically. Ronny was a good friend. The hysterical creature had almost scratched out one of his eyes. "Anything else, Commissioner?"

Van In glowed. "Have her brought upstairs."

Deschacht hesitated. "She fell asleep moments after we locked her up, Commissioner. Wouldn't it be better to let her sleep it off?"

"Nonsense, Deschacht. Tell them to throw a bucket of water over her. I want her sober, and I want her now."

Deschacht didn't respond. Letting someone cool off in a cell for twenty-four hours was one thing, but this was pushing it.

"You can't be serious," said Versavel in disbelief.

"You bet I'm serious. And if you're not up to it, then I'll do it myself."

"Can I do anything else, Commissioner?"

"No, Deschacht. You can go."

The officer turned on his heels in an instant.

"Come with me, Guido," said Van In. "It's time Sleeping Beauty got a wake-up call."

"Sorry, Pieter, but that sort of game doesn't float my boat." The days when drunks were strong-armed back to sobriety and then treated to a good hiding were a thing of the past. "De Kee will be furious if he—"

"De Kee will cover me. That's what chief commissioners are supposed to do."

"I wouldn't count on it," said Versavel. "He's more likely to issue sanctions for unlawful detention."

"No one ever died from a bucket of water, Guido. She's gasping for a drink and a cigarette. This is my only chance to get her to talk."

"Your funeral, Pieter. I'm heading home." He clicked his heels together. "*Sieg Heil, Herr Kommissar.*"

Versavel grabbed his jacket and left the room. This time Van In had crossed the line.

Van In treated the departing sergeant to his middle finger. He expected to have the loose ends tied up by the following morning. Then they would all be lining up, including De Kee, to congratulate him for forcing a breakthrough in the case.

Hannelore arranged slices of sizzling calf kidney in a large frying pan. A jar of green peppercorns and a carton of cream stood ready on the kitchen counter. She had found a dusty bottle of Vin de Cahors in the cellar, which now enjoyed pride of place in the middle of the dining table next to a romantic candle. *Pieter deserved a little extra,* she thought. She hadn't thought he would hold out for more than a couple of days on her Spartan diet, let alone three months. The festive menu was her way of saying thanks for his efforts.

She glanced at the clock on the wall. *He'll be here in twenty,* she figured. She browned the slices of kidney then added the peppercorns and cream. With a bit of luck, his favorite dish would be ready just as he walked in the door.

Then the phone rang. If the telephone rings when you're expecting someone, it's usually bad news. Still, Hannelore turned down the heat and made her way over to the phone, unsuspectingly.

"Hannelore Martens."

"Hi, honey." Van In never said "hi." "Sorry, I'm on duty tonight. Don't worry about me. I'll grab a sandwich later. See you when I get off."

Hannelore wished him a fine evening, blew out the candle, and tossed the kidneys in the trash.

6

Yves Provoost made his way up the gravel path leading to Lodewijk Vandaele's villa. The flat Belgian landscape to which the great Jacques Brel once pledged his heart was on the point of slipping into a misty sleep. The temperature in Flanders that afternoon had been unbearably warm, but now a September chill had risen up from the centuries-old canal in front of the house. Changeable weather was as much a part of Belgium as fries and chocolate. The crowns of the trees bowed down as if this bogus herald of an advancing fall was a danger to their foliage. Here and there a wisp of blue smoke hovered above an isolated farmhouse set off against a cotton candy sky. Provoost shivered. The short bicycle ride hadn't done him any good. He was chilled to the bone.

Johan Brys, Vandaele's other guest, had parked his jet-black BMW in front of the villa. Provoost noticed the license plate.

Brys liked to follow fashion. He had replaced the ministry license plate with his private number, a tactic the majority of dignitaries were inclined to deploy these days. It made their excellencies a little less obvious when they were tearing along the highway at double the speed limit.

"Yves. Come inside, quickly. The evenings are getting colder, don't you think?"

Lodewijk Vandaele welcomed his visitor with a broad smile. Provoost took off his jacket and followed his host into the living room. Four large blocks of oak crackled in the fireplace. The flames from the expensive fuel roared gently.

Brys was much more reserved and restricted himself to a formal handshake. Provoost concretized the coolness of the greeting by standing as far from Brys as he could. There was little left of their old friendship. Both men had agreed to meet out of their own self-interest, and Vandaele was well aware of the fact. He tried to lighten the atmosphere.

"So, I guess we could all use a drink."

Before waiting for a response, the former building contractor crossed to the liquor cart and filled three glasses. Vandaele was anything but miserly with the expensive Exshaw. "Here," he said in what sounded like a command. "This'll perk you up. What possessed you to come by bike?"

Provoost gulped down the contents of the glass like a giraffe that had finally found water after four hours of searching. Instead of raising it to his mouth, he had leaned over and tilted the cognac to his lips at an unusual angle.

"There's no need to worry, Yves. I have the whole business under complete control. Johan's been on the phone to the prosecutor-general. In a couple of days the investigation will be dead in the water and we can all get on with our lives."

Brys nodded when Vandaele turned to him but didn't seem entirely convinced. Counselor Lodewijk lived in the past. The days when a government minister could put pressure on a prosecutor-general were dead and gone. The scandals that had shaken the judiciary in recent years had left an indelible mark. But he wasn't about to tell Counselor Lodewijk that of course. The old man was still convinced that every crime could be covered up for the sake of discretion.

"And what about Aerts?" Provoost asked.

Vandaele rested his right elbow on the mantelpiece. The intense heat of the fire did his rheumatic bones a world of good.

"I have reason to believe that Aerts's departure has nothing to do with the case," he said, his tone reassuring.

Brys swirled the Exshaw in his glass. "What makes you think that, Counselor Lodewijk?"

Vandaele smiled. He liked to be called "counselor."

"William and Linda are always at each other's throats. He's left her a dozen times. Give him a couple of days. He'll be back. I'm convinced of it."

"I wonder if the police would share your opinion," Brys grunted. "If they connect Aerts with the Love, his departure will raise questions."

Vandaele sighed. Aerts was indeed the weakest link, and it

didn't look as if either Provoost or Brys were about to swallow his argument that the man's departure was backpage news. "And do you think our wonderful Bruges police will be able to make the connection?" he asked condescendingly.

Provoost emptied his glass in a single gulp. "They've put Van In on the case."

"Surely you're not afraid of a policeman, are you, Yves?" Vandaele was completely certain the prosecutor-general was going to call Van In to heel.

"Don't underestimate Van In," Provoost protested. "The man stops at nothing and no one. I don't have to remind you how he took on Degroof and Creytens."

"Degroof committed suicide, and Creytens was taken out by some crazy Mafioso," Vandaele retorted.

"Pretty convenient if you ask me. Am I the only one to notice that the guilty rarely make it to court when Van In's on the case?"

Brys nodded. Provoost was right. As a local, he had followed both cases closely.

"Come on, Johan. Surely you don't believe that a second-rate commissioner like Van In would take the law into his own hands."

Vandaele sensed he was losing his hold on Brys and Provoost. "Van In doesn't have a leg to stand on," he said, trying to placate them.

"So why did you ask me to pressure the prosecutor-general?"

Vandaele was speechless for an instant.

"I think we should account for the possibility that the police will track Aerts down," Brys insisted.

Like every politician who had been around the block a couple of times, Brys had learned that the human factor was the most unreliable.

Vandaele was unable to disagree, but he wasn't about to give up on Aerts without a fight. "The most important thing is that we all tell the same story if there's a confrontation. The corpse was found on my property, remember. Technically, that makes me an accessory to murder."

An oppressive silence filled the room, only to be interrupted by the sound of a block of wood collapsing in the grate in a shower of sparks.

"Everything depends on Aerts," said Brys, hammering his point. "If he starts shooting his mouth off, we're all in the shit."

Provoost poured himself a second drink. The cognac was both fast and merciless. Another sip and he would be drunk.

"If it ever comes to that, I'll see to it that Aerts disappears once and for all," said Vandaele resolutely. No one could accuse him of not trying to save Aerts's skin.

Brys and Provoost completely agreed with the provisional sentence. They knew that the counselor was a man of his word.

"Then I can finally stop paying the bastard." Provoost sighed after his slip of the tongue, for which the Exshaw was clearly responsible.

Vandaele frowned. Brys studied the bottom of his glass.

"Would you mind repeating that, Yves?" Vandaele asked.

Provoost glanced knowingly at Brys, but his former friend had nothing to say.

"Aerts has been blackmailing us for years. The bastard claims to have videotapes of the incident."

Vandaele abandoned the comfort of the fireplace, lit a cigar, and started pacing. He didn't like it when people kept him out of the loop.

"Tell me now," said Vandaele.

"We didn't want to cause you any embarrassment," Provoost whispered. "I was convinced he was blackmailing you too. Didn't Johan tell you?"

Brys glared at Provoost. That was a step too far.

Vandaele hawked like an old mineworker, and the cigar wasn't to blame. His nerves had gotten the better of him. He was willing to forgive the fact that Aerts had buried the body on his property, but blackmail was a different matter altogether.

"I'll take care of it right away," he said in a toneless voice. "Our William has been a little too greedy."

Vandaele now understood why Aerts had disappeared in such a hurry. He had known damn well that the boss would punish him.

Van In needed two buckets of water to wake Linda Aerts. The result wasn't a pretty sight. Linda looked like a wet kangaroo, and she started to race around her cell like a madwoman, cursing and swearing at the top of her lungs.

Van In was safely ensconced behind the door. He smoked

one cigarette after the other. It was only a matter of time before she reached the point of no return.

Every half hour he opened the hatch and peered into the cell. Around midnight, the frequency of her temper tantrums diminished. The quieter it became, the more often he opened the hatch to take a look. Linda was hunched up on her wooden bed, her teeth chattering, a coarse stinking blanket draped over her shoulders. Earlier that evening, Van In had asked the assistance of a female officer who had helped Linda out of her wet clothing. He didn't want her to catch pneumonia.

Around two thirty he sent a young officer to buy cigarettes at the convenience store. There wasn't much time. This was his only chance to force her to her knees.

Van In lit a cigarette, opened the hatch, and puffed a cloud of smoke into the cell. Their eyes met for a couple of seconds. The stimulating smell of the cigarette smoke roused her from her lethargy. She jumped like a cat with its tail on fire. "Pervert fucking shit packer!" she screamed. "Lousy baton fucker, cock sucker, pile driver, limp-dicked, sour-faced canary fucker, piss drinkin' cum dump . . ."

The expletives kept on coming. Van In smiled and continued to blow smoke into her cell. The sight of his grinning face was the last straw. Linda charged at the door, a finger pointed and ready to do some damage. Van In took a step backward, sat in his chair, and listened as she thumped the door. She kept it up for a good ten minutes, then she collapsed, burst into hysterical tears, and tossed the blanket on the floor. If Van In had entered the cell at that moment, he would have risked immediate suspension. No chief commissioner would cover for him if there was evidence he had spent more than ten seconds alone in a police cell with a naked woman.

Carine Neels offered Linda back her clothes, which she had dried to the best of her ability over an electric heater. They were still damp, but Linda had no complaints. The temper tantrum had left her completely empty. She got dressed like a zombie. The shock treatment had also screwed with her sense of time. How long had she been in the cell? When would they let her go?

"She's ready, Commissioner," said Carine when Linda was fully dressed. "Do you want me to stay?"

She had cause for concern, and she knew her presence could spare the commissioner a headache or two.

"I'd appreciate it, Miss Neels."

Carine nodded. She liked it when Van In addressed her formally. In spite of the rumors circulating about the commissioner, she had a soft spot for him.

Van In took a deep breath. He wasn't one to take young officers into his confidence, but he didn't have much of a choice. It was three forty-five, and time was of the essence.

"But then you have to promise me one thing: whatever you see or hear remains strictly confidential."

Her heart pounded. She once smoked a joint as a student. The tingling feeling now running up her back was at least as much fun.

"Goes without saying, Commissioner."

Van In smiled. The girl was as green as a pool table, and in this situation, that was more an advantage than a disadvantage.

"We're pretty sure Mrs. Aerts has information that might prove indispensible for winding up the case. Do you understand, Miss Neels?"

Of course she understood. She had been following the business with the skeleton step by step.

"Please, call me Carine," she whispered conspiratorially.

Jesus H. Christ. Here we go again, thought Van In.

Linda followed them to Room 204 without protest. A dormant desperation glazed her eyes. Her self-confidence had taken some serious blows. Forced abstinence was beginning to take its toll as the merciless demon drink cranked up its final offensive. If Van In had told her at that moment that she was going to be locked up in jail for six months, she would have believed him without condition. The thought almost drove her out of her mind; locking a person up was the worst thing you could do to them.

When Van In offered Linda a chair, she almost thanked him for it. The jargon junkies liked to call that kind of reaction the Helsinki Syndrome, a concept that emerged in the 1970s when endless hostage takings plagued the TV screens. Psychologists observed that a sort of friendship evolved during hostage situations between the victims and their captors. Twenty years ago, it took a few days for such a special relationship to evolve, but in today's instant society, of course, a lot less time was needed.

Linda took a seat, bowed her head, and folded her hands in her lap. Carine Neels stood at attention, her back like that of a sentry. There was something Eastern European about the whole scene. All that was missing was a leather jacket and a piercing desk lamp.

"Mrs. Aerts," said Van In in a dulcet tone. "I'm afraid I still have a couple of questions to ask."

Linda barely reacted. She was terrified. She remembered seeing a movie in which a female guard suddenly turned into a crazed, bloodthirsty sadist.

"I want to know the names of the men your husband escorted to Mr. Vandaele's little house in the country."

Linda raised her eyes. William had always made her promise never to mention names.

"I kept out of it."

"Come, come, Mrs. Aerts. Mr. Vandaele's special guests all used to meet in the Cleopatra, where you were tending bar."

In the old days, when men appreciated a firmer chunk of flesh, she was a welcome sight in the Love. But most men tended to prefer stuffed skeletons these days, and William had degraded her to barmaid.

"That's possible," she said, her self-confidence on the return. "I may have taken care of the drinks, but I never asked for IDs. They say that's the police's job."

Carine snorted indignantly. *What a liar,* she thought.

"Of course, ma'am." Van In consciously emphasized the word *ma'am*. "But don't tell me there were no regulars, people you knew by name."

Linda shook her head stubbornly. "You'll have to ask my husband. If you can find the bastard."

"Fine," said Van In frostily.

He leaned back in his chair, opened a drawer, and produced a bottle of whiskey and a glass.

"If that's the case, then you might as well go back to your cell."

The gurgle of the whiskey in the neck of the bottle had the same effect on Linda as a bag of blood to a waking vampire. Her nostrils trembled. She had to fight not to drool.

Van In raised the glass to his lips and took a sip. *If this isn't an excuse for a drink during working hours,* he thought.

"Care for a little nightcap, Mrs. Aerts?"

Carine raised her eyebrows. Had the commissioner lost his mind?

Linda stared longingly at the bottle of Haig. Van In fished a second glass from the drawer and filled it halfway. He lit a cigarette and placed the pack in the middle of his desk. Linda hit it like a diving duck. Carine grabbed her arm, but Van In gestured that she should let go. He was holding a lighter in his left hand.

"A light, Mrs. Aerts?"

He held out the flame. Linda cradled the useless cigarette in her quivering hand. This was too much. *What the fuck,* she thought, *half of Bruges knew who frequented the Cleopatra. And what went on in the Love wasn't a crime.*

"Yves Provoost, once every two weeks."

"The lawyer?"

"Who else?" she snapped.

Van In pushed the whiskey closer. Linda grabbed the glass and emptied it in a couple of swigs.

"Now that wasn't so hard, was it, Mrs. Aerts?"

Van In held out the lighter and poured a second drink. He then took out a pen and a sheet of paper. The page filled with names as the bottle emptied.

"Hah, Alexander De Jaegher. Now who would have expected De Jaegher?"

"*Doctor Blowjob*," Linda sneered. "He sometimes came twice a week."

In the space of thirty minutes, Van In had filled two sheets of a legal pad. He now realized precisely why Vandaele had installed an electric gate. Some of the Love's "clients" were so well known they demanded the utmost discretion. Speedy entry and exit was an indispensible condition for guaranteeing their celebrity privacy.

Van In crossed the Zand in the center of Bruges. The square was bathed in an unearthly light. The open surface dotted with wrought-iron street lamps reminded him of a Paul Delvaux nude. The association wasn't so crazy; this was where the train station used to be and a naked woman was now sleeping off her hangover in a cell around the corner. A chilly east wind made him shiver. He stuffed his hands in his pockets, bent his back, and braved the cold fall breeze. He had struggled through many a night shift in his life and had learned that those who held out till five a.m. rarely wanted to go straight home. So he made his way to the Egg Market only to find everything closed. His only option was Villa Italiana.

Mario the barman recognized Van In at a glance. "On your way home or on your way to work?" he asked in a thick Bruges accent.

He mixed two measures of Glenfiddich with half a bottle of Coke. Four listless fortysomethings were making fools of themselves on the dance floor. Their wooden movements were in complete contrast to the infectious beat of the place's signature disco music. Fortunately there was no one to hiss at them.

"One for the road," said Van In dryly.

He took a sip. Mario knew his trade. The drink cleared his head. Question one: How was Hannelore going to react to his nocturnal escapade when he got home? Question two: What kind of hornet's nest had he stirred up? The answer to question one was imminent, but it was question two that bothered him most. Lodewijk Vandaele, one of Bruges' most respected citizens, had run a luxury brothel in the vicinity, and the cream of West Flanders had made use of its services. Twenty-four hours after the discovery of Herbert, William Aerts, one of Vandaele's sidekicks, had skipped town.

Van In emptied his glass. A drop of whiskey could be inspiring at times. Mario was on the ball and promptly mixed a filler.

"From the *patron*," he said, grinning.

Questions, more and more questions. If Vandaele knew there was a corpse buried on his property, why did he hand it over to a charity like Helping Our Own? Or was it Humping Our Own? What was the charity all about? And what role did Benedict Vervoort have to play, the realtor with the air of a washed-out Mafioso?

Van In scribbled his thoughts on the back of a beer coaster. That way he was sure to remember the day before the morning after. Or was today already the morning after?

"Coffee, sweetheart?"

Hannelore was about to leave for court when Van In arrived home more dead than alive. Luckily there were no mirrors around. His face was puffy and swollen, and the bags under his eyes were big enough to house a garrison.

"Please," he said, yawning.

"A pleasant night?" She prodded his ribs none too gently. "Did the water torture have the desired effect?"

Van In rubbed his eyes.

"Guido called me yesterday," she said dryly. Her engaging smile made way for grim determination. "He asked me with his usual politeness to put an end to your medieval shenanigans."

"What shenanigans?"

Van In sipped the coffee. It tasted thin and watery.

"If I were you, I'd want the ground to open up and swallow me."

"Why didn't you send in the feds?"

An argument was brewing. Hannelore took off her jacket and sat down at the table opposite Van In.

"I considered it, Pieter Van In. Have you lost your mind completely?"

"She was completely smashed," Van In retorted.

"Look who's talking."

"I'm tired," he protested. "Versavel's exaggerating. No one ever died from a drenching. In the old days—"

"In the old days they took a beating as well," she said. "Those days are gone for good."

Van In understood what she meant. Twenty years ago the police extracted confessions, the magistrates evaluated them, and they did their best to mimic the wisdom of Solomon by delivering sentences that were acceptable to both parties. Nowadays, the judiciary had to account for public opinion. The jury of the people, ten million strong, was no longer willing to acknowledge that arguments were more important than emotions—and not without reason. It had been demonstrated more than once in the past that the same arguments had been used to serve the interests of the moneyed, propertied classes. The ordinary man or woman in the street was subjected to the letter of the law.

"You have to admit the old-fashioned approach can be productive," said Van In as he fished the list of names from his inside pocket and slipped it across the table. He then got to his feet and tossed the undrinkable coffee into the sink.

Hannelore examined the sheets of paper. Men were depraved

creatures by nature, and she was aware that the odd black sheep had been spotted among the so-called upper crust, but this suggested a flock.

"Did Linda Aerts give you all these names?" she asked in amazement.

Van In grinned. It took a lot to impress Hannelore. She grabbed a cigarette without asking.

"I thought you were in a hurry to get to court."

He kicked off his shoes and snuggled into the sofa. Hannelore smoked her cigarette, headed into the kitchen, spooned four large measures of coffee into the percolator, and half filled it with water.

"We have a problem!" she shouted from the kitchen.

"What's new?"

"Didn't you get my fax yesterday?"

"What fax?"

Hannelore stood in the doorway. "What's with you?" she grumbled.

Van In listened to her story about Koen Versnick, the police doctor's loose-lipped assistant, without opening his eyes.

"If De Jaegher's been deliberately withholding evidence, he has to have had a good reason. I'll check it out in the morning," said Van In.

"According to Versnick's father, it should be pretty easy. Plastic surgery was still in its infancy back then, and operations of the sort our Herbert underwent were few and far between."

"Excellent," said Van In. "Sounds like the perfect job for Chief Inspector Baert. If he screws up this time, I have a good excuse to send him to Siberia."

"Siberia?"

"Lost and Found, Hanne. Didn't I explain that to you before?"

Hannelore ignored the dig.

"But De Jaegher is small change compared to the other names on the list," she said, concerned. "Provoost is a prominent lawyer, and Brys is the minister of foreign affairs. If the case is moving up to a different level, I'm not sure if—"

"Don't let it worry you, Hanne. The judiciary isn't inclined to protect government ministers as much as they were in the past. One imprisoned excellency more or less makes little difference. The public can't get enough of it."

In contrast to the boarding school coffee he had poured down the drain, Hannelore's second attempt was like liquid tar.

"Drink . . . it'll sober you up," she said, her tone authoritarian. "I want my holiday in Portugal, and you need to get your act together and get down to Hauwer Street in half an hour."

Van In stirred three lumps of sugar in the coffee. Hannelore didn't comment.

"Vervoort's also on the list," he said in passing.

"Who's Vervoort?"

"The treasurer of our distinguished charity and administrator of Lodewijk Vandaele's property portfolio."

"Jesus," said Hannelore.

"Don't let it bother you, honey. If it all goes wrong, we can always appeal to the king for clemency." Van In gulped his coffee, and his stomach reacted as if it were nitric acid.

7

Yves Provoost stared at Linda Aerts and shook his head. Her ruined hairdo and lack of makeup made her appear even less appealing than usual, if that were possible.

"Your story is in very bad taste, Mrs. Aerts."

Provoost gritted his teeth, causing all the color to drain from his face.

"First you sully my good name, and then you ask me to start proceedings against a senior police officer because he threw a bucket of water over you."

"Is that allowed?"

"Of course not," Provoost growled. He was in an awkward predicament. The Belgian public didn't give a damn when the powers that be overstepped the mark now and then. There wasn't a case to answer, and the press wouldn't touch it. The Love's clients were among the elite of Bruges society.

There wasn't a single chief editor who would even think of publishing an article with the names of those involved. Constructing a scandal on top of a scandal wasn't enough these days to make heads roll. Without evidence, her story was just a rumor, and people could handle rumors. It was also clear that Linda Aerts had made her statement under pressure, making it more or less worthless. But his primary concern was that Van In might dig his teeth into the case. If the commissioner made a connection between the orgies and the discovery of the corpse, there was every chance he would keep digging.

"You should never have made a statement, Mrs. Aerts. I wonder what William will have to say about this."

"William left me," she grunted.

"Come now, Mrs. Aerts. Let's be serious for once. It's not the first time William has taken off for a few days. He's sure to reappear."

Provoost was certain that no one was ever going to see William Aerts alive again.

"With sixteen million in his pocket," she said, sneering. "Why the fuck do you think I called the cops? The bastard robbed me, and I want my money back. I don't give a fuck about the other stuff."

"Sixteen million." Provoost whistled.

"Exactly, your honor, as if you didn't know where he earned it."

Provoost gulped and did the math in his head. Over the years he had coughed up almost an eighth of that amount.

"I can't compensate you for the full amount of course, but what would you say if I were to write you a check for a hundred thousand francs? You could take a vacation. Enjoy yourself a little."

Provoost tried to conjure an engaging smile. Playing for time seemed to be the best strategy.

Linda didn't budge an inch for a moment or two. His generous offer seemed to have warmed her. Provoost produced a pen from his breast pocket and opened the top drawer of his desk, where he kept his checkbook.

"I want that baton fucker dragged into court," Linda hissed.

Provoost closed the drawer and returned the pen to his pocket.

"Of course, Mrs. Aerts."

The hag suddenly gave him a brilliant idea.

"Why don't you tell me again what happened last night, Mrs. Aerts, and don't spare the details," he said with a demonic grin.

Linda liked his change of tack. She stretched out her legs and started to talk.

Versavel heard the news that afternoon. Linda Aerts had submitted a complaint to the federal police accusing Van In of assault and attempted rape. In Van In's absence, he decided to call Hannelore but to no avail. Deputy Martens was unavailable, the operator told him with a hint of malicious delight. Versavel didn't insist, resigned to the fact that the public prosecutor's office always gave the brush off to anyone below the rank of officer. Van In appeared just as he was hanging up. He looked like Perseus ready to confront Medusa.

"Versavel." Van In rummaged in his trouser pocket and tossed a handful of coins on the floor. "Should be thirty pieces or thereabouts, Judas."

Versavel waited until the last coin had stopped clattering. "I considered it my duty to inform Hannelore of your outrageous behavior, Pieter. You crossed the line last night."

Van In shrugged his shoulders. Versavel was right, but it was too late to tell him that.

"Linda Aerts submitted a complaint this morning to the federal police. She's accusing you of assault and attempted rape," said Versavel, nervously rubbing his mustache.

"So what?" Van In grumped. He lit a cigarette and sat down at his desk.

"You're in serious shit, Pieter. Judges don't like this kind of mess these days. Times have changed . . . don't you get it?"

Van In didn't underestimate the problem. He recognized it, but admitting he was in the wrong was a different kettle of fish.

"I didn't touch the woman, Guido. You know that as well as I do. Anyway, I conducted the entire interview in the charming company of Carine Neels. So I'm not as crazy as you think—"

"Yves Provoost is planning to defend Mrs. Aerts," Versavel interrupted. "Everyone knows he rarely loses a case."

"Provoost's still milking his father's success. He's not as good as he'd like us to believe. And don't forget, he's anything but invulnerable. So do me a favor and spare me the patronizing talk. I can wet-nurse myself." Van In dug deep into his trouser pocket. "I spent the entire afternoon going through the commercial court archives."

He handed Versavel a thin bundle of papers. "This is a copy of the memorandum of association submitted by Helping Our Own. It makes interesting reading, I can assure you."

Versavel read the names of the executive board, all of them from the list dictated by Linda Aerts: Vandaele, Provoost, Brys, Vervoort, and De Jaegher.

"Impressive."

He didn't sound convinced.

"Jesus H. Christ. Think about it, Guido. Our friend Vandaele sets up a charity with a few intimate buddies. The organization's goal is to support the poor. After Herbert is killed, Vandaele hands the charity a dilapidated farmhouse, a gift he can deduct from his tax return. One remarkable detail: the farmhouse functioned for years as an exclusive brothel where the members of the board used to enjoy a bit of slap and tickle on a regular basis."

"Remarkable indeed," said Versavel dryly.

Van In was on marshy ground. The complaint Linda had put together against him was more serious than a couple of public figures having a bit of fun with the ladies.

"Don't you see the connection?" asked Van In in amazement. "According to its latest annual report, the charity has more than one hundred and eighty million in assets. If that doesn't stink, Christ knows what does. They spend twelve million a year on printing, twenty on trips abroad for the poor and destitute, and a little more than ten on training for the handicapped. No one in his right mind would believe that."

"Stranger things have happened . . ."

"Cut it out, Guido." Van In didn't understand why Versavel was being such an ass. "Strange indeed, Guido, and it gets stranger. I called a couple of other charities. No one's ever heard of Helping Our Own. There's no trace of their activities."

"So what have they been spending their assets on?"

"I've been asking myself the same question, Guido."

Versavel rubbed his upper triceps with his left hand, something he often did when he was nervous. "If I'm not mistaken, Vervoort's one of the FLASYC heavyweights. Maybe we should check them out."

Van In looked at his friend in astonishment. Flanders Show Your Claws was a faction within a right-wing political party that had grown in popularity in recent years. It was known in the meantime that the FLASYC boys weren't averse to a bit of violence. "Tell me you don't mean it, Guido."

"FLASYC has to get its money from somewhere," said Versavel.

"Let's pray our Herbert wasn't a Moroccan."

Van In was reminded of the summer of 1996, when the Dutroux child abuse case turned Belgium on its head. The witch hunt that followed was still fresh in his memory.

"At least it'll give us an excuse to give those sickos a good going over," Versavel growled.

Van In tried to imagine what would happen if Versavel's hypothesis was right. "It's certainly a line of inquiry we can't ignore. It wouldn't be the first time a so-called charity was manipulated to serve a 'higher' goal."

"Vandaele never hid his rightist sympathies," said Versavel. "And Provoost isn't exactly a fan of Karl Marx."

Van In got to his feet and started pacing. Hypotheses were tempting because they inclined investigators to think in a specific direction and only focus on elements that supported the proposed theory. "So where does Brys fit in to the equation?"

The minister of foreign affairs was a socialist. He had his faults, but even Versavel figured that a secret alliance with the extreme right was a bridge too far. "Perhaps he knows nothing about it. You know what socialists are like. When someone stokes the embers, they plead collective memory loss." The sergeant was an apolitical being. As far as he was concerned, politicians were all the same.

Van In tried to line up the facts. One: Herbert murdered. Two: the connection between the killing and the clients at the Love. Three: potential financial connections between FLASYC and Helping Our Own. More parameters and even more unknowns.

"What if we order a review of the charity's accounts," he blurted out.

"That would take too much time, Pieter. While we're waiting for permission, they'll just tidy up the books. Most of these organizations keep two sets. And they'll be ready with a reasonable explanation for every transaction."

"Other ideas?"

"An unannounced visit can sometimes do wonders," said Versavel. "Didn't you mention something about the charity running a center for the homeless?"

"Now that I think of it . . . What did Vervoort call the place?"

"Care House. I found the address yesterday in the telephone directory."

"OK, let's check them out. One of us needs to inform Baert."

Versavel shrugged his shoulders. "His wife called him in sick this morning."

"Nothing serious, I hope."

"She said he needed a couple of days' rest. Poor guy has back trouble. Too much time on the phone if you ask me."

"And he only takes two days off?"

"His doctor is one of the new boys, determined to help clean up the social security system. His patients have to be half-dead before he's willing to prescribe a week's leave."

"Shame."

"Shame?"

"That Baert can't find himself an old-fashioned doctor."

Versavel laughed. "Shall I requisition a car?"

"No," said Van In. "A police vehicle would attract too much attention. Is Devos on duty?"

"I think so," said Versavel. "He's manning reception."

"Good. Then I have a question for him before we go any further."

Van In made his way to the door but stopped and turned halfway. "Give Carine Neels a call. Ask if she can spare a couple of days to work on the case. I want her to call the plastic surgeons."

Versavel was taken aback.

"Herbert had one of those nip and tuckers give him a face job. Sorry, Hannelore dug it up yesterday and I forgot to mention it in all the commotion."

Van In opened the door.

"Pieter."

"Yes, Guido."

"I'm wondering why you know Carine Neels is on duty today but had to ask me if Devos was in the building."

Van In stopped and gripped the door handle. Versavel's question cheered him immensely. "Because *I* know where the pretty girls hang out, Guido."

In contrast to the Love, Care House was a neatly renovated farmstead surrounded by an abundance of well-maintained green. Visitors had to admit that Helping Our Own was anything but amateur. The place looked like an expensive spa where sagging middle-class ladies would sign in for six months to tighten their skin. But appearances can be deceptive. The tiny pavilions scattered here and there across the property offered a home to ten or so families who, for one reason or another, had found themselves on the fringes of society.

Ilse, a well-spoken social worker who appeared to be in charge, gave Van In and Versavel the grand tour.

"The charity's main concern is the fate of families," she said with a smile that any advertising agency worth its salt would have been happy to purchase. "Initially, we try to offer people a chance to rest. We only get down to real business after two weeks. A team of specialists explores the issues and suggests appropriate solutions, which are then passed on to our clients. After a thorough evaluation, we employ a strategy designed to ensure our clients' reintegration. Our success rate is well above the national average."

Van In had stopped listening halfway through her pitch. The social worker had a fine pair of legs, and he could see through the flowers on her linen summer dress that she didn't buy her underwear at the local supermarket.

Versavel took notes, fortunately not distracted by such details.

"That was an extraordinarily interesting tour, Miss . . ."

"Vanquathem, Doctor," she said. "But call me Ilse."

Versavel tried to keep a straight face. Impersonating doctors was Van In's idea, a tried and tested tactic. The adepts of Hippocrates still commanded respect. Ilse Vanquathem was convinced that Dr. Dupont and Dr. Praat wanted to set up a similar project in the neighborhood of Turnhout near Antwerp. Even the mangled Antwerp accent Van In had conjured up for the occasion didn't arouse her suspicions.

"It might help if we had the opportunity to chat with a couple of clients, Miss . . . eh . . . Ilse," said Van In.

The radiant smile froze on her lips.

"I'm afraid we're not allowed to improvise in such delicate circumstances, Doctor. Confrontations of the sort you are suggesting require preparation. But I'll certainly discuss the matter at our next staff meeting."

"That would be kind of you, Ilse. I'm sure you understand that whatever information we can acquire about this wonderful project would be most welcome."

He handed her his card.

Ilse glanced briefly at its elegant lettering: Professor Dr. Pieter Dupont, Psychiatrist. Versavel had fifty similar cards in his pocket. There was a machine in the local post office where you could print them for two hundred francs. In a gesture of overconfidence, he also produced his credentials.

"Thank you, Dr. Praat," said Ilse with a hint of admiration. She had a weakness for older academics in good physical shape. "Can I perhaps offer you a cup of coffee?"

Ilse accompanied her visitors to the main building and asked one of the clients to make coffee. Versavel feigned an urgent need to use the facilities while Van In launched into an extensive tribute to Helping Our Own and its work. He was so convincing that Ilse didn't notice that Versavel was absent for more than fifteen minutes.

When they were taking their leave at the front door, Van In bumped into a tall, lanky man in overalls. The workman's icy gaze left Van In with a feeling of unease. The garden shears in his hand triggered an image of Freddy Krueger from *Nightmare on Elm Street*.

"What time is it?" asked Van In as they waited at the traffic light.

"Four thirty," said Versavel.

"Excellent. Devos has no need to worry."

André Devos was a colleague and a sucker for expensive cars. In spite of his modest rank in the force, he drove an impressive Alfa Romeo. Van In had borrowed it for a couple of hours to add plausibility to their visit to Care House.

Van In slowly released the clutch and hit the gas. The nervous Italian reacted accordingly, leaving the competition far behind.

"Feisty," Van In snorted.

"You're doing eighty, Pieter, and this is a thirty zone."

"And not a cop in sight to write a ticket." Van In grinned.

Versavel held his tongue. His main hope was that Van In would get the car back to Devos in one piece. It would kill the man otherwise.

Van In was at the stove watching four quails simmering in a pan. The table was set with glistening glasses and washing-line fragrant table linen. But there was a hint of tension in the air that became even more tangible when Hannelore slammed the front door. The obligatory candle quivered in the neck of an empty wine bottle, its flame flickering ominously.

"Don't tell me you're angry, sweetheart."

Hannelore tossed her handbag into a chair, breathtaking in her turquoise dress. Being pregnant made her seem younger every day.

"You're such a moron, Pieter Van In. What in God's name am I to do with you?"

She said nothing about the aroma of simmering quails that wafted through the house. The events of the last few days had shifted the diet obsession onto the back burner.

"I asked if you were angry."

There were times when Hannelore wanted to curse the doggish look in his eyes more than anything else. But she hesitated, and Van In seized the moment. He left the quails to themselves and threw his arms around her. Hannelore's protest wasn't convincing, and when he insisted, she accepted his kiss.

"I should have had you locked up yesterday. Everyone's talking about you at the courthouse. Even the receptionist asked how you were and didn't hold the condescension. Ask anyone."

"Don't let it bother you, Hanne. I know what I'm doing."

She wriggled out of his embrace. "I'll have Prosecutor Beekman down my neck before you know it."

Van In grinned. "You can handle it, Hanne. Anyway, Mrs. Aerts just wants the attention. No one is going to believe her. And Provoost? He seems to have forgotten that he was one of the horny bastards that stopped by to balance his hormones at Vandaele's farm on a regular basis. If push comes to shove, he'll back off."

"Are you sure?"

Hannelore tipped the lid of the pan. The bouquet of golden-brown quails made her dizzy. She had missed lunch that day and was pining for a bite to eat.

Van In opened the refrigerator, grabbed a half-full bottle of Moselle, and removed the quails from the heat.

"I have a statement from Mrs. Aerts, don't I?" he said unperturbed.

"Provoost will trash it."

Hannelore sat down at the kitchen table and asked herself why he always managed to cook her favorite dishes on days when she was totally pissed off.

Van In poured a couple of glasses of wine, spilling a drop on the tablecloth in the process.

"I don't understand why Provoost agreed to defend her. If it ever gets to court, his name is bound to be connected with his activities at the Love."

"Provoost knows that his name is likely to crop up sooner or later. If you ask me, his using Linda Aerts is a diversionary tactic. A police commissioner molesting a naked, defenseless woman is more likely to attract public attention these days than a lawyer who likes a bit on the side," said Hannelore.

"Wait a minute. I didn't even get close to molesting the bitch," Van In protested.

Hannelore dried the foot of her glass with a paper napkin and took a sip.

"And I'm supposed to believe you?" she mocked.

Anxiety suddenly took hold of him. When people questioned his good intentions, he could explode like a batch of illegal fireworks.

"I didn't lay a finger on her." He slammed the table with his fist to underline his claim. The thud knocked over his glass, and he watched it roll across the table and smash to pieces on the kitchen floor.

"What's the matter with you?" Hannelore screamed.

She was usually ready for his angry outbursts, but that evening she was tired and irritable. She jumped to her feet. The splashing wine had stained her dress. She crossed to the sink and held a towel under the faucet.

Van In sat motionless for a couple of seconds. To his great surprise he felt his rage ebb away. Was it true after all that three months of sobriety had had a positive effect on his explosive temperament?

"Is it bad?" he asked, crestfallen, crossing to the sink in his socks.

"Be careful!" she shouted, more concerned than angry. "There's glass all over the place."

"Sorry, sweetie."

Hannelore dabbed her dress with the corner of the wet towel.

"I'm thankful it wasn't red," she said in a conciliatory tone.

Van In slid submissively into his slippers, grabbed a brush, and swept the pieces of broken glass together, leaving a sticky trail of wine on the polished tiles.

"Shall I pop your dress in the washing machine?" he suggested, trying to be helpful.

"You wish."

Hannelore spotted the wronged look in his face and burst out laughing.

"So you believe me?" asked Van In.

"Of course I do. But the questions is: Will the judge believe you?"

"We'll cross that bridge when we come to it," said Van In. "It'll be my word against the word of a hooker. And speaking of hookers, it wouldn't surprise me if Helping Our Own turned out to be a cover for a prostitution network."

Van In told her all about his visit to Care House.

"So while I was drinking coffee with the manager, Versavel took a look at their computer."

Hannelore had told him time and again that evidence procured illegally would be rejected by the courts, but she was too tired to repeat it.

"And guess what he found."

Van In didn't wait for her to answer. This was the moment he had been waiting for all evening. He fished a sheet of printer paper from his trouser pocket. "What do you think?"

Hannelore examined the sheet of paper. Twenty names, give or take.

"Look at the header."

"Available," she read innocently.

"Check the dates of birth."

After each first name on the list there was a six-figure number. She didn't get it.

"None of the women are a day over thirty-five," said Van In.

"You're not serious," Hannelore blurted out.

"They have to get their girls somewhere," said Van In cynically.

"But you said Vandaele closed the Love in 1986."

"True. And a couple of months later, our charity takes over Care House. Coincidence?"

"After Herbert was killed."

"Exactly."

Hannelore gulped down some wine from her glass.

"Aren't you exaggerating a little? A list of names doesn't prove anything. You wouldn't even be able to check their identities. Maybe it's a list of staff the charity has been paying under the table."

"Guess what. I've got just such a list," said Van In. "And guess who's on it. John Catrysse, the man with the motorcycle who drove into Vandaele's Mercedes. He seems to be a bit of a gardener, and I can assure you, the accident didn't do him any good at all. The man looks like Quasimodo's younger brother."

"Come on, Pieter Van In. Nobody's responsible for the way they look."

"OK, but he still deserves a place of honor in Cesare Lombroso's cabinet of curiosities," Van In teased.

"Lombroso's theories were debunked half a century ago,"

she snorted. "There's no connection between people's physiognomy and their potential criminal inclinations."

"Did I say Catrysse was a criminal?"

"No, but you insinuated it."

"But some American scientists still claim—"

"Some American scientists still claim that Elvis is alive and kicking."

Van In shrugged off her response. He wasn't in the mood to needle her any further. A strained silence filled the room.

"But I still think we need to take a closer look at the charity's activities," Van In insisted as he yawned a few minutes later.

Listlessness took him unawares, as if someone had tapped him on the head with a rubber hammer. His thoughts blurred like watercolor paint on a sheet of coarse-grained paper.

"I think it's time for dinner," he said.

Hannelore didn't press the point. They'd both had a trying day. She had an appointment with her gynecologist the following morning, but she didn't see the point in reminding him about it.

"They're showing *Metropolis* on Arte in ten minutes. Care for a TV movie?" she asked.

Hannelore knew he was partial to the classics and wasn't surprised at his enthusiastic response. He jumped to his feet and headed for the kitchen.

"In that case, it's supper in the salon, madam."

•   •   •

The shortened and digitally colored version of Fritz Lang's masterpiece didn't impress.

"Proof if proof be needed," said Hannelore. "When Hollywood screws with art, there's not much left worth looking at."

She gnawed at the bones of her second quail.

"They're broadcasting *The Birds* tomorrow," said Van In. "Hitchcock's never a disappointment."

Van In zapped to the BBC as Hannelore snuggled up against his shoulder. They landed in the middle of a documentary, with David Attenborough commenting expertly on a couple of paring anteaters.

"It's enough to put you in the mood if you close your eyes and just listen," said Hannelore contentedly.

Van In pushed his plate to one side and switched off the television.

"That can be arranged," he said eagerly.

Jos Brouwers had earned a small fortune in a relatively short period of time. After leaving the federal police six years ago, he went into business for himself and added a zero to his annual income. His private detective agency had a sound reputation among those with more right-wing inclinations, and Lodewijk Vandaele was one of his most faithful clients. Brouwers knew the former building contractor as a man who always got what he wanted, by whatever means necessary.

He parked his rusty Renault on a side street adjacent to the Damme Canal and continued on foot for the remaining three hundred yards. Vandaele could be generous, but in exchange he demanded absolute discretion.

Brouwers pressed the doorbell at nine o'clock sharp. Virginie, Vandaele's elderly housekeeper, obviously beyond her pension age, opened the door before the bell stopped ringing. Not bad for an old lady doubled over from rheumatism. She greeted the late visitor with a toothless smile and informed him that Mr. Vandaele was expecting him in the conservatory.

Vandaele welcomed Brouwers with exaggerated gestures, testifying more to his sense of authority than his hospitality.

"Take a seat, Jos. Thanks for coming. Cigar?"

Brouwers didn't say no. Vandaele only smoked Davidoffs, a prohibitive luxury even for a prosperous ex-cop.

"Coffee?"

"Please."

Brouwers took a cigar, helped himself to a strip of cedar wood, lit it with a match, and rolled the tip of the cigar above the yellow odorless flame.

"How's Greta?"

"She's traveling," said Brouwers dryly. "Martinique . . . as if Belgium isn't good enough."

"Women." Vandaele sighed tellingly.

The men chatted until Virginie had served the coffee. Brouwers loved the aroma of freshly ground Colombian beans. Virginie shuffled back to the kitchen and returned with a tray of petit fours, a delicacy Brouwers particularly enjoyed. He attacked them uninvited.

"From Nicolas?"

"Of course," said Vandaele affably.

Nicolas was renowned for his refined patisserie.

"Thanks, Virginie."

On Vandaele's lips, even a word of gratitude sounded like an order. The elderly housekeeper disappeared without a sound.

"I'm looking for someone," said Vandaele when Virginie closed the conservatory doors. Brouwers nodded, swallowed half a cookie, and fished a notebook from his jacket pocket.

"No notes, Jos. There's some unpleasantness involved."

The ex-cop returned his notebook to his pocket and helped himself to a second cookie. *Unpleasantness* was one of Vandaele's euphemisms for taking someone out.

"For the usual fee?"

Vandaele poured the coffee and added a dash of whipped cream. Brouwers passed on the cream. He was forty-six, had the body and condition of a thirty-year-old, and wanted to keep it that way. Only cookies from Nicolas and a good glass of beer were worth the occasional sin.

"Naturally, Jos. Plus a bonus of half a million if you finish the job within the week."

Brouwers raised his eyebrows. *An attractive offer,* he thought, *and hard to refuse.*

"The man I'm looking for is an awkward customer, Jos, exceptionally slippery. He disappeared without a trace a couple of days ago. I wouldn't be surprised if he's already out of the country."

"Not an issue, Mr. Vandaele. It's a small world. They always leave a trail, if they want to survive."

Vandaele smiled. Brouwers was a professional. It wouldn't be the first time he'd managed to complete an almost impossible assignment.

"Are the police also looking for him?"

"Most likely, Jos. Hence the bonus. It's essential that you get to him before the cops do. Don't worry about expenses. I'm happy to reimburse everything."

Brouwers was about to ask Vandaele what he meant by *everything*, but the old man beat him to it.

"If you have to use the Concorde to track him down, don't hesitate. And if the thing is flying too slow for you, have a word with the captain and tell him to hit the gas. D'you get my drift, Jos?"

Brouwers puffed at his cigar. He quite fancied the idea of a trip on the Concorde.

"Let's hope our man likes long-distance travel," he said with a grin.

"So I can assume you're willing?"

Vandaele got to his feet and crossed to the mahogany liquor cart. It was time to seal their agreement with something special. For once, Brouwers didn't say no.

"I'll need some additional information, of course," he said. "The more I know about the target, the quicker I'm likely to find him."

"There's information in abundance, Jos. I've known William Aerts since he was a toddler."

• • •

Jos Brouwers was already a little tipsy when he said good-bye to his client around midnight. The sky above the polders was exceptionally clear. Trillions of stars illuminated his path. But Brouwers didn't notice the chill in the air. He ambled to his car. Shame Greta wasn't going to be there when he got home.

Van In kissed Hannelore good night in their home alongside the old Vette Vispoort almshouse. Only an hour earlier, no one would have been able to convince him that a documentary about mating anteaters could be so stimulating.

8

Van In was up with the birds the following morning. An insipid sun did its best to penetrate the grime on his office windows. Cutbacks announced by the city council a year ago were beginning to take their toll. Building maintenance had been reduced to a minimum, and only the rooms that were open to the public were cleaned on a regular basis—not that Van In cared. The film of dirt on the windows offered a certain privacy. It was more or less impossible to tell from the outside if people still worked in the place.

Versavel took care of the coffee as usual. Van In was stretched out in his chair with his feet on his desk. He'd had a turbulent night. After a bout of animal sex with Hannelore, he had fallen into a deep, deep sleep. But Morpheus had only granted him a couple of hours of oblivion. He woke with a start at three thirty that morning soaked in sweat. He had spent the rest of the night tossing and turning and fretting. Linda Aerts's accusations were hanging over his head like the sword of Damocles. And the sword was a real one. He had seen it in his dream, swaying back and forth like the giant sickle in Edgar Allan Poe's infamous story in which a poor prisoner only just survives the horrors of the pit and the pendulum.

Van In had lined up all the arguments, and the more he thought about it the more convinced he was that he wasn't going to get off scot-free. Uncertainty gnawed at his soul like waves crashing against the white cliffs of Dover.

"I wonder what made Aerts take off in such a hurry," said Versavel out of the blue.

"Do you suspect him of something?"

Van In had to admit that he hadn't been paying much attention to that line of inquiry. Perhaps he'd been concentrating too much on the Love and its clients.

"People with nothing to hide don't just disappear and leave everything behind."

"Leave everything behind?" Van In echoed. "He took sixteen million with him. That's not exactly what I'd call 'everything.'"

Versavel wasn't fazed by his boss's argument. He poured him a cup of coffee as Van In sat upright in his chair. It wouldn't have been the first time he'd spilled boiling coffee on his shirt while trying to drink it semihorizontally.

"An APB on the television wouldn't go amiss," he conceded.

Versavel looked at him expectantly.

"Unless you have other suggestions, Guido."

"It might make sense to warn the airports and the border crossings."

Van In shrugged his shoulders. "And don't forget the federal boys," he said with more than a hint of sarcasm. "Feel free to warn the entire country, Guido. Heaven forbid the public gets the idea we were careless."

Van In took a taste of Versavel's always excellent coffee. The sergeant had gotten the message and had decided to ease back. It clearly wasn't Van In's day, and it was better not to get on his nerves.

"Did you manage to get Carine Neels involved?" asked Van In after a few moments of silence.

Versavel nodded. "She was on the line all day. The telephone company's bound to be wondering what we're up to."

"With a bit of luck it'll help us identify our Herbert. Once we know who he is, the rest should be child's play."

Van In flipped his legs back onto his desk. It promised to be a quiet day, but he was visibly taken aback when the telephone rang. His cup was half-empty, but he still managed to spill coffee on his shirt.

"Hello, Pieter."

Van In immediately recognized Hannelore's voice. "Do you miss me already?" he asked.

"Don't be an asshole, Pieter Van In." She sounded tense. "The Groene Rei, on the double. Somebody killed Provoost, and believe me, it's not a pretty sight. His secretary found him half an hour ago."

Van In sat in stunned silence for a full ten seconds after Hannelore hung up, the receiver still pressed to his ear.

"Something wrong?" asked Versavel.

"There is a God after all, Guido. Somebody just did me a massive favor."

"Did they find Aerts?"

"No." Van In laughed. "This is way better."

The late Yves Provoost's secretary opened the door and let Van In in. The woman was still trembling, and her face was whiter than hotel linen.

"Prosecutor Martens is waiting for you in Mr. Yves's office," she said with a sniffle.

In spite of the seriousness of the situation, Van In was having trouble suppressing a smile. In legal circles, deputies were always referred to as prosecutors. Vanity, after all, was no respecter of rank.

The Provoost house on the Groene Rei had been completely renovated a couple of years earlier. Van In had a hard time thinking of a historic building in Bruges that hadn't been given a professional once-over. In contrast to many a restoration project, however, Provoost had spared neither money nor effort to return his parental home to its former glory. In addition to the skillfully sanded facade, he had also renovated and refurbished the interior. The entrance hall alone contained a fortune in antiques.

Van In followed the elderly secretary down the corridor.

Yves Provoost had inherited Miss Calmeyn from his father with the rest of the furniture. Eudoxia Calmeyn had worked for the family for close to forty years and was planning to retire in six months. She was old school: dutiful, efficient, and loyal. Van In observed her violin-shaped contours. Miss Calmeyn was wearing a gray calf-length skirt, an opaque white blouse, and heavy denier, flesh-colored nylons. The sound of her flat, sensible shoes shuffling along the tall, narrow corridor only added to the gloom. At the end of the corridor she opened one of two double-padded doors and motioned for him to go inside. She herself remained in the corridor.

"Hello, I'm here," Van In chirped. He looked around in surprise. "Where's everyone else?"

Hannelore was standing by the fireplace, a neo-Renaissance monstrosity. Van In crossed to her, and she kissed him absently on the lips.

"Miss Calmeyn called the public prosecutor's office," she said. "I'm expecting the rest of the circus in ten minutes or so."

"Excellent. So, where's our friend?"

Hannelore pointed to a futuristic sofa, almost invisible behind a forest of indoor plants. Van In spotted the sofa's back legs through a screen of ferns and ficuses with a set of steel handcuffs attached, similar to those used by the police.

"Don't laugh," Hannelore chided when Van In turned to her with a twinkle in his eye.

Provoost was on his back, stark naked, with a ball of fabric in his mouth.

"And I'm not supposed to laugh?" Van In clenched his jaws. "Jesus H. Christ. Is that a clothespin on his nose?"

Hannelore had kept a safe distance. The entire scene disgusted her, but not Van In.

"Looks like our eminent legal expert has been playing a deadly little game. What shall we call it? Clothespin sex?"

Hannelore said nothing, not out of indignation, but afraid she too might burst out laughing. That was Pieter's fault, but now she wanted to cut off the comical commentary. "No one puts a clothespin on his nose before cuffing himself, Pieter."

Hannelore did her best to stay objective, but she couldn't deny that the scene excited her a little. Pieter's observations only served to fuel her fantasy. She tried hard to suppress the perverse images that filled her imagination but to no avail.

Van In circled the sofa with caution. At this stage in the investigation, it was extremely important not to screw up the evidence. It was almost as if Versavel had whispered those words in his ear. "Not a pretty sight, eh?"

"I told you that already on the phone," Hannelore quipped.

She moved a step closer, trying not to look at the naked male on the floor. She had limited success. Now that Van In was here, the corpse seemed to exert a morbid attraction on her. She had once attended a postmortem in college, determined not to give her male classmates an excuse to ridicule her for the rest of the year. But as a magistrate her situation was different. This was a professional matter, so she forced herself to look. Or was she using her authority as an excuse to satisfy what she herself considered a morbid curiosity? She observed inadvertently that the expression *rigor mortis* didn't apply to every part of the male anatomy. She'd heard different claims about men who hanged themselves.

"I wonder what Dr. De Jaegher will have to say."

"He's not likely to miss the clothespin, that's for sure," said Hannelore, confused. She couldn't keep her eyes off the body. Provoost was fatter than his expensive tailored suits suggested. Even lying on his back his belly stuck out above his chest, evidence that the dead lawyer didn't sweat the calories at a gym. Hannelore didn't want to be reminded that Van In once looked the same. He suddenly leaned over and rummaged in a pile of crumpled clothing hidden out of sight between a jet-black filing cabinet and a terra-cotta planter, in which a giant cactus stubbornly braved its unnatural biotope.

"Find something?" she asked, moving even nearer.

Van In picked up one of the pieces of clothing. Provoost had good taste. The olive-green pajama pants sported the label of an expensive tailor, and the dressing gown was enough to make any self-respecting Brit jealous. The color and pattern matched the ball in Provoost's mouth to perfection. It had to be a matching scarf. Without it his stylish outfit wouldn't have been complete.

Was it the deceased's awkward position on the slanting arm of the postmodern sofa, or was it a final muscular spasm? The grisly thud with which Provoost's legs hit the floor, tugging the body onto its side, made them both jump. Hannelore swallowed a squeal and grabbed Van In. Her body was on fire. Van In peered over her shoulder at Provoost as he dangled grotesquely from the sofa.

Hannelore squeezed him so hard she almost crushed him. It was a strange sensation. A few feet away death had staked its claim, yet in her frightened body he could feel the throb of new life.

"Don't be afraid, Hanne." His words sounded biblical. With a little reverb they could easily have been the words of the angel at the grave of Jesus. "It's pretty common for recent corpses to do weird things."

Hannelore had had enough in spite of his attempt to calm her. She crossed to the window and gazed over the embankment at the dark waters of the Groene Rei, trying to restore her emotional balance. Was it her hormones? Why was she feeling embarrassed? Was she any better than the criminals she helped to put in jail every day, people they labeled perverts? Was she just lucky to have been born into different circumstances, easier circumstances? Was it all a question of fate?

The doorbell announced the arrival of the expected visitors. Miss Calmeyn didn't leave the judicial authorities waiting for a second more than necessary. She raced to the door and let them in: Dr. De Jaegher, Leo Vanmaele—there to takes photos of the scene—and two officers from forensics.

"We meet again, Dr. De Jaegher," said Van In lightheartedly. De Jaegher raised his hand in recognition and turned immediately to Hannelore. A magistrate, and especially a pretty magistrate, was more in keeping with the dignity of his position than a half-baked police commissioner.

Hannelore had to put up with an old-fashioned kiss on the back of her hand. The wrinkled Don Juan clearly wanted more, but with Van In in the neighborhood, he had to watch his step.

"This isn't good for the crime figures," said Leo cynically. "One more corpse this week and we'll be on par with Brussels and Antwerp combined."

His sharp eyes registered every detail, searching unconsciously for the ideal corner and best light to take a couple of decent photographs.

"This one's got more flesh on his bones," Van In mumbled a little too loudly.

Leo glanced tellingly in the direction of Dr. De Jaegher, who fortunately hadn't heard the remark. He was too busy sweet-talking Hannelore.

"I wonder why the killer stripped him and cuffed him," said Van In in a neutral tone. "It makes me think of a couple of gays settling accounts."

Leo was inclined to endorse the suggestion. He opened his bag and snapped a twenty-eight millimeter lens onto his Nikon. Van In let Leo get on with his work. He made his way to the front room, where De Jaegher was still doing his best to impress Hannelore. Like every male of the species, Van In sensed a need to mark off his territory. In an effort to dispel any doubts, he took her hand in his. The gesture was enough to remind De

Jaegher of his obligations. The police physician excused himself and began his business. He flipped Provoost onto his belly and popped a digital thermometer in his anus in an attempt to determine the victim's time of death. The reliability of the method was dependent on a number of different parameters, and the result of the measurement had to be interpreted by a specialist. This was a textbook case. The ambient temperature was constant, and the corpse was fresh. Even De Jaegher had to be capable of making a reasonably accurate diagnosis. According to Van In's guess, Provoost hadn't been dead for more than twelve hours.

Leo took photos of the cuffed hands. De Jaegher then called on the assistance of the forensics guys to remove the handcuffs. He scraped under the victim's fingernails and placed the gunk in plastic bags. Tissue or blood from the killer was often found under the nails. Such genetic fingerprints had led to more than a few convictions in recent years.

"So when did he die, Doctor?" Van In asked.

De Jaegher waited to be asked again before formulating a reluctant answer.

"In this instance I can be quite specific, Commissioner. The man was probably killed between three and four a.m."

Van In noted the time of death. He wasn't in the mood to argue with De Jaegher, but he couldn't help noticing the contradiction between *specific* and *probably*.

"Cause of death?"

De Jaegher looked at Van In indignantly. He considered the

commissioner a mere pawn and himself the king. It was time the police learned to respect some of the elementary rules of politeness.

"What did the man die of, Doctor?" Van In insisted. It was a stupid question. A child could see that Provoost had choked to death, but it had to be officially confirmed by the police physician.

"Suffocation, Commissioner."

Van In noted the cause of death next to the time of the murder. He would read the rest later in the autopsy report. He suddenly felt an ice-cold hand on his arm.

"Can you wangle a glass of water, Pieter?"

Hannelore looked far from her best, and her voice sounded like a death rattle.

Van In jumped and threw his arm around her.

"What's the matter? You look so pale. Shall I . . . ?"

He pointed toward De Jaegher. Hannelore vigorously shook her head. Van In was pleased. The very idea of that quack laying a finger on her . . .

"A glass of water and a breath of fresh air and I'll be fine," she whispered hoarsely.

Van In helped her to the door. The air in the corridor was already enough to perk her up. She smiled and squeezed his arm.

"Thanks, Pieter. Don't worry, I'm fine, really."

"Are you sure?"

"I'm sure."

Hardly three seconds later, Miss Calmeyn appeared from an adjacent room. She had been keeping a patient look out while the doctor and his team went about their business.

"Do you have a glass of water, Miss? Deputy Martens isn't feeling too well."

Miss Calmeyn didn't ask unnecessary questions and hurried to the kitchen. *What in God's name made them saddle such a young creature like that with a murder inquiry,* she thought bitterly. *They've no respect these days.*

Hannelore emptied the glass as the color returned to her cheeks. Van In held her hand firmly in his.

"I skipped breakfast this morning," Hannelore confessed.

Eudoxia Calmeyn shook her head disapprovingly.

"Come, child," she said, her tone suddenly familiar. "I made some cheese sandwiches in the kitchen. You could use a few calories by the look of you."

Van In raised his eyebrows in surprise when Hannelore thanked Miss Calmeyn and followed her to the kitchen. Corpses made little impression on him these days, but he was sure of one thing: they didn't give him an appetite.

Eudoxia Calmeyn made a fresh pot of coffee as Hannelore dug in to the sandwiches. Van In would have bet a month's wages that she was munching on the late Yves Provoost's breakfast. Eudoxia turned to look at her every now and then. A sublimated form of the maternal instinct she had consciously suppressed for the last forty years glowed in her eyes. *Had she known that the frail creature beside her was a self-assured woman who had treated many a lawyer to a sleepless night she might have looked at her differently,* Van In thought with a hint of perverse delight.

"Just what the doctor ordered, eh?" asked Van In.

"Delicious," Hannelore replied, clearly enjoying every morsel. "You don't happen to have a jar of gherkins by any chance?" she asked the elderly secretary.

Eudoxia looked her up and down. Van In figured Miss Calmeyn was checking for signs of pregnancy, but she would have to be patient. Hannelore's belly was still relatively flat.

"Did Mr. Provoost live here alone?" he asked when Eudoxia placed a plate of mini gherkins on the table.

"Mr. Yves lives in Knokke," she responded in the present tense. "In his parents' villa."

She poured the coffee and joined them at the table.

"He only stays here when it's busy at the courthouse," she said, nimbly anticipating Van In's next question. No one had to know that Mr. Yves only went to Knokke on the weekend. He did it for the children, nothing more.

Van In dropped two lumps of sugar into his coffee and stirred it carefully with the silver teaspoon Eudoxia had set beside him.

"Do you have a key to the house, Miss Calmeyn?"

Eudoxia was an experienced secretary, so she wasn't about to let such a question throw her off balance.

"Of course I do," she said, her head held high. "Both Mr. Gaetan and Mr. Yves trusted me completely."

"Gaetan Provoost was Yves's father," Hannelore explained between bites. "The man was an institution. There's still a photo of him in the courthouse."

Eudoxia smiled approvingly. She was warming to the girl, little by little.

"So it was evident that you would be the one to find Mr. Yves," said Van In.

Eudoxia sipped nervously at her coffee and then blew her nose. The horrific picture was engraved forever in her memory. "I'm supposed to start at nine, officially," she said with a lump in her throat. "But most of the time I'm here by eight."

"To make breakfast for Mr. Yves," said Van In with an affable smile.

"Yes, of course," she replied. "I mean, not every day. Only when Mr. Yves spends the night."

Miss Eudoxia had walked right into his trap, and she spotted it immediately. Hannelore looked away. Fortunately, Van In didn't push the issue. He knew what he wanted to know, and that was enough.

"Mr. Yves likes to get an early start," said Miss Calmeyn in a worthy effort to save the situation. "When I'd heard nothing by eight thirty, I went to his study and knocked. And when he didn't answer, I . . ."

Her voice faltered. She picked up her damask napkin and dabbed her eyes. Her sadness was genuine. Hannelore stopped guzzling. The elderly lady did her best to control her emotions, but she didn't protest when Hannelore put her arm around her shoulder.

"What a terrible shock that must have been, Miss Calmeyn," she said comfortingly. "I can't imagine how I would feel in your shoes."

"Heaven forbid, child. I still don't understand it. The times we're living in . . ." She started to sob out loud and hid her face behind a lattice of bony fingers. It had finally hit Miss Calmeyn that Yves Provoost was truly dead.

Van In thought it best to leave the two women alone for a while.

Dr. De Jaegher had finished his work in the study. The two forensics experts were busy searching for clues, an activity Van In hated with a vengeance. For him the atmosphere at the scene of the crime and the reactions of those involved were more important than all that messing around with fingerprint spray and handheld vacuum cleaners. Material evidence was only necessary when perpetrators refused to confess. But the perpetrators had to be tracked down first, and that for him was what made crime prevention so interesting.

De Jaegher was gathering his things. Van In felt it would be hypocritical to shake the man's hand and quietly left the room. It was time he explored the rest of the house. A steep flight of stairs in the corridor led to the first floor. His curiosity got the better of him, and he made his way up. The walls were covered with miniature paintings in pretentious gilded frames, all of them still lifes by unknown nineteenth-century masters. Such work fetched astronomical prices at the antique fairs. A sketch of a pile of overripe fruit in a porcelain bowl could set you back the best part of a hundred thousand francs. On the landing, which was twice the size of his own bedroom, there was an excessively adorned Dutch mirrored cabinet, a piece of furniture that actually belonged in a museum. The first floor had two spacious bedrooms and an English-style bathroom with an abundance of mahogany and ornate but impractical facilities. The room on the street side functioned as a guest room. The air was musty, and the white sheets on the bed seemed a little yellowed. The walls were so chock-full of artwork it was barely possible to see the floral wallpaper behind them. Van In counted twenty-three paintings, watercolors, etchings, and drawings. Gaetan Provoost had been an "art" collector all his life.

The second bedroom was less tidy and clearly something of a bachelor pad. Books and magazines were scattered everywhere. A glass and an open bottle of Glenfiddich graced the nightstand next to a box of anxiety pills.

The bedside lamp, a bronze monstrosity from the previous century, shed its insipid glow over the turned-down quilt. A wide-screen mastodon of a TV on an elegant console served as a sort of dividing wall between the bed and the rest of the room. Two piles of videocassettes towered on each side. The titles spoke for themselves, evidence that Provoost was inclined to swing both ways. On the basis of what he saw, Van In tried to form a picture of the man lying downstairs on the sofa. Yves Provoost was a respected attorney with clients he had inherited for the most part from his forefathers. He had, in fact, been born into a family of eminent lawyers and had more or less been brought up in the business. Together with the name, he had also inherited a significant family fortune. Even without his legal qualifications he would have had no problem maintaining a flamboyant lifestyle.

Van In explored the room. The wardrobe contained a variety of suits, all of impeccable quality. He then inspected the sideboard. Its drawers were stuffed with an extensive assortment of expensive underwear and cotton pajamas.

"Commissioner."

A flash of lightning once succeeded in knocking Saint Paul from his horse, making him see the error of his ways. Miss Calmeyn's voice mimicked the same special effect. Van In shuddered, turned, and tried to smile innocently. The secretary of the late Yves Provoost wasn't about to be mollified by a fake smile. She glared at him, her eyes filled with the fury of a tropical storm. Hannelore kept her distance and did her best to keep a straight face. She thought Eudoxia was the ideal mother-in-law, the type men are scared of.

"Excuse me, Miss Calmeyn. I was thinking . . . in the interest of the investigation . . ."

"No one is allowed into Mr. Yves's room without my permission," said Calmeyn. "I know the law. Without a warrant this is forbidden territory."

Miss Calmeyn knew well enough that Provoost guzzled whiskey on the quiet and watched porn. She may not have approved, but that didn't mean just anybody had the right to come poking their nose into his business.

"I understand, miss, but—"

"No buts, Commissioner. If you do not leave the room this instant, I shall call the federal police."

Van In sighed. He'd heard that argument before somewhere.

"As you wish, Miss Calmeyn. We're on our way. But don't come complaining in a month that the police haven't done their job."

Hannelore bit her lip as she watched Van In beat his retreat like a chastened dog.

Jos Brouwers was in luck. Thanks to detailed information he had received secretly from Vandaele, he had rushed to knock on the door of Dominique Verhelst. As the slippery assistant manager of Bruges' commercial bank, Verhelst promised to do whatever was necessary, and right away. Brouwers had saved Verhelst from an expensive divorce after his wife brought in the police in an attempt to catch him in flagrante delicto with another woman. Brouwers had informed Verhelst in advance, and he had canceled the party.

Verhelst called him less than two hours later. "Hello, Jos. Good news I think."

Brouwers grabbed his notebook and pen. This was promising to be easier than he had expected.

"William Aerts withdrew half a million in cash at the beginning of the week and then transferred the rest to an account at the Banco Condottiere in Rome."

"The rest?"

"Sixteen million."

Brouwers underlined the amount. Our friend wasn't planning to come back anytime soon. "Excellent. Can you check if he withdrew the money in Rome?"

"Is that important?" Verhelst inquired cautiously.

Passing on confidential client information to a third party was pretty reprehensible. As assistant manager, he had a degree of leeway and within the bank he was more or less immune, but international transactions were a different matter altogether, and the risks couldn't be underestimated. In reality, there was relatively little chance that the bank in Rome would respond to his request for information.

"Would I ask if it wasn't important?" The sudden silence between them only served to emphasize Verhelst's frustration. "If it hadn't been for me, you would have been forced to sell that villa of yours in Montpellier, Dominique."

That was enough to settle it.

"I'll see what I can do," said Verhelst. "But I can't promise anything."

"That's fine, Dominique. I'll call you tomorrow at two p.m."

9

So what do you think?" asked Hannelore.

The waiter at the Mozarthuys served two cappuccinos. An early group of tourists paraded across Huidenvetters Square under a cotton wool sky.

"Let's wait for the forensics report," said Van In sullenly. In the preceding week, he had been kicked out twice by women, and it still bothered him, as did the fact that the case had more or less ground to a standstill. He needed an Arthur to pull Excalibur from the rock. Van In had ordered a door-to-door inquiry in the neighborhood, but he wasn't expecting much to come of it. Provoost had been murdered in the middle of the night. The chance that a witness had seen the killer enter or leave Provoost's house was exceptionally slim.

"Don't tell me you haven't formed an opinion. I know you better than that, Pieter Van In, and I can read your face like a book. I can see all the cogs turning feverishly in that handsome head of yours."

Van In dipped his nose into the cappuccino's creamy froth. "Is there a reason why I have to drink coffee, by the way? It's eleven fifteen, for Christ's sake. I bet a Duvel has fewer calories."

"I thought we'd come to an agreement," she said, her tone rigid.

Van In lit a cigarette and blew the smoke defiantly in her direction.

"It's your funeral," she said with a nasty grin. The smoke reminded Hannelore of her own weakness. She had also given in to temptation. *One Duvel wouldn't do him any harm,* she thought. "Unless we break the rules for once."

Van In pushed the sweet cappuccino to one side and signaled the waiter. The man had been following the conversation.

"A Duvel, sir?" he asked with a smile.

Hannelore profited from the situation and stole a cigarette. "Quid pro quo," she teased.

Van In didn't react. He figured a Duvel for a cigarette was fair exchange. "If De Jaegher's to be believed, Provoost was killed between three and four a.m., but if you ask me, the killer must have arrived a lot earlier."

"What makes you so sure?"

"No signs of a break-in, so we have to presume that Provoost let his killer in. I'm guessing it's unlikely Provoost would have visitors after midnight."

Hannelore raised her eyebrows in surprise. "Aren't you jumping the gun a little? Maybe Provoost got up because he heard a suspicious noise."

"Also unlikely," said Van In. "If I hear a suspicious noise in the middle of the night, I don't put on my dressing gown first."

"Of course you don't." She grinned. "You don't have one."

"OK. Provoost was the aristocratic type. He hears a strange noise and puts on his dressing gown."

"Sounds logical to me," said Hannelore.

"And a scarf?"

The waiter arrived with a frothy Duvel. Van In grabbed the glass and gulped greedily.

"I hadn't thought of the scarf," Hannelore admitted. "But how do you know that Provoost was wearing a scarf at the time of the murder? The killer could have taken one from the dresser."

"Then he must have done it in Provoost's bedroom. I checked the drawers in the dresser and found piles of them, all neatly folded. Someone looking for a gag isn't likely to head for the bedroom and carefully remove a silk scarf from a pile in a drawer without making a mess. I'm not convinced. If you ask me, Provoost was expecting someone. His bedside lamp was still on for one, and I'm pretty certain the silk pajamas and matching scarf weren't just a coincidence."

Hannelore shook her head.

"He only had one pair of silk pajamas, Hanne. Men tend to buy these things for a reason."

"They do?" she asked.

"I mean certain men. Women apparently find silk to be a turn on."

"Why don't you have a pair?"

"Because silk pajamas cost at least fifteen thousand francs, and I can't afford such excesses."

Van In emptied his Duvel in a single gulp and immediately ordered another. Hannelore didn't insist on a second cigarette.

"I'm afraid you've lost me, Pieter, unless you're trying to suggest the killer was a woman."

"Everything is pointing in that direction," said Van In with a scowl.

Hannelore admired him in spite of her confusion. The way he picked up on things even made her a little jealous. Van In wasn't burdened by the academic limitations that weighed down the majority of intellectuals. He reasoned on instinct.

"OK, let me run through it again," she said resolutely. "Provoost is expecting a female visitor in the course of the evening. He spruces himself up, puts on his fanciest pajamas, and waits in the bedroom until his guest rings the bell. He lets her in. The woman overpowers him, slaps on the cuffs, and kills him a couple of hours later."

Van In nods. Her analysis was spot on. "Half of Provoost's porn collection is hardcore S and M, so I'm not surprised he was found in cuffs. But the killer needed time, and that bothers me."

"Why should it? Those S-and-M games can go on for hours, or so I'm told," said Hannelore, unable to understand why the time element troubled him.

"Because I think there's a link between the death of Provoost and our Herbert. If Provoost succumbed to a sex game that got out of hand, then his death was an accident, and I find that hard to believe. I'm convinced Provoost was murdered in cold blood, and if I'm right, the killer didn't have to stretch the execution for several hours."

"A remarkable hypothesis," said Hannelore. "Do you think we'll ever find the truth?"

"If we want the truth, then we have to take a close look at the charity," said Van In resolutely. "A search warrant would give Versavel the chance to hack into their computer files. Can you arrange one?"

"You know it's not as simple as that," she retorted. "There isn't an examining magistrate in the country who would write out a warrant on the basis of a couple of vague suspicions. And God knows what would happen if Versavel's extrajudicial computer antics got out."

When Hannelore used words like *extrajudicial*, Van In knew it was better not to push the point.

"Then our only option is to infiltrate the charity," said Van In flatly. He had devised a plan that same evening to put an undercover officer into the charity.

"Can't you think of anything legal?" Hannelore asked, raising her voice.

"I'm open to suggestions," he said submissively. He knew there was no alternative, and so did Hannelore. The list of names Van In had dragged out of Linda Aerts was worthless. The men who figured in it hadn't broken the law. William Aerts, who probably had useful information to offer on the Love and what went on there, had disappeared without a trace, and the connection between the murders and Helping Our Own was based on little more than conjecture. It was common knowledge that Lodewijk Vandaele's empire was founded on crooked practices, but no one had been able thus far to bring charges against the man and make them stick.

"Did you have someone particular in mind?" she inquired with caution.

"It has to be a woman, of course," said Van In. "And preferably good-looking."

Hannelore smiled. He wasn't exactly subtle, but what did it matter? A compliment was a compliment. "OK, Pieter. But before you get started, let me run it past the prosecutor. If he gives his blessing, then I'll give it a try."

Van In realized he had made an unforgivable blunder. "I had a different sort of good-looking in mind." He grinned sheepishly.

"You mean another woman."

"Don't get me wrong, Hanne. You're pregnant, and besides, this is police business."

"Is she under thirty-five?"

There was no point in messing with her any longer. "Carine Neels is twenty-three and specially trained for this sort of job,"

Van In lied. Her age was the only thing that tallied. Carine Neels had just completed two years at the police academy. The kind of criminals she'd had to deal with so far were illegal parkers and pensioners who hadn't paid their dog licenses.

"And you're sure this Carine person isn't pregnant?" Hannelore asked innocently.

"Carine is a lesbian," Van In lied a second time.

"Aren't lesbians allowed to get pregnant?" Hannelore glared at him ready for a fight. *Sweet talking SOB*, she thought to herself. *Next thing she'll have a beard and a mustache.*

Van In hadn't missed the sarcasm in Hannelore's question. "Carine Neels also suffers from vaginism," he whispered. "I found out for myself the day before yesterday."

Hannelore said nothing. She didn't want to get his hackles up.

Jos Brouwers unfolded a map of southern Europe. Dominique Verhelst had just called him back. The sixteen million was still in the bank in Rome. Brouwers tried to put himself in the shoes of his prey. According to Vandaele, Aerts was a cunning bastard. So there had to be a connection between the city of Rome and the fugitive's hiding place. The ex-cop carefully removed the cellophane from a packet of peppermint gum, tore open the foil, and popped a stick into his mouth.

Most investigators invariably make the same mistake. They think that the solution to a problem has to be in proportion to its complexity. But nothing could be further from the truth. Complexity is nothing more than a collection of simple elements. Jos Brouwers knew that a correct analysis of a problem constituted half the solution. He had inherited a talent for numbers from his father. Brouwers senior had spent most of his working life as a junior bank clerk. No one had ever seen him using a calculator. His ultimate dream was that his son would become a civil engineer. He worked himself to the bone day and night to make his dream a reality. But fate can be capricious, and plans are always human creations.

Brouwers finished his first year at college magna cum laude, and his father died the same day from a heart attack. Welfare provisions weren't enough in those days to pay for college, so Jos Brouwers was forced to interrupt his studies. He applied for a job with the federal police, completed their rigorous training program, and submitted himself to the humiliations and arbitrariness of his superiors. For more than ten years he handed over his wages to his mother. His brothers and sisters went to college in his stead, and when they graduated they turned their backs on him, ashamed that their older brother was "only" a cop. But every tragedy has its turning point, its catharsis, as the Greeks call it. Six years earlier he had decided to retake control of his life. He resigned from his job and swore revenge on his stuck-up family. The only way to achieve his goal was to become richer than his brother Jacob, the ophthalmologist; acquire more prestige than Bert, the soap actor; more freedom than Christa, the sculptress; and more influence than Kathy, the local government representative. When it came to wealth and freedom, he had succeeded summa cum laude. He enjoyed prestige and influence in certain circles, and that was enough for him.

Brouwers took a pair of compasses, checked the scale of the map, and drew a three-hundred-mile circle around Rome.

Versavel looked nervously at his watch and rubbed his mustache. Van In had left his beeper in the office as usual. Intentionally unavailable, yet again. Chief Commissioner De Kee called every half hour, insisting that Van In report to him the minute he got in. Versavel did his best and called around. Miss Calmeyn assured him that the commissioner and Deputy Prosecutor Martens had left more than an hour ago. Leo Vanmaele suggested he call his favorite café, l'Estaminet, and the clerk at the courthouse informed him that Deputy Martens was away from her desk.

Versavel tried the same people a second time before checking in with De Kee. The diminutive chief commissioner was furious. Versavel swallowed the abuse and promised he would contact Van In before the day was out. The chief commissioner could rest assured. Versavel had left a message on Van In's answering machine.

When Van In hadn't appeared by noon, Versavel threw in the towel. Frank was waiting with a delicious lunch.

"Hello, is this Lodewijk Vandaele?"

Vandaele recognized Brouwers's voice and attached a scrambler to the telephone. They always followed the same procedure. "Jos. What's new?"

Brouwers immediately noticed that Vandaele sounded tense.

"Is there a problem?" His direct question was met with a moment of silence.

"Provoost is dead," said Vandaele. "Murdered, apparently."

"Messy, sir. Do you want me to investigate?"

"Out of the question," said Vandaele decisively. "I'd rather hear what's been going on with you."

Brouwers sensed that the old man was hiding something but didn't push the matter. "Aerts is in Malta," he said.

"Malta. What makes you think that?"

"Because I have evidence to support it, sir."

Vandaele didn't ask any unnecessary questions, giving Brouwers the opportunity to develop his hypothesis.

"Aerts transferred sixteen million to an account with the Banco Condottiere in Rome. If he's as savvy as everyone claims, he knows well enough that the transaction was traceable. If he doesn't want to leave a paper trail, he'll have to withdraw the money in person. That's why he started off with half a million in cash, money he needs to survive while the situation cools down. Aerts is presuming that the judiciary will forget about him after a couple of months. I would have done the same, and I would have picked out a safe hiding place to wait out the storm."

"Sounds plausible," said Vandaele. "But why Malta of all places?"

Brouwers had expected Vandaele's response. He had asked himself the same question. "I presumed that Aerts would prefer familiar territory to go underground and preferably not too far from his money. If it were me, I would opt for somewhere I knew."

"Continue, Jos."

"Malta isn't part of the European Union, and it's been growing in popularity of late as a tax haven. The island is less than three hundred miles from the Italian mainland. Anyone with anything resembling a boat can make the crossing without being noticed. And of course, Aerts has been there on vacation a couple of times."

Brouwers had called dozens of travel agencies in search of information when he struck gold with the last one on his list. He had a good story, and he told it with vigor. His brother-in-law, William Aerts, had recommended an apartment hotel on Malta, but he'd lost the address, and his brother-in-law was temporarily out of reach. All he could remember was the name of the travel agency where William made the reservation. He needed the name of the hotel. Would they mind checking?

"How did you know Aerts was staying in an apartment hotel?"

"I made it up." Brouwers grinned. "But his name was in their computer, and that was the important thing. According to the guy at the travel agency, William booked his first trip to Malta in 1988. He opened the account at the Banco Condottiere a year later. I'm guessing he's been planning his disappearance for quite some time. I also wouldn't be surprised if he got to know someone in Malta."

"Aren't we getting ahead of ourselves, Jos?"

"I'll be able to answer that question in a couple of days, sir."

Brouwers had the half million bonus in mind, promised by Vandaele if he managed to liquidate Aerts within the week.

"So you're going to Malta," said Vandaele.

"If that's OK with you, sir."

"Of course, Jos. But keep me posted."

"Of course, sir. I'll call every night between eleven and twelve."

Van In arrived at the Hauwer Street police station around two-fifteen. He had enjoyed a healthy lunch with Hannelore on the terrace outside the Mozarthuys. Meat roasted on a lava stone grill was an acceptable alternative for people on a diet.

Versavel was peering through the window and barely reacted to Van In's cheerful greeting. "Problems, Guido?"

Versavel turned and sat down at his word processor without saying a word.

"I'm the one with the depression issues, don't forget." Van In laughed.

Versavel didn't respond. The silence was heavy, like a wet bath towel on dry skin.

"Is there something going on with Frank?"

Versavel reached for his mustache and rubbed his nose with the palm of his hand. Van In joined him at his desk. His arm floated aimlessly through the air for a couple of seconds then landed a little awkwardly on his friend's shoulder.

"Nothing serious, I hope?"

Versavel appreciated the gesture. He turned to Van In with eyes full of sadness and despair. "Frank's gone. There was a note on the table when I went home at lunchtime. He took his clothes and his kitchen stuff—that's it." He sounded as if he was still reading the note.

"Has Jonathan got anything to do with this?"

"Frank felt cheated, like he was nothing more than my house slave."

Van In had been through a lot in his life, but a jealous fifty-six-year-old man was a first, and it pushed him to his limit. "Jeez, Guido," was all he could think to say. "Just like that?"

Versavel shook his head. He'd seen it coming, and he cursed the day he set eyes on Jonathan again after so long.

"It's my fault, when you think of it," said Van In submissively. "If I hadn't asked you . . ."

"I made the suggestion myself," Versavel protested.

"D'you want me to take you home?"

Versavel looked at his friend, his eyes filling with tears. Van In felt a lump in his throat. "Not home, Pieter. It would drive me crazy."

Versavel took his boss's hand. He was the only man alive who could get away with it. "A breath of fresh air wouldn't go amiss, Pieter."

Carine Neels was taken aback at the sight of both men holding hands. Two days earlier she would have been sure to knock before entering Room 204, but now she felt like part of the team, a full member of Bruges' Special Investigations Unit.

"Sorry," she said. "I didn't know . . ."

"No need to apologize," said Van In, making no effort to let go of Versavel's hand.

"I thought you'd like to hear my report," said Carine.

Her telephonic odyssey hadn't been very successful. Five minutes ago she had talked to Dr. Verminnen, the last plastic surgeon on her list, but like the others, he too was unable to remember a young man having his jaw set back for aesthetic reasons. Much to her surprise, Van In didn't seem to be bothered.

"Perhaps you could make yourself useful in another way, Carine."

Her heart beast faster when Van In used her first name. "At your service, Commissioner," she responded with enthusiasm.

"Are you free this evening?"

"Depends for what," she said in a neutral tone.

Van In let go of Versavel's hand and invited Carine to sit at his desk. "Do you know what an undercover agent is, Carine?"

Of course she did. She never missed an episode of *NYPD Blue* or *Hill Street Blues*.

"Then you know the risks involved?"

She nodded and tried to conceal her accelerated breathing by folding her arms macho-style.

"Good," said Van In. "I want you to take the rest of the day off and . . ." He gave her a number of detailed instructions. "I'll expect you at my place around eight. Then we can go through the rest of the operation."

Carine Neels floated out of the office like a madonna on a cloud. She wanted to broadcast her happiness for all to hear, but she knew that wasn't a good idea. If she did, she would blow her cover.

Gray clouds amassed above the towers of Bruges. After a long, warm summer, September was showing signs of an early winter. Van In headed toward the coast in the hope of catching a few final rays of sun. Versavel said nothing the entire journey, just stared ahead absently as if they were driving toward the end of the world.

Van In parked the Golf near the marina in Blankenberge, a busy seaside resort where the gray fall sky had made way for azure blue. A pleasant breeze wafted in from the sea. The people here seemed friendlier than in stuffy Bruges. The air was pure, and the murmur of the sea was enough to crush even Versavel's stony silence.

"You're a good man, Pieter," he said out of the blue.

Van In rested his arm on his friend's shoulder. "I know, Guido," he said with a laugh. "And it's good to hear it from someone else for a change. But you really knocked me for a loop back there. You and Frank? After so many years?"

Versavel filled his lungs with tepid sea air. In the car on the way from Bruges to Blankenberge, he had tried to find an explanation for the tragedy that had torn his orderly life to pieces.

"I should have known," he said. "I couldn't keep up with him, I mean sexually. It must have been painful for him. He alluded to it more than once in the last few months. It made me want to prove myself. The affair with Jonathan was the last straw. Frank's gone and I'm alone and old."

Van In had experience with depression. Comforting words rarely helped heal the wounds, but silence made no sense either. "Spare me the nonsense, Guido. You don't look a day over forty. There's a big wide world out there, and you're handsome, kind, intelligent, and . . ."

Van In told Versavel the things *he* didn't want to hear from his well-intentioned friend when *he* had hit the bottom. Then he did something he could never have imagined doing in his wildest dreams. He turned and looked Versavel in the eye.

"And to cap it all off, you're my best friend, Guido, and I love you."

Even Versavel was taken aback when Van In embraced him. A kiss on the cheek eased the pain if only for a moment. Day-trippers gaped, but Van In paid no attention.

"Hannelore would have done the same," he said. "We both love you a lot, Guido. Don't forget it."

Versavel looked up at the sky, at a loss for words to express his feelings. He stroked his mustache Versavel-style, and Van In read it as a good sign. "I think we both deserve a Duvel," said Versavel unexpectedly.

"We?"

"I think I could use one too, especially today," said Versavel.

A shrimp boat sailed into the harbor with a swarm of seagulls in its wake. It turned left at the lifeboat station and headed toward the eastern pier.

At the end of the pier there was a wooden warehouse that served as a café cum restaurant. The terrace out front was packed with hikers enjoying the late fall sun.

Van In just managed to secure a table where a group of four cackling Germans were arguing about the price of the sangria. He took advantage of their confusion, and the waiter clearly didn't mind. He smiled knowingly when the Germans continued their "alcohol-free stroll."

"Two Duvels," said Van In. "Ice-cold if possible."

When a stately yacht sailed past the pier, everyone on the terrace turned right, and the cameras started to click. This was the highlight of the day for many of them. An original photo would be evidence to those at home that the day-trip hadn't been for nothing.

"Feeling any better?" Van In asked.

Versavel rolled up his shirtsleeves and loosened his tie. No one would have guessed he was a cop. "De Kee wanted to talk with you this morning," he said.

"For Christ's sake, Guido, relax."

"I'm relaxing, Pieter, I'm relaxing. My work is all I have right now. It keeps the ghosts at bay."

The waiter—friendly, fortysomething—served the Duvels with the usual thick head of froth. When Versavel took out his wallet to pay right away, the man held up his hand. That suited Versavel down to the ground.

"Any idea what the old bugger wanted to talk about?"

Versavel gulped down the high-octane beer as if it were mineral water. Tufts of froth glistened in his mustache. "He read your report, Pieter. I think he's pissed about the list you managed to squeeze out of Linda Aerts. De Jaegher's a board member at De Kee's rotary club."

"I can imagine some of the names will give him nightmares," said Van In. He was thinking of Johan Brys, among others, the ambitious minister of foreign affairs. When guys like that reach a certain level, all that matters is money and sex.

"Whoever Herbert is, he must have been quite a special man," Van In murmured.

"D'you think there's a connection between Brys, Provoost, and Herbert?"

"Two of them are already dead," said Van In.

"So you're planning to move in on Brys?"

Van In had asked himself the same question a thousand times in the last forty-eight hours. Crucifying government ministers had become fashionable of late, but if he wanted to grill Brys, he would need proper evidence. The occasional visit to an obscure farmhouse for a bit of slap and tickle wasn't a crime. "Some of the other names on the list are interesting too, Guido."

Versavel nodded. Bringing in the minister of foreign affairs for questioning on the basis of a forced confession from a brothel keeper wasn't worth the risks. The idea of turning up the heat on Brys by smoking out some of his cronies sounded a great deal safer.

Van In ordered another pair of Duvels and a plate of cheese. The light lunch he had enjoyed with Hannelore had clearly been a little too light.

"We have to find the weakest link, Guido."

He fished a copy of the list from his inside pocket, and they reviewed the names together. After discounting the magistrates, they were left with a dozen or so politicians, a retired federal police colonel, four industrialists, a priest named Deflour, a couple of senior civil servants at the Ministry of Finance, Vervoort, and De Jaegher. Van In was certain that the list was far from complete. Linda Aerts only knew the names of the regulars. He took a pen and underlined the names of the Helping Our Own board members: Vandaele, Provoost, Vervoort, Deflour, and Muys.

"Let me deal with the canon," said Versavel enthusiastically. "Priests aren't supposed to lie, or so they say."

Van In circled the name *Deflour*.

"Then I'll take Muys," he said grinning.

"Why Muys?"

Van In took a swig of his second Duvel. "Isn't it obvious?" He laughed. "Muys rhymes with mouse rhymes with whorehouse."

Versavel finished his second Duvel in almost a single gulp. The effects of such an overdose were immediately apparent. "I have to tell Europol right away," he slurred. "I'm pretty sure they don't have that particular method of inquiry in their database."

Carine Neels had to ask directions a couple of times before she finally arrived at the Vette Vispoort. The man she spoke to on Saint Jacob Street offered her five thousand francs for an hour at his place. Her metamorphosis had clearly worked. Carine caught sight of her reflection in a shop window. *Pretty sexy,* she thought.

10

Melchior Muys was a corpulent man, his ice-cold cobra eyes bulging behind the convex lenses of his expensive designer glasses. His receding hairline was typical of a genuine bureaucrat. Such premature baldness was once considered a sign of wisdom. Now people knew better. Men were bald because their maternal grandfathers were bald.

Van In knew that Muys was forty-four. Without that information he would have said the senior auditor was at least ten years older.

"Good morning, Commissioner."

Muys offered him a chair. A tray with a thermos and two cups was evidence that the man had been expecting him. In spite of the obligatory NO SMOKING sign, Van In lit a cigarette with the intention of showing Muys who was boss before they got started. Muys was quick to react. He pressed the button on his intercom and asked his secretary to bring an ashtray.

"I'm here about the Yves Provoost murder," said Van In coolly.

Coming straight to the point had its advantages. The initial reaction of the person being interrogated was often invaluable, certainly if he was pouring coffee at the time. The timing was perfect. Muys spilled coffee in the saucer.

"An unfortunate affair," Muys conceded.

The senior auditor tried to keep his trembling hand under control.

"You knew him well, I presume."

Muys returned the thermos to the tray and sat down at his desk, where he felt a great deal safer. "Professionally, yes," he said with obvious caution. "Yves was a valued colleague. His death has touched me deeply. Such a brutal killing—"

"Provoost was liquidated," Van In interrupted. "According to the present state of the investigation, we're assuming it had to do with his regular visits to the Love."

Muys folded his arms under his chin, a bearing intended to absorb the shock caused by Van In's reference to the Love.

"If I'm not mistaken, you visited the place yourself, Mr. Muys?" Van In inquired, sipping his coffee and pretending to look out the window while keeping Muys in view from the corner of his left eye.

"Excuse me, Commissioner, but I'm afraid I don't follow you," said Muys, his voice composed. The shock effect had clearly worn off.

"You were never there?"

"Never," said Muys.

The senior auditor had recovered his balance. Like so many middle management civil servants, he had learned by trial and error that truth was a relative concept. Denial was always better than admission. "Another coffee, Commissioner? Or a cognac perhaps?"

He was about to get up when Van In gestured that he was happy with another coffee, but Muys wasn't taking no for an answer. The filing cabinet was where the majority of civil servants kept their stash of booze.

"Yet there are witnesses who swear you were a regular," said Van In. "Which isn't a crime, of course," he added immediately.

Muys selected an unopened bottle of Otard from an extensive assortment. "I wonder who such witnesses might be, Commissioner," he said.

He poured Van In an immense glass of Otard, a tried and tested technique that almost always worked. Food and drink was the cheapest form of corruption in Flanders.

Van In recognized the maneuver. His thoughts turned to Linda Aerts. He understood why she'd lost her bearings. A night in a police cell could be a grisly experience, especially after learning that your partner has taken off with your savings. Van In didn't consider himself an alcoholic, but the amber liquid had a strange attraction. *One glass wouldn't do any harm,* he thought. "I'm afraid I can't say, Mr. Muys, but we have evidence to suggest that . . ." Muys gave him the glass of cognac.

"Cheers, Commissioner."

Van In took a sip. Only a week ago, this sin would have filled him with remorse. But today the flavor of wood and fire was sheer pleasure, pure and simple.

"This is an informal interview, Commissioner," said Muys. "Off the record, if I understand you correctly?"

Van In nodded. He felt like a coachman losing control of the reins, his horses on the verge of bolting.

"I'm pleased to hear it." Muys smiled. "Otherwise I would be obliged to consult my lawyer."

He sipped victoriously at his glass. The man's malicious reptilian gaze brought Van In back to his senses.

"I wonder what your lawyer would advise if I were to let him see the videos, Mr. Muys. Unless your wife doesn't mind her husband messing around behind closed doors."

Van In realized that this was a major gamble, but the way Muys's fingers tensed around his glass spoke volumes. His knuckles turned white, and in the business, that was called a bull's-eye.

"Videos, Commissioner?"

"Every married man drops his pants now and then, Muys. I don't expect the taxman's slaves to be any exception."

Muys focused on the Otard and gulped greedily at the bait he'd set out for Van In. "It's all so long ago, Commissioner," said Muys after a few moments of silence. "I was there twice, max."

"Twice?"

People always lie by degrees, thinking they'll get off cheaper if they minimize the frequency of their misdeeds.

"You mean twice a month," said Van In sternly.

The senior auditor took another gulp of the first-rate Otard, which he drank like lemonade. Muys searched in desperation for the best way to limit the damage.

"But that's not why I'm here, Muys. I'm more interested in Provoost and Brys."

Muys was visibly distressed. His reptilian eyes narrowed into thin bloodless slits. He knew there had been problems in the eighties. Vandaele had shut down the Love without warning, and there were rumors going around that something bad had happened in the place. Provoost and Brys had also been mentioned, and it had taken a full year before activities could restart in another location. "Civil servants aren't saints, Commissioner. Sometimes we have to be pragmatic, if you get my drift."

Van In swirled the cognac in his glass and inhaled its aromas as a connoisseur would. "You mean the taxman's always open to suggestions."

Muys tried to defend himself as best he could. The lie had burst open like a festering ulcer. "Sometimes there are other factors we have to account for," he said with caution.

"Such as?"

Van In permitted himself the air of an inquisitor. His illustrious predecessors had demonstrated that the very sight of instruments of torture could have the same effect as actually using them.

"Jobs, Commissioner. If we were to tax every company to the limit, then . . ."

"Then what?"

Muys poured himself another drink.

Van In enjoyed watching the senior auditor walk into his own trap.

"Everyone knows that taxes in this country are inhumanly high. That's why we're instructed not to be too strict with the minor evaders. At least that's what it used to be like," said Muys.

"And in exchange for your silence, you get some free ass on a regular basis at the Love?"

Van In grabbed the Otard and made a show of pouring himself a second glass. Victory had to be celebrated. Muys reminded him of a character in a Fellini movie. The senior auditor was nothing more than a quivering pile of fat in a tailor-made suit.

"It wasn't uncommon back then," Muys whimpered. "That sort of thing was tolerated in the eighties."

"And you've changed your ways," Van In observed sarcastically.

Muys looked at him imploringly, like a pig face-to-face with its slaughterer.

"So you have no information on Brys and Provoost?"

Muys shook his head vehemently. One word about Brys and he could kiss his career in the ministry good-bye.

"Vervoort perhaps?"

A vacant expression took hold of Muys's face. Vervoort was dynamite. He had warned Vandaele about him years ago.

"You know Vervoort, don't you? He's on the board of Helping Our Own if I'm not mistaken, and according to the information I have at my disposal, you are too."

Van In had been saving this observation for last. The talk about Provoost's murder was designed to bring Muys to his knees.

"That's correct, Commissioner."

Muys pressed his lips together, which made him look like a cobra. "The charity was Mr. Vandaele's initiative. The organization's goal is to support people in need."

"Our own people?"

"Flemish people in need, Commissioner. Everyone is welcome."

"No conditions?"

"No conditions," Muys confirmed. "We verify our clients' stories, of course. We don't want people abusing the system."

Muys gulped. His Adam's apple wiggled almost invisibly. He shouldn't have used the word *abuse*.

"Remarkable," said Van In. "I've been told that people who want the charity's help have to be card-carrying FLASYC members."

It was a reasoned guess. Van In had no hard evidence that the charity only offered help on the basis of ideological inclination.

"Out of the question, Commissioner. FLASYC heads a political movement, and we work with them from time to time. Of course, I can't deny that many of the people we assist end up joining the movement on their own initiative."

Van In knew exactly how to play the winning hand. "Are you a revisionist, Mr. Muys?"

The senior auditor was manifestly shocked at the question. The vein meandering across his forehead visibly swelled. "I don't have to answer that question," he said stoically.

Van In gauged the hostility in the man's words. "So you admit it," he said. "I wouldn't be surprised if the millions the charity spends on printing every year is intended to convince the innocent that the concentration camps were a fable and that the Jews who didn't return died of lung infections and dysentery."

"You have no right . . ." said Muys, his pent-up rage visible in the same ugly pulsing vein on his forehead.

Van In felt the time had come to let go. "What gives you the right to mislead people in need? Your sort makes me sick. And let me promise you one thing: I'm going to enjoy cuffing you, Mr. Muys. Soon!"

Van In glanced at his watch. "But now it's time for a breath of fresh air."

He got to his feet and left the senior auditor a blubbering mess.

Versavel was waiting for Van In in Room 204. His visit with Canon Deflour had taken less time than he had planned.

"The flesh is weak," said Versavel when Van In asked him about his conversation with the priest. "I came away with the impression that the poor soul was happy to be able to confess his sins."

In different circumstances Versavel would have grinned at that point. But this time he delivered his report as if he was carrying the pain of the planet on his shoulders.

"Did he have anything to say about Provoost?"

"Negative."

"Brys?"

"Not a word," said Versavel. "Deflour seems like an honest man."

"FLASYC?"

"Deflour swears by all the saints in heaven that he has no access to the charity's accounts."

"That's crap. There are more Catholic priests with extreme right leanings in this little country of ours than you'd think."

"What if we're on the wrong track?" Versavel asked.

Van In had also asked himself that question. The connection between Herbert, Provoost and FLASYC was extremely fragile. If Provoost hadn't been murdered, he'd have abandoned the hypothesis long ago. "If the phone tap brings in nothing, then it's time we started looking elsewhere," said Van In resignedly.

Versavel's eyes widened.

Van In freed a last cigarette from his crumpled pack. "I wasn't planning to mention it, Guido, but . . ." Van In filled his lungs with smoke. "I know a guy . . . who happens to owe me big-time."

Versavel raised his hand to his forehead. "You're playing with fire, Pieter. Does Hannelore know about this?"

"She's determined to go to Portugal." Van In sighed. "If I go the legal way, it'll take at least two months to get permission to tap their lines."

"Tell me about it," said Versavel pointedly. He and Frank had been planning a trip to Turkey. The very thought of it pained his heart. "Why not put a wire on Vandaele and Brys?"

Before Van In could answer, the telephone rang.

"Hello."

Van In grabbed a pen, scribbled a couple of sentences, and asked a couple of questions Versavel didn't understand. The conversation lasted three minutes. Van In appeared exceptionally upbeat.

"Well?" asked Versavel.

"Vandaele and Brys both have scramblers on their phones," said Van In, confused.

"That's not what I meant, Pieter."

"Wasn't that what you asked?"

"Yes, that's what I asked, but now I want to know who you were just talking to."

Van In pretended he didn't notice Versavel's curt tone. The sergeant was on edge. The positive effects of the visit to Blankenberge hadn't lasted long. Frank's departure had aged him five years in the space of a couple of days. "Muys called Vervoort less than five minutes after I left. He asked about the charity's accounts, whether they were up to a serious audit. If Vervoort's reaction is anything to go by, Muys can relax. There isn't an examining magistrate in the country who would dare to issue a warrant on Helping Our Own."

"He might be right, Pieter."

Van In shrugged his shoulders.

Leo Vanmaele was renowned for his perfect sense of timing, invariably appearing when no one expected him.

"Am I interrupting?" The diminutive photographer grinned.

"You? Interrupting? Impossible, Leo. Grab a chair. Any coffee left, Guido?"

Versavel grunted, got to his feet, and fetched him some coffee.

Leo snuggled into one of the new office chairs. He liked the fact that he could adjust the height when he was already sitting down. It was a bit like a Big Dipper ride. But even at its lowest setting, his feet still didn't touch the ground. "Provoost's last hours were pretty ugly," he said, making a long face.

Van In nodded. The idea of choking to death with a clothespin on your nose didn't seem like a pleasant way to shuffle off this mortal coil.

"It looks as if the killer tickled him first for a while."

Versavel turned in surprise.

"Explain yourself," said Van In.

"There was a floor lamp in Provoost's study, one of those expensive Italian jobs. You know what they're like. Cost a bloody—"

"Get to the point, Leo, to the point!"

"OK, OK. The cable had been cut close to the base and the bare wires deliberately tucked back under. The technical crew found a fragment of insulation in the siphon under the sink and tiny splinters of copper in Provoost's pubic hair."

"Welcome to Latin America." Van In whistled.

He now understood what Leo's reference to tickling meant. He had recently seen a movie on TV in which a prisoner was tied to a metal bedspring. A man in a doctor's coat poured water over the poor bastard and laid into him with electrodes. Music by Schubert could be heard in the background. Van In thought instinctively of Linda Aerts. Perhaps she had also seen the film and her night in the cell had left her terror-stricken.

"Isn't that a bit far-fetched for your average S-and-M fan?" asked Versavel.

"Of course," said Leo. "Most S-and-M aficionados have a code. If the pain is too much to bear, they stop . . . love-play over. Sadists on the other hand . . ."

"Have no limits," Versavel finished his sentence.

Van In thought about Linda again. He felt a little guilty, and he also had to admit that he had enjoyed the moment when she succumbed to the full effects of his method. "Unless Provoost's killer was looking for information. That's what torture's for, isn't it?"

"Every sadist has the same excuse," said Versavel dryly.

"Torture is one of the classic methods for extracting information," said Leo matter-of-factly.

"Or a confession?" said Versavel. For a brief moment he forgot the harrowing pain that was threatening to tear open his chest. He was happy that the discussion had been able to distract him.

"Do you think Provoost killed Herbert?"

Leo and Versavel turned to Van In in surprise. Why hadn't they thought of that?

A pale bolt of lightning illuminated the purple sky. A few seconds later, a clap of thunder rolled over the rooftops. Day suddenly turned into night as a legion of clouds covered the city in darkness. Versavel rushed to the window and slammed it shut. Van In rolled his chair closer to his desk, as if he was safer there.

"In that case, Pieter . . ."

"I know, Leo. If Provoost killed Herbert, the shit will hit the fan. The other clients at the Love will sense the threat and close ranks."

Leo belonged to the judicial police, which fell under the public prosecutor's office. His reaction was understandable. There had been so many scandals of late and yet another would be likely to shut down his department for good. The public prosecutor's office was under serious fire these days.

Van In tried to defuse the situation. "Gentlemen, let's focus. If heads have to roll, then I'll take care of it myself."

Versavel nodded. He knew what Van In meant. The commissioner had exposed some major players in the past, and in a pretty unorthodox way. All the same, Versavel was determined to defend his boss.

"Could William Aerts be behind this?" asked Versavel. The

sergeant thought that Van In hadn't given enough attention to Aerts as a line of inquiry.

"Aerts is a pawn, Guido. He organized the orgies at the Love. I'm interested in the big fish, not the small ones."

"But small fish catch big fish," Versavel insisted. "If you ask me, Aerts knows the whole story. Why would he disappear in such a hurry otherwise?"

Van In couldn't simply ignore the question.

Forked lightning and crackling thunder followed in quick succession. A curtain of rain limited visibility to less than a couple of yards.

"Guido might be onto something," said Leo, filling his cup with coffee.

Van In covered his face with both hands. In democracies the majority always had the last word. But whether they had the right word remained open to question. "OK, OK," he said with barely concealed sarcasm. "I hereby declare hunting season to be open. Do whatever you think is necessary. Inform Interpol, call the federal boys, pray to Mother Teresa. I don't give a rat's ass what you do, but I think we need to make the best of what we have."

"So we should start with the clients who frequented the Love." Versavel sighed. "That's good news for Herbert, but what about Provoost? Who took him out? The same clients?"

"Pretty unlikely," said Leo. "Why would they get rid of their buddy?"

"An outsider then?" asked Versavel, unconvinced. "But who else had access to the Love's membership list?"

Van In had never touched an electric eel before, but he had a fair idea what it would feel like. Provoost had been killed the day Linda spilled the names, and she had consulted with Provoost that same day.

"Linda Aerts," said Van In under his breath. "But why?"

Leo scowled and gulped his coffee. "By the way . . . our forensic friends discovered something remarkable at Provoost's place. The killer apparently took the time to vacuum the entire house and mop the floors."

"You're kidding . . ." said Van In.

Leo nodded, sure of his information. "Someone also removed the vacuum cleaner bag, and Miss Calmeyn insists that one of her mops is missing. You should check it out in the file. Killers sometimes take the time to vacuum the scene of the crime, but I've never read anything about mopping."

"A woman after all," Van In hissed.

"Or someone who's well informed about the methods we use to detect evidence," said Versavel matter-of-factly.

Van In was on the ball. "I'll call Hannelore," he said. "If this isn't enough to make the public prosecutor issue an arrest warrant on Linda Aerts . . ."

Just as he was reaching for the phone, it rang.

"Van In."

He could hear hysterical screaming in the background.

"Mr. Vermast, good afternoon. How are you?"

"I'm fine; thanks, Commissioner."

The screaming in the background continued unabated and didn't incline Van In to ask after the rest of the family.

"Sorry to disturb you, Commissioner. It's probably nothing important," said Vermast hesitatingly. "But . . ."

"You can never tell what will be important, Mr. Vermast. And you're not disturbing me at all." Van In made a weary face and an obscene gesture. What did the blundering garden gnome want this time?

"Well . . . it's like this, Commissioner. Just before the police arrived, my daughter took a couple of bags from the grave. We only found out this morning."

Van In gestured that Versavel should listen in. Judging by his boss's widening eyes, something serious was going on. Leo poured himself a third cup of coffee.

"Tine hid her discovery from us all this time," Vermast continued in an apologetic tone. "Perhaps—"

"Would you mind coming to the point, Mr. Vermast?" said Van In, his patience thinning.

Versavel heard the poor man gulp.

"Tine found two small bags. My wife thinks they're breast prostheses," said Vermast, not entirely sure of what he was saying.

"Jesus H. Christ."

"What was that, Commissioner?"

"Breast prostheses?"

"Isn't that what I said, Commissioner?"

Versavel stroked his mustache. *Pure Kafka,* he thought.

"Never mind, Mr. Vermast. We'll be there in ten minutes."

The Air Malta 737 landed at the Luqa airport at two thirty p.m. The aircraft taxied over the bumpy tarmac and parked two hundred yards from the modern terminal. Jos Brouwers waited until it emptied its load of sun-seeking tourists. An overtired flight attendant urged him to get a move on. Brouwers grunted. It wasn't the first time he'd been on a plane. She didn't have to lump all the passengers in the same box.

The heat embraced him like a dry sauna, but it didn't take long before the sweat was running down his back. The breeze was warm and did nothing to help.

He passed through customs without a hitch. The island was clearly begging for tourists. It took less than fifteen minutes for the pack of impatient vacationers to fill the colorful buses awaiting them and disappear.

Brouwers walked through the terminal, happy the Maltese had discovered the advantages of air-conditioning. Inside, it was bliss. When the stream of tourists had come to a standstill and tranquility had returned, Brouwers inspected the building. The Avis car-rental office was no bigger than the illuminated red-and-white company logo that announced its presence. The clerk in attendance compensated with a broad smile.

Brouwers opted for a compact Suzuki. The friendly Avis clerk waved him off. Brouwers had read in a tourist guide that the Maltese were crazy for ready cash, but that wasn't the main reason he had paid for the car with hard currency. Credit cards and checks left an electronic trail, and that wasn't smart for someone traveling on a false passport.

The trip from Luqa to Valletta, the island's capital, took less than fifteen minutes. The divided highway was broad, and the road signs were pretty clear for the Mediterranean, but that changed when he drove into the city. Its chaotic streets and traffic reminded him of Athens.

Brouwers had bought a map of the city before leaving Belgium. He had studied it in detail at home but lost his way within minutes. Driving on the left was the biggest hurdle. Luckily the locals reacted politely when he took a bend too wide or veered too far to the right. They appeared to be used to foreigners and their clumsy driving. And they had devised an ingeniously simple way of spotting them in the traffic. License plates of rental cars all started with an *X*, which made them easy to identify even from a distance.

Van In sounded his horn when they arrived at the Love. Versavel was about to get out and open the gate, but Van In held him back.

"This is the twentieth century, Guido."

He might just as well have said "open sesame." Before Versavel had relaxed back into his seat, the ten-foot-wide gate swung open as if by magic.

"Time was always of the essence." Van In grinned. "When the big boys wanted a quick screw, every second counted."

"I've never really understood what a quick screw is all about," said Versavel, his mind drawn back to endless evenings with Frank, grilled lobster, and cool almond oil.

Van In maneuvered the Golf over the bumpy terrain. "Those guys fuck like they talk," he said. "Too fast and without passion."

"How come you know so much?"

"Because I'm a commissioner, of course. What did you think?"

"So you see yourself as one of the big boys?"

"Big is relative."

"So this is a size thing?"

"Let's not go there," said Van In. "You're the last person I want to have *that* conversation with."

Hugo Vermast welcomed the gentlemen of the police with a nervous smile. "That was fast," he said. "I hope I didn't bother you for nothing. I'm sure it's not really so urgent."

Van In held up his hand. "The police are here to serve, Mr. Vermast," he said. "It's our duty to investigate every tip."

His words appeared to put Vermast at ease. Versavel bit his bottom lip. Van In was clearly in one of his manic dips. Or did he have his tongue in his cheek?

"I normally pay no attention to these things, but my wife—"

"Your wife is a nurse," said Van In before Vermast had the chance to remind him.

"Nice of you to remember, Commissioner."

Vermast led them into the kitchen. It was tidier than the last time. The bags were lying on the table like a pair of deflated balloons. "That's what she found," said Vermast.

Van In picked up one of the bags. It felt like jelly wrapped in thick cellophane. "Hard to believe that women are willing to pay a small fortune for these things," he said.

Versavel resisted comment. He had never understood what attracted men to breasts.

"Joris hid them in his secret box. He's crazy about special objects. Did I mention that Joris is on the autistism scale?"

Van In nodded emphatically, hoping Vermast wouldn't stray from the point.

"The intellectual capacities of people with autism are often underestimated," said Vermast, straying from the point. "Have you seen *Rain Man*?"

Vermast was a proud father. Joris was a special boy because a clever screenwriter had elevated an exception to become the norm.

"With Dustin Hoffman?" asked Versavel diplomatically when Van In didn't respond.

"That's the one." Vermast turned to Versavel. "Unbelievable, don't you think? Our Joris has a long way to go, but he'll get there."

"I thought it was your daughter who found the bags," said Van In, letting the blubbery bag slip through his fingers. Vermast's initial unease appeared to have vanished. He seemed more self-assured than ever.

"Tine knows that her brother likes to collect unusual things. That's why she took them from the grave and gave them to him. She wanted to do Joris a favor. No one can blame her."

"Of course not," said Van In.

Vermast beamed. "Coffee, gentlemen?"

Versavel jumped at the chance, not catching Van In's glare. Vermast grabbed three cups and an oversized thermos from the kitchen counter. The coffee tasted like stewed chestnuts.

"Is there still a drop of cognac, Hugo?"

Van In used Vermast's first name deliberately. His host smiled conspiratorially.

"Leen won't be back for another hour. Let me see what I can do."

He disappeared into the living room. Van In poured his coffee into a planter containing a sickly looking sansevieria. Versavel followed his example without blinking.

Jonathan Brooks, a tall, blond Brit, had served in the SAS for eleven years. He was one of the commandos who took out a couple of IRA heavyweights in Gibraltar back in the day. The entire affair created such a political commotion that the four-man SAS team was forced into early retirement. Brooks had accepted the golden handshake offered by Her Majesty's government, but he wasn't happy about it. Six months after the incident, he set himself up as a private investigator in Valletta. His choice was no coincidence. Malta had been part of the British Commonwealth until only recently. British culture was still part and parcel of everyday life, and the weather suited him down to the ground.

Jos Brouwers parked his rented Suzuki in a working-class suburb of the capital, not far from the harbor. A couple of children ran past him, whooping and having fun. The narrow streets, scruffy café terraces, and loud advertising billboards reminded him of Naples. The smell at least was unmistakably Neapolitan: urine, rotting food, and heating oil.

Jonathan Brooks lived in a spacious villa looking out over the docks. Its flaking façade—typical of southern European houses—concealed the cool opulence of whitewashed walls and efficient air-conditioning.

"Hello, Jos. How are you? How was the flight?" he shouted from the balcony.

Brouwers wiped the sweat from his brow, waved, then joined his hands together to form a cup.

"Thirsty?"

The Brit let out a full-throated laugh. He and Brouwers had first met at an SAS training camp. Brouwers was part of a delegation representing the Belgian federal police. After the wave of terrorism in the seventies, the police were in search of a way to respond to the meaningless violence threatening to destabilize society. The politicians had decided to set up a counterterrorism unit. Brouwers had been part of the elite special interventions squadron—SIE, or Speciaal Interventie Eskadron—from the outset, and no one was surprised that it followed the British model. After all, the SAS was generally considered the best anti-terror brigade in the world. And that was without exaggeration.

"I've got Jupiler," said Brooks as the two men shook hands. "Ice cold."

Carine Neels hadn't ridden a bicycle in years. She had chosen the most rickety thing she could find in the warehouse where her colleagues stored stolen two-wheelers awaiting collection by their rightful owners. But owner and bike were rarely united.

The bicycle fitted her new image to a tee. Its frame was covered in rust, and the chain squeaked like a nestful of abandoned chicks. Perfect for a woman on welfare.

Care House was in a wooded estate outside the city, about three miles from the Hauwer Street station. The wind was cold and in her face the entire journey. It took her the best part of twenty minutes to get there. Carine was exhausted and out of breath when she cycled up the driveway to the house.

Ilse Vanquathem watched Carine arrive from behind her office window. More and more women in need had been finding their way to Care House of late, and the boost in her annual bonus was tangible to say the least. This time providence had sent her a magnificent specimen. The girl on the bike had long shapely legs, a cute little face, and broad shoulders. Her thin jacket barely concealed an ample pair of breasts.

"Come inside, miss," said Ilse as she stood in the doorway.

She winked hospitably and welcomed her in. "No need to lock the bike. All the people who work here are honest to the core."

Ilse found it hard to imagine that anyone would want to steal such a pile of scrap.

Versavel spent the entire journey from Sint-Andries to Hauwer Street staring vacantly through the windscreen, only half-listening to the monologue being delivered by his boss.

"All this time we were trying to identify a man," Van In rattled on. "Herbert's a damn transsexual. That explains the aesthetic surgery and the mouthful of porcelain teeth. Why didn't we think of it? It's back to square fucking one with phone calls and doctors. Jesus H. Christ. Lucky there aren't too many quacks into that kind of business. What man would get it into his head to . . ."

Van In glanced at Versavel out of the corner of his eye. The sergeant looked like a wax statue recently escaped from Madame Tussauds. "You all right, Guido?"

Versavel didn't move a muscle.

"Is it Frank?"

Van In knew it was a stupid question, but what the fuck else could he say? "D'you want me to take you home?"

Versavel had been stroking the holster of his pistol for the best part of five minutes. Van In hadn't been paying much attention, but suddenly the sight of it filled his mind with unwanted images.

"I'm taking you home," he said. "And I'm staying with you until you get back to your old self."

11

The atmosphere at the breakfast table was tense to say the least. Hannelore was in a mood because Van In had arrived home in the middle of the night.

"Guido was in the pits, Hanne. Without Frank he's as useless as a . . ."

"Husband without a phone? You at least could have called," she snorted.

Van In took the swipe chin on. Hannelore had an appointment with the gynecologist that afternoon for an amniocentesis. He had a good idea how she was feeling. Images of what could go wrong had haunted his own thoughts for the best part of two days. Of course he should have called her, but when Versavel broke down after their visit to the Vermasts, Van In had brought his buddy home, and they had talked into the wee small hours. By the time he realized how late it was, he didn't want to wake her.

"Just call next time, no matter how late it is."

Hannelore pushed her toast to one side. Since dinner at the Heer Halewijn, there hadn't been much movement in her belly. *What if...*

"You believe me, don't you?" Van In waved his hand in front of her eyes. "Are we good?"

The concerned expression on his face made her smile involuntarily. When Van In showed signs of compassion, that meant he was in emotional turmoil himself. If something happened to her, he would be capable of anything, even putting a bullet through someone's head.

"Next time you should bring Guido back here. We can talk about his problems together."

Van In didn't feel like explaining that some conversations were man to man only. "Guido would appreciate that," he lied.

Hannelore tolerated a kiss. Men would never understand how worried women can get.

"By the way," she said moments later, "Miss Neels was here last night. She wanted to report back on her visit to Care House."

"Shit," said Van In.

"You're forgiven, Pieter. If you leave two good-looking women in the lurch for Guido, then it must have been serious."

"Did she say anything?"

"What do you think?" Hannelore smiled. "The girl is convinced she's working undercover and the only person she has to answer to is her immediate boss."

Van In wisely held his tongue. Her mood had clearly changed for the better, but he still didn't figure it was time to ask her to issue a warrant for Linda Aerts's arrest.

Mdina is the jewel of Malta—no ifs, ands, or buts. The old Moorish-looking city dominates the island's arid interior like a much honored holy place on a hill.

Brooks parked his Land Rover—he detested Japanese cars— on the square dividing the historic capital from the more modern town of Rabat.

"As I mentioned yesterday, there's only a handful of Flemish expats on Malta," he said with the self-assured air of a Brit in exile.

Brouwers was still a little groggy from the Jupiler. They had lavishly celebrated their reunion the night before—he with beer, Brooks with red wine. "And a good thing too." Brouwers sighed.

If his hypothesis was right and Aerts was indeed on Malta, it was only a question of time before he traced him and took him out. Once the job was done, Brooks would bring him to Sicily in a speedboat. In exchange for the favor, the ex-commando had offered his friend a commission of one thousand Maltese pounds. It was a lot of money, but crumbs compared to what he'd have had to pay to persuade a Concorde pilot to fly faster that Mach 2.2.

"Plets has lived here for more than fifteen years," said Brooks. "If anyone knows anything about Flemish people on the island, he's your man."

The sudden clatter of hoofs took Brouwers by surprise. A cheerfully decorated coach raced past the Land Rover, missing it by inches. A middle-aged couple waved enthusiastically, as tourists are inclined to do. The coachman droned dutifully on, but the couple in the back weren't interested in his story. Brouwers noticed the man pour a drink for his wife—a triviality, but it moved him. A happy retirement in the company of a woman was a dream he would never experience.

"Most people in Mdina are pretty well-off."

Brooks grabbed Brouwers by the arm. The myth that Belgians were insatiable beer drinkers was highly exaggerated. His friend didn't look well at all. "Most of them are descendants of old Maltese families. The city is an open-air museum that attracts hundreds of thousands on a yearly basis."

Brooks steered Brouwers across the sun-drenched square. It was so hot that even the tourists had sought shelter in the meager shade of a solitary palm tree, where it was at least ten degrees cooler.

Both men entered the massive gate. The city was surrounded by a tall fortified wall that sucked up the Mediterranean heat like a cactus in the desert. The moat had been filled in, and a bunch of well-tanned teenagers were enjoying a snappy game of soccer. Mdina was more of a fortress than a city—imposing and invincible.

Jeroen Plets was Flemish and heavyset, with a beer belly and blushing cheeks. He had the air of a contented gentleman farmer who didn't need to work and hadn't for years. When Brouwers explained in West Flemish that he was looking for a fellow countryman on the island, Plets invited them in with a gesture of welcome. Brooks knew Plets's wife was native Maltese. They had met twenty years ago at a jewelry fair in Milan. Plets was a buyer back then for a renowned Antwerp jeweler. His bride to be was heading the Maltese delegation and presenting her own exquisite collection. It was love at first sight. They courted by correspondence and phone for sixteen months and vowed eternal fidelity in the winter of 1979. She now supervised fifteen jewelry shops on the island. The fast-growing tourist market hadn't done the enterprising couple any harm, and their exclusive den in Mdina was clear proof, if any was needed.

"We haven't had someone from the old country on a visit for ages." Plets laughed. "Is this your first time on Malta?"

Brouwers nodded.

"Jane, we have visitors!" their host shouted in evident good spirits.

Jane turned out to be a heavy-boned, slightly timid woman. Her smile, on the other hand, was more disarming than the best-trained photo model.

She greeted Brouwers and Brooks each with a solid hand-shake. Her fingers were bedecked with the most magnificent silver rings Brouwers had ever seen. "May I offer you some white wine?" she asked without imposing herself.

Brouwers was dying for a glass of water. He was normally

pretty reserved when it came to alcohol, and he had already broken the rules twice in the preceding week.

"That's very kind of you, ma'am," said Brooks, saving his friend from an unforgiveable blunder. On Malta, refusing such an offer would have been a humiliation.

Jane smiled and disappeared as the men planted themselves in cushioned wicker chairs scattered around the courtyard. The historical building's patio fulfilled its purpose to perfection, as it offered shade and refreshment.

"Make yourselves at home, gentlemen," said Plets, still clearly delighted to have visitors.

His wife took care of refreshments, setting a tray on the table and leaving the rest to her husband as an exemplary hostess should. She seemed exceptionally sweet in her long cobalt-blue dress, which subtly camouflaged a number of surplus curves. The curvaceous Maltese looked like a well-fed Arabian princess. Her gray eyes were intelligent, and the stunning jewelry with which she was adorned jingled with every movement.

Plets took a chilled bottle of white wine from the ice bucket and served his guests.

Brooks leaned back in his chair and tasted the excellent vintage. He was familiar with Maltese hospitality and was looking forward to a lazy afternoon.

"You mentioned that you rarely have Flemish visitors, Mr. Plets," Brouwers commented. "No family or friends then?"

Brooks noticed Jane's eyes cloud over. Plets was just as ruffled. He raised his glass without answering and stared for several seconds at the deep blue sky through the sparkling wine. The dancing kaleidoscopic colors seemed to interest him more than his guest's inquiry.

"I presume you still have contacts back home," Brouwers cautiously insisted.

"No, I don't," said Plets dryly.

Brouwers sensed the unease and tried desperately to pick up the pieces.

"Please excuse my indiscretion, sir."

"My family rejected me twenty years ago," said Plets after a nerve-racking silence. The confrontation with the past had torn open old wounds, but he had no reason whatsoever to conceal the truth. "You couldn't have known that, of course, but take it from me, the man you're looking for isn't family."

"The thought hadn't entered my head, Mr. Plets."

Brouwers deftly capitalized on the new turn in the conversation. "The man I'm looking for is a notorious crook, and I have reason to believe he's somewhere on the island. It seemed logical to assume that a man on the run from the law would seek contact with his fellow countrymen. According to Jonathan, you're one of the few Flemish people living on Malta, so—"

"I understand, Mr. Brouwers," Plets interrupted. "But believe me, you're the only other Flemish person I've seen around here in the last ten years."

Plets rubbed the stubble on his chin. Brouwers reminded him of his family. The notorious crook Brouwers was looking for suddenly acquired Plets's complete sympathy.

Jane lifted the skirt of her dress and crossed her legs. Brooks thought it was time to be going.

"I'm not claiming you know the man," said Brouwers, trying to put a good face on the situation. "But Malta is a small island. Perhaps you've heard rumors?"

"If you want rumors, then Amand's your man."

"The restaurant owner on Gozo?" asked Brouwers.

Plets nodded. "If anyone can help you, Amand can. He knows every foreigner on the island."

Jane refilled the glasses and returned the bottle to the ice bucket upside down, a clear signal that she considered the visit to be over.

Fifteen minutes later, Brooks and Brouwers drove off in the swelteringly hot Land Rover heading for Gozo, the second largest island in the Maltese archipelago.

"What did I do wrong, Jonathan?"

"Just bad luck," said Brooks. "I didn't know the family thing was so sensitive."

"Next stop Gozo, I suppose." Brouwers sighed.

Brooks glanced at his watch. "No problem," he said enthusiastically. "Gozo's crawling with good hotels."

Brouwers didn't ask why Brooks wanted to spend the night on Gozo, but he wasn't in any hurry.

Chief Inspector Dirk Baert was feverishly thrashing his keyboard when Versavel arrived.

"Good morning, Sergeant."

Versavel ignored his superior's greeting and didn't reciprocate with the usual "How are you?" He wasn't in the best of shape himself. For the first time in almost forty years, he hadn't shaved, and he'd been wearing the same shirt for two days in a row.

"We received some important information on William Aerts yesterday," said Baert after a moment or two. The silence irritated him. He also thought that Van In and Versavel were being unprofessional.

"I tried to reach you all day yesterday," he added with an accusatory tone.

Versavel sniffed at his armpit and made a face. He then focused his attention on the coffee machine.

"William Aerts took a chartered flight last Tuesday to Rome. Don't you think we should follow up on this, Sergeant? If you ask me, people who leg it in a hurry have always got something to hide."

"Leave the decisions to Van In," Versavel growled. Baert was right, of course, but Versavel preferred to die than admit it.

"Can we expect the commissioner today?"

"Do me a favor, Baert?"

The chief inspector turned. "A favor, Sergeant?"

"Shut the fuck up, and leave me in peace," Versavel snarled.

Baert reacted like a man with Parkinson's. He wanted to move, but his limbs refused to listen. When he finally managed to get to his feet, the door flew open. Van In thought for a second he'd walked onto a film set where the director had just roared "Cut."

"I forgot my ID card, and the clown at reception wouldn't let me in."

Versavel grinned. Van In used the same excuse at least once a week.

"A rookie?"

"Still wet behind the ears." Van In sighed, shrugging his shoulders. He tossed his jacket at the coat stand, ignoring Baert, and poured himself a cup of coffee. Since one or another idiot introduced the concept "sense of civil insecurity," the various police forces across the country had been competing with one another for new recruits. The public had to feel safe, and that meant more uniforms on the streets. The next idea would be a private cop for every family. No one gave a damn about serious crime. That was reserved for the TV.

"Who was it?" asked Versavel.

"Robocop thirty-six or thirty-seven. Jeez, Guido. I can't tell them apart anymore."

"The boys at the desk are only doing their job," Baert protested. "People used to walk in and out of the station unchallenged. It was high time something was done about it."

He was referring to the new security procedures Chief Commissioner De Kee had set up at the entrance to the building. Visitors had to identify themselves at reception, and the staff had to use a card with a magnetic strip that opened the bulletproof-glass door.

"Then they should have done a better job," Van In sneered.

Everyone knew that the bulletproof-glass door had been wrongly mounted. One tick with a hammer and the whole thing would shatter into a thousand pieces. To make matters worse, the door between reception and the hallway was made of pressed cardboard. A sturdy toddler could force it open with no trouble. And if that didn't work, someone could grab a riot gun from the arms room, which was next to reception and thus outside the "secure" zone.

Baert swallowed the critique in silence. His fingers trembled above his keyboard. His brain manufactured a strange hormone cocktail that transformed his blood into a churning mountain stream. "William Aerts has been spotted in Italy," Baert hissed. "But no one appears to give a shit."

"Hmm." Van In sniffed. "I have to admit that our friend William has pretty good taste, but Hannelore insists on Portugal. Sorry, Baert."

Versavel stared at his boss in disbelief. One day Van In was going to go too far and Baert was going to explode like an over-inflated balloon.

"Let's go, Guido. Poirot here has work to do. First stop home to collect my ID."

Versavel didn't hesitate. Before Baert had the time to recover from his second surprise, the two men were chuckling in the corridor.

• • •

Van In parked the Golf on Burg Square, a privilege granted only to the police and a handful of apparatchiks. He loosened his tie and tossed the choking thing onto the backseat.

"De Kee's expecting me in his office at eleven," he said nonchalantly. "But first we need to talk."

"So you don't trust De Kee either."

Versavel tapped the dashboard as if he were playing an invisible piano.

"Dirk Baert is a sucker, and they say suckers can be vindictive. It wouldn't surprise me if our chief inspector is reporting back to the big boss every day, and the very thought drives me up a wall," said Van In.

They wrestled their way through an almost stationary sea of people blocking access to Blinde Ezel Street like a herd of dull-witted cattle.

"I presume we're looking for a quiet café terrace," Versavel figured.

"Needs must, my friend. The Duvel supply at home has dried up, so I'm forced to be unfaithful."

"Huidenvetters Square?"

"Too much yackety-yak, Guido. I prefer l'Estaminet at this hour of the day."

Van In wormed his way through a horde of hysterical Spaniards. A well-mannered family man who was just about to take his best ever video shots called him every name in the book. Van In didn't give a damn. He had walked into the occasional cameraman's field of fire on purpose.

• • •

Queen Astrid Park is sometimes referred to as the green lung
of Bruges, a nickname it doesn't really deserve since it has little
more to offer than a dozen unhealthy trees, a silted-up pond,
and two hundred square yards of parched grass. Van In couldn't
help agree as he walked past the listed facade on the Pandreitje,
an adjoining street. The old prison had been demolished five
years earlier, and the undeveloped land had been transformed
into a cheerless parking lot after a political wrangle that seemed
to take forever. The ad hoc urban intervention hadn't done anything to improve the view of the park. The city fathers might
just as well have planted a power station on Burg Square. But
the disharmony between nature and commerce offered one
positive advantage: tourists avoided the place like the plague.

It was pleasantly warm on l'Estaminet's covered terrace. A group
of about fifteen handicapped youngsters with almost as many
supervisors had commandeered the lion's share of the tables.
The atmosphere was friendly and good-natured. Van In reveled in being surrounded by real people for once. A young man
with palsy treated him to a huge grin. His face was covered in
chocolate sauce, and it clearly delighted him.

Van In chose a table in the corner of the terrace, and Versavel joined him. Like Van In, he too enjoyed the sight of the
handicapped youngsters having such fun.

"I wanted to have a word about the Pamela Anderson connection," said Van In, coming straight to the point.

Versavel was a stranger in the hetero world, and Van In could read it in his eyes.

"The silicon boobs, Guido."

Johan, the proprietor of l'Estaminet, wiped the table with a damp cloth. Unlike Versavel, he knew exactly who Pamela Anderson was, and her silicon boobs didn't bother him in the least. "Two Duvels?" he asked.

"A Perrier and a Duvel," said Van In when Versavel waved the offer aside.

Johan beat a professional retreat. He wasn't in the habit of eavesdropping on his clients' conversations.

"The prostheses are no use to us, Guido. There's no way we can trace where they came from. All they tell us is that our Herbert was a transsexual, and that sheds a whole new light on the case. Until yesterday we presumed Herbert was a man and his connection with the orgies at the Love was unclear. But as a woman, he fits perfectly into the little network Vandaele and his consorts created. Whores get bumped off every day."

Versavel nodded. He had to admit yet again that Van In's intuition was not to be mocked. The commissioner had been following the right tracks from the outset. Herbert's death had a direct link with the parties at the Love.

"Are you thinking what I'm thinking?" asked Van In as he curled his thirsty lips around the frothy Duvel Johan had just served.

"That things got seriously out of hand at one of those parties?" asked Versavel.

"Gold star, my boy! Front of the class!" Van In grinned.

One of the handicapped girls responded to his grin with a fitful grimace. The young man with the face full of chocolate sauce was sitting beside her. A supervisor wiped his mouth, which he clearly didn't like. He stamped his feet and demanded another ice cream. Paid charity was clearly an ersatz solution, but Van In still admired the patience with which the supervisors interacted with the youngsters in their care. If he had been a believer, he would have said a prayer there and then, and begged God for a healthy baby.

"I can't imagine too many sex-change operations were carried out in Belgium in the eighties," said Versavel. "I'm guessing only a couple of places were equipped back then for that kind of business. Why not have Baert call the university hospitals. We'll know who Herbert is before the day's out."

"Baert's already called every specialist in Flanders," said Van In. "And besides—"

"You don't trust the man."

"How did you guess? If Dirk Baert identifies Herbert, he'll be on the phone to the press in a heartbeat to take credit for a breakthrough in the investigation."

"Ask Carine then."

Van In shook his head. "Carine's got other business to attend to."

He briefed Versavel about the undercover operation. "Social services agreed to help. If someone from Care House asks for information on Carine Neels, they'll get a social worker on the line with a fake story. According to their files, Carine Neels is on benefits. Her husband left her with a pile of debt, and if she doesn't pay up in a couple of months, she'll be evicted from her apartment."

Versavel looked at Van In with surprise. "Does De Kee know about this?"

The group of handicapped youngsters was getting ready to move on. At least they could rely on the safe shelter of a properly functioning institution, something most ordinary people had to do without. Van In waved when the ice-cream-guzzling young man treated him to another lopsided smile.

"Jesus H. Christ. Didn't I say De Kee was expecting me at eleven?"

"You did," said Versavel. "And you've got ten minutes. Shall I call a taxi?"

Van In emptied his glass in haste.

"I'll walk, Guido."

He jumped to his feet.

"And I'll settle the bill." Versavel grinned.

Van In turned.

"Relax, Pieter. I'll make the university hospital calls when I get back to the office."

"Thanks, Guido."

The jingle of keys arrested his movement.

"The car's parked around the corner," Versavel said.

"Jesus H. Christ," Van In groaned. "Couldn't you have said that earlier?"

Versavel took two hundred-franc notes from his wallet, left them on the table, and followed his boss.

"Hello, Amand." Jeroen Plets's voice sounded tense. Jane was standing at his back. "Jeroen here. There's something I have to tell you."

Amand looked at the busload of hungry Germans noisily storming his restaurant. "I don't have a lot of time, Jeroen. It's busy as hell here."

"Two minutes," Plets begged.

Chief Commissioner De Kee was deep in the shit. Dr. De Jaegher was a good friend who overstepped the mark once in a while. No big deal. Most men grabbed a bit on the side when they could. The problem was that the doctor's name had appeared on a list Van In had acquired by improper means. De Kee was faced with a dilemma. If he rapped Van In's knuckles for his unorthodox methods, the insubordinate commissioner would accuse him of bias. If he said nothing, then De Jaegher planned to go public with an old secret, and De Kee was determined not to let him. No one had to know that he had gotten a young officer pregnant ten years before and that De Jaegher had skillfully disposed of the result of his fleeting moment of passion.

Van In waited at the door until the clock in the corridor struck eleven. He straightened his tie and knocked.

De Kee jumped to his feet and instead of pressing the *enter* button on his desk he opened the door himself. "What a pleasure to see you, Pieter," said the chief commissioner a little too emphatically.

They shook hands. De Kee sat down at his desk and invited Van In to take the seat opposite him. The office had a familiar feel to it, as if De Kee had never been away. Van In looked around. Everything was back in its place—the framed university diploma, the photo of De Kee with the king, the artwork he had been given as a gift by the Belgian football association, an etching of city hall, and a baseball hat with the logo of the American Police Federation.

"And how is the Provoost case progressing?" De Kee folded his arms, rolled back his chair, and stretched out his legs, just like the legendary J. Edgar Hoover had been in the habit of doing.

"I think there's light at the end of the tunnel," said Van In.

"Explain, Pieter."

"We're focusing on the first murder for the moment," said Van In. "And we're expecting a breakthrough anytime now."

De Kee maneuvered his chair closer and leaned over his desk.

"I'm not interested in the mysterious John Doe, Pieter Van In," he whispered. "Take my advice and leave that line of investigation be for a while. It's a nasty bag of worms, and it could drag you in before you know it. There are names on the list you gave me—important people, people with influence. There's a strong possibility—"

"Dr. De Jaegher doesn't need to worry."

Van In stared the chief commissioner in the eye.

De Kee got to his feet. It was clear from his tightening jaw muscles that he was doing his best to contain himself. "And why might Dr. De Jaegher have reason to worry?" he asked.

"I can't say. We all make mistakes, Chief Commissioner, and if we were to drag everyone who ever crossed the line before the courts, the prisons would be full of decent citizens." Van In allowed himself an arrogant smile.

De Kee sat, joined his hands behind his head, and stretched. The message was loud and clear. Van In would keep his hands off De Jaegher if the Linda Aerts incident was allowed to fizzle out. "A reasonable way of looking at things, Pieter."

His voice was much milder than it was minutes earlier. It wasn't the first time he had underestimated Commissioner Van In's shrewdness. "Don't think I'm trying to influence your investigation, Pieter. My main concern is the welfare of my team. That's why I felt it my duty to discuss a number of delicate issues with you. But now that our strategies would appear to be aligned, let's hope both murders can be resolved to our mutual satisfaction. In fact, I'm looking forward to it with bated breath. Let justice be done."

Even seasoned politicians would think twice before uttering such crap, but De Kee thought he'd fended for himself pretty well given the circumstances.

"Will that be all, Chief Commissioner?"

"One last thing, Pieter. As far as I'm concerned, the Linda Aerts affair is closed but only on the condition that you leave her alone. As long as she's not being indicted on charges, keep your hands off her. Is that clear?"

Van In didn't blame the old bugger for wanting the last word. "You can count on it," he said, relieved.

De Kee got to his feet and accompanied his subordinate to the door. The conversation had lasted no more than ten minutes, and both parties were satisfied with its outcome.

As soon as Van In was out of his office, De Kee called Dr. De Jaegher.

"Psst."

Van In was about to walk into Room 204 when Carine Neels drew his attention with another *psst*. It may not have been particularly original, but it worked. Van In turned, and Carine gestured that she wanted to have a word. The young policewoman looked far from sexy in her uniform.

Van In played the game. They walked together to the first floor where there was a room that was tailor-made for clandestine encounters.

"Big news," she whispered excitedly.

Van In locked the door behind him. The poor creature was quivering like a hummingbird.

"You were right, Commissioner. Care House is a front for a prostitution network. I tried to reach you yesterday but—"

"Calm down, Carine," said Van In. He wondered if he had done the right thing when he gave her the job. Carine sat down.

"Ilse contacted me this morning. She said that they were

looking into a solution for my problems and asked if I would stop by."

Carine was in such a hurry to tell her story she sounded more and more flustered by the second. "The charity is prepared to settle my debts and pay my rent in arrears in return for a small favor."

Her cheeks blushed.

"You didn't agree to anything, did you?" said Van In.

"Ilse took a couple of photos," she said provocatively.

"Nude photos?"

She nodded.

"Ilse then explained what was expected of me. I have to make myself available for six months. During that time I can be called for a maximum of twenty sessions."

"Sessions? You don't mean . . ."

Carine giggled nervously. Van In had the impression that the whole operation was turning her on.

"No sessions," he said. "Absolutely out of the question."

Carine shook her head, unconvincingly.

"Those guys have got a lot of nerve."

Hannelore emerged from the shower, knotted a white towel around her head like a turban, and wrapped herself up in a thick bathrobe.

Van In was in the adjoining bedroom. "The ball's in your court," he said.

Hannelore sat beside him on the bed. Her bathrobe bulged

a little. "I get your frustration, Pieter. But how many times have I told you that we have to stick to the rules? There isn't an examining magistrate in the country who would issue a search warrant on the basis of unlawfully obtained evidence."

"Because a couple of their colleagues appear on the list," Van In observed. "Double standards across the board! The letter of the law and the spirit. It all depends who you know and how much you can pay."

Hannelore shrugged her shoulders, loosened the towel around her head, and started to dry her lustrous hair.

"According to the law, I'm first obliged to ask that poor girl to prostitute herself before I can submit a complaint." Van In sighed.

"Out of the question. Even a mediocre lawyer would win the case for the charity. Carine is a police officer, and as such, she's not allowed to incite a crime. It wouldn't even surprise me if they turned the tables and charged her with incitement. Anyway, where would it get you? Maybe Ilse is a lesbian who takes advantage of her position to hook a girlfriend now and then."

Van In lit a cigarette, tetchy. It was the last of his daily ration.

"It's time to revisit that criminal law course you took." Hannelore smiled. "I'm guessing you've forgotten a bunch of stuff."

Van In got to his feet and started pacing up and down. The investigation had ground to a standstill and had nowhere to go. He had been relying on the identification of Herbert, but there was still no new information. A couple of hospitals had promised to report back the next day, but what if their responses were negative? All they would have left would be hospitals abroad, and that would be like looking for the proverbial needle in a haystack.

At dinner, Van In made a tentative attempt to return to the subject of Linda Aerts. "If the public prosecutor's office is afraid of the powers that be, maybe we should go to work on the outcasts," he said sarcastically.

"Communism is dead, Pieter. And even when it was still alive it followed the same principles. No one is truly equal before the law. People are egocentric creatures, and there's no system I know that can change it. Magistrates are human too. We're all walking a shaky tightrope, Pieter, and we're all doing our best to stay balanced."

Hannelore tucked in to a slice of fried calf's liver.

"I didn't want to get into ideologies, Hanne."

"I guess you didn't," she said between bites. "What you want is for me to have Linda Aerts arrested."

Hannelore popped the last morsel of liver into her mouth. Van In offered her a napkin.

"Linda Aerts is a suspect in the Provoost case. I have evidence . . ."

"Evidence, Pieter? I need proof."

Van In stared longingly at the empty pack of cigarettes. He had a good mind to go to the convenience store and then get drunk somewhere. "You can't prove anything these days," he said sullenly. "Everybody lies to save their own skin, and it takes two witnesses to refute a lie."

"Good thing too," said Hannelore. "And I don't have to tell you what the alternative would be. If it was up to FLASYC, we'd be arresting suspects on the spot, handing out long prison sentences, and not worrying too much about their right to defense."

Hannelore was clearly agitated. She found it hard to believe that her husband would flirt with right-wing ideas.

"That's not what I meant, sweetheart."

Van In tried to stay calm, although he was fighting with a demon that threatened to tear him to pieces.

"Isn't it?" she asked.

With these two words of condescension, the devil in his soul broke free of its chains. "You shouldn't have said that." Van In felt like a champagne bottle about to pop. Why was she doing this? She knew he would explode if she kept it up. "I thought we were both on the same side," he whispered.

"Of course, but . . ."

Hannelore grabbed her belly. The twinge of pain was so intense it forced her to arch her back. Van In's guardian angel pushed the champagne cork back into the bottle. The demon prudently withdrew.

"What's wrong?" he asked.

"Don't worry, Pieter. I guess it's not my day today."

Hannelore massaged the sides of her thighs. Van In could see the pain in her eyes and pulled up a chair beside her.

"It's all my fault," he said apologetically. "I know it's no excuse, but I've had a tough day too. The investigation's going nowhere, and you know how much I want to take you to Portugal."

Hannelore nestled her head on his shoulder. "That's sweet of you." She ran her fingers through his hair. Van In always got goose bumps when she did that. "I'm sorry I compared you with those FLASYC sickos," she said.

Van In was happy that his rage had receded. He had almost forgotten that she had been to the gynecologist that day. Having an amniocentesis wasn't exactly a day at the circus. He considered asking her if everything had gone OK but decided not to. If she wanted to talk about it she would, and he had to respect that.

"Maybe I should have a word with Mrs. Aerts myself," said Hannelore after a moment.

Van In drew hearts on her back with his finger. "If I can carry the bucket of water," he said grinning.

Carine Neels looked a picture in her floral nightgown. Her old-fashioned fountain pen scratched elegant letters in the fluffy pages of her diary. "I ignored Commissioner Van In's orders. I checked in with Ilse at ten o'clock. She was really excited and asked if I wouldn't mind doing a camera test before we got down to the real thing. She said I had a beautiful body and that I didn't need to pose naked if I didn't want to. She took me to a studio, fully equipped, and asked if I minded that a man was present. She knew nothing about cameras. I quite liked being in the spotlight. It was exciting. The cameraman didn't come near me. He just stood there in the dark and didn't say a word for the entire shoot. But one thing struck me about him: the man smelled of toilet cleaner, a mix of lemon and lavender."

12

William Aerts had hidden himself in Amand's bedroom, where he could keep a close eye on the cars parking in front of the restaurant. Waiting was for demented pensioners. If they made it an Olympic discipline, Aerts would be first in line to hand out the medals. For him, waiting without knowing what was going to happen was torture. He counted the seconds, added them up into minutes, and cursed the hour hand of his wristwatch.

Aerts had lived in a state of euphoria for two days—two days that had seemed to last no longer than a nanosecond.

Brooks and Brouwers arrived at Amand's restaurant shortly before noon. The Englishman was in the best of humor, having spent the night with his girlfriend, Penelope. Brouwers had met her the day before in the lounge of the King George Hotel. From that moment he understood exactly why Brooks insisted on spending the night on Gozo. Penelope was a sophisticated woman in her early forties with smooth, soft breasts and wide, sad eyes. She reminded him of the closing scene of Homer's *The Odyssey*. As in the blind Greek poet's epic, this Maltese Penelope had an irresistible charm that attracted middle-aged men. Brouwers had masturbated twice that night in his hotel room, a very rare occurrence.

Aerts recognized the former federal policeman immediately. What he didn't understand was how Vandaele's bloodhound had managed to trace him so quickly.

Amand was collected, in control. He welcomed Brooks and Brouwers with a professional smile. "A Belgian," he said when Brouwers introduced himself. "Few and far between around here. Welcome to my restaurant, gentlemen."

Brooks and Brouwers opted for a table on the terrace under a linen parasol. A refreshing breeze blew in from the sea. On Gozo, the sea was never far away.

"I'm told you're from West Flanders," said Brouwers affably.

"That's right," said Amand. "I was born in Knokke."

He handed them each a menu. Brouwers didn't recognize any of the dishes. "I can recommend the smoked swordfish as a starter," Amand suggested.

Brooks licked his lips. Amand had the best swordfish on Malta. He nodded enthusiastically. Brouwers went along with Amand's suggestion, and both men ordered *fenek* as his main course.

"Rabbit," said Brooks when Brouwers asked for an

explanation. "The Maltese are keen hunters. They shoot whatever moves, just about. If you spend any length of time here, you'll realize that Malta has very few birds."

The swordfish rivaled the best of Scottish salmon. The structure was a little less refined, but the mild flavor of the meaty slices gave it a definite edge.

Aerts poured himself a nip of whiskey. Amand had promised to keep him posted. What was he up to for Christ's sake? He emptied his glass in a single gulp. *Why had Vandaele sent a hired killer after him*, he asked himself in desperation.

Provoost had probably spilled when they dug up the body. Aerts grabbed the bottle and poured himself a second glass. He was having trouble thinking straight. If Vandaele had pronounced the death sentence, then it made no sense to keep running. Brouwers would catch up with him sooner or later. They didn't call the ex-cop the pit bull for nothing.

The terrace in the meantime was beginning to get busy. A battery of waiters scuttled nervously back and forth. Amand served the steaming chunks of *fenek* personally from a casserole dish. The smell was mouthwatering.

"Will there be anything else, gentlemen?" Amand asked.

Brouwers looked at him searchingly. Amand's broad smile froze. "I'm told you know all the foreigners on the island, Monsieur Amand. I'm looking for someone . . . perhaps you can help me."

Brouwers fished a recent photo of Aerts from his jacket pocket.

Amand examined it for a couple of seconds, wrinkling his brows to give the impression he was searching his memory. "Sorry," he said.

"A client?" Brouwers inquired further.

"Not possible. I can count my Flemish customers on one hand. If the man was ever in my restaurant, I'd have recognized him immediately."

"Sorry," said Brooks. "Not much of a harvest, but at least the food was worth it."

A waiter brought a tray with a pot of strong coffee, some thin slices of cake, and two snifters of cognac. The drinks were on the house, he said.

Brouwers took off his sunglasses. "Do you think so?"

Brooks swirled the cognac in his glass. "Tell me, you little devil," he said grinning.

Brouwers shoed the flies from the cake, tried a bite, and returned it to the plate with a grimace. "Dentists must make a fortune around here. That crap is so sweet it makes my dentures twinge."

"You get used to it," said Brooks. "But tell me what you discovered," he insisted. Brouwers was flattered by the SAS man's pushy curiosity.

"Isn't it obvious, Jonathan? *Primo*: Amand used the word *Belgian* when we arrived, but when I showed him the picture of Aerts, he suddenly shifted to Flemish. He also didn't ask why we were looking for Aerts, which is strange for a man who rarely gets visits from his fellow countrymen. *Secundo*: from the moment Amand knew why we were here he let a waiter take care of our table. And *tertio*: I have a nose for liars. If you ask me, Aerts isn't far from here. So I think I'll hang around for a while if you don't mind."

Brooks didn't mind in the least. The prospect of a second night with Penelope set his heart pounding.

"I'm Deputy Martens, public prosecutor's office," said Hannelore when Linda Aerts opened the door. "I'm here about the complaint you filed against Commissioner Van In."

She had parked her Renault Twingo on the driveway under an overgrown briar—*sub rosa*, just like her mission.

The villa was a mix of art deco and Austrian *heimatstil* and had served until the sixties as the status symbol of a hyped-up artist. When the man took his own life one somber winter evening, his greedy family auctioned off the "property." It's generally known that a house with blood on its walls never fetches market prices. Lodewijk Vandaele snatched it for next to nothing and turned it into a discreet whorehouse. He named the place the Cleopatra for lack of anything better.

Linda Aerts might once have rivaled the Egyptian princess in beauty, but now she looked more like a bloated mummy. "What complaint?" she croaked.

"Assault and battery," said Hannelore. "According to your declaration, the police molested you."

Hannelore's no-nonsense approach was enough to rouse Linda from her alcohol-induced daze. She raised her eyebrows and looked Hannelore up and down, the daze still evident in her eyes. "Do you mind if I come in, Mrs. Aerts?"

Linda ruffled her bedraggled hair, shrugged her shoulders, and stepped aside. "Why not."

The inside of the villa smelled of musty cushions, stale cigarette smoke, and flat beer.

"I was just having breakfast," said Linda. "Want a coffee?"

Hannelore nodded. She followed Linda through the bar into the kitchen. *Even Van In would've found the place too grimy,* she thought. Mold battled it out in the sink on piles of unwashed plates. Stuffed ashtrays soiled the air with microscopic particles. The litter box hadn't been cleaned in weeks, and the smell of piss was enough to choke an army. Hannelore focused for a moment on her prenatal gymnastics classes and tried to survive on short, shallow breaths.

"That fucker threw two buckets of water over me. It was like the Middle fucking Ages! What's wrong with that picture?"

Linda rinsed a cup under the faucet. Hannelore regretted having said yes to the coffee. She recognized the smell of boarding school coffee left too long on the burner.

"The public prosecutor's office is taking your complaint very seriously, Mrs. Aerts. Ill-treatment and sexual harassment are unforgiveable, especially when a police officer is involved."

"Sexual harassment?" Linda cackled. "They can fill my bucket anytime, as long as they pay for the pleasure."

"Your bucket, Mrs. Aerts?"

"Sweetheart! Men always exaggerate. They unload a teaspoon and they think they shot a bucketload."

Hannelore slid her cup of coffee to one side.

Linda grinned, then collapsed into a chair and filled her cup with Elixir d'Anvers. "Milk?"

Hannelore shook her head.

"A drop of Elixir?"

Without waiting for an answer, Linda got to her feet, took a glass from the kitchen cabinet, and filled it with the sweet liqueur.

"Do you already have a lawyer, Mrs. Aerts?"

Hannelore nipped at the glass for appearance's sake and tried to suppress her disgust. One sip was worth it if it helped gain Linda's confidence.

"*Pff.*"

Unbelievable how much contempt a tiny meaningless word could convey. Van In could count his lucky stars. Without a lawyer she didn't stand a chance.

"Provoost got what he deserved. I don't need the bastard. He was no better than the others."

"The others?"

Linda laughed. "Vandaele's a pig. De Jaegher's a frustrated worm, Vervoort deserves the chair, and Deflour can jump from his choir loft for all I care."

"And Brys?"

Linda stiffened. "Johan was a sweet boy," she sniveled.

"Was?"

Hannelore looked the withered woman in the eye. There's nothing sadder than an emotional alcoholic. Linda grabbed the bottle and refilled her cup. Her eager gulps were evidence that she was in the final stages. "So you knew him well?"

Linda wiped a tear from her eye. She had worshiped Johan Brys. If she'd accepted his proposal back in the day, she'd now be living in a mansion with servants, spending exotic vacations abroad. That was what she dreamed about every night when she was a girl. "Johan stopped by now and then," she said. "Before he got the ministry post, of course."

Hannelore nodded understandingly. She pinched here eyes shut and took another sip of the sweet Elixir. It was pleasant enough in the mouth, but it left a trail of fire as it went down.

"A top up?"

Linda was beginning to like the sophisticated bitch. She filled Hannelore's glass to the brim. "I was a beauty queen once." She got to her feet and staggered toward the ramshackle kitchen dresser.

Hannelore was shocked at the blue varicose veins and the hard perished skin that clung to her plump calves. "Do you still see each other?"

The question sounded almost trivial. Linda turned and threw open her housecoat. Her cotton nightdress barely concealed her sagging body. "What would you do if you were a man?"

Hannelore tried to hide her compassion by taking a sip of Elixir. "Fortunately I'm not a man," she said.

Linda knotted her housecoat and concentrated on the contents of the dresser. "Where is that fucking thing?"

"There's no need, Mrs. Aerts."

Linda crouched in front of the dresser. "I was Miss West Flanders in 1979," she groaned. "Where is that fucking cup?"

The clatter of crockery drowned out her lamentations.

"I believe you, Linda. You haven't lost it completely."

Linda calmed down when she heard her first name and abruptly ended her pointless quest. "D'you mean it?"

A spontaneous smile lit up her sunken cheeks as she stood and returned to the table.

"Johan has good taste, and he's intelligent too. His appointment as government minister never surprised me." Linda had completely forgotten about the cup.

Hannelore raised her glass and winked. She hated what she was doing, so to punish herself she emptied the glass in a single gulp. She hoped the baby had inherited Pieter's alcohol genes.

"What a bunch they were," said Linda nostalgically.

"They?"

Linda rummaged nervously for a cigarette in a crumpled pack. Hannelore pushed her glass to one side, fished a packet of John Player's from her handbag, and offered Linda a cigarette.

"Thanks. I was just out."

"So who were *they*?"

"Johan, Provoost, and William. I chose the wrong one, of course."

"Keep the pack," said Hannelore.

"Join me?" Linda asked.

Hannelore didn't resist the temptation. *In the interest of the case,* she thought. Pieter used the same excuse often enough when he was up to no good. "So you had a choice," said Hannelore.

The Elixir had started to do its business. The combination of sweet liqueur, an empty stomach, and a glorious cigarette gave her a sense of euphoria she hadn't experienced since her student days.

"Johan, Yves, and William were bosom buddies." Linda giggled.

"Yves Provoost?"

"Mr. Respected Lawyer Provoost. God rest him," she snorted. "I could have had all three. My body drove them crazy."

"Typical men." Hannelore smiled. "Good-looking women always get the short end of the stick."

"You're telling me."

Linda's speech started to slur. She lit one cigarette after the other and left them to burn themselves out in one of the stinking ashtrays.

"They'd been friends for years?"

Linda nodded enthusiastically. Her eyes were glazed, and Hannelore wasn't sure if she should continue. This was just as cruel as the water treatment Linda had so vigorously complained about. "Johan was the smartest, Yves was the richest, and William had the biggest. You get my drift?"

"But you haven't done so badly," said Hannelore.

William Aerts had set aside sixteen million francs over a period of fifteen years. In business terms he was far from a failure.

"*Pff.* This place still doesn't belong to us. That's Vandaele's fault. The bastard never lets go of his prey, and every favor has its price. I once sent him a video of *The Godfather*. You know the film?"

Hannelore nodded.

"I included a letter asking if Marlon Brando had used him as an example."

Linda was on a roll. "Vandaele rules his disciples with an iron fist. He steered Johan into the party, and Provoost would've been in jail years ago if it hadn't been for him. If you want to point the finger, point it at Vandaele."

"What makes you think that?" asked Hannelore, unruffled.

Linda treated herself to a generous gulp of Elixir d'Anvers. She started to stammer. "D-don't tell me the j-judiciary knows nothing about the sh-shit. I'm not f-falling for that one. E-everybody knows what that f-fuck's been up to."

Linda lit a match and suddenly lost her grip on it. It all happened in what felt like a split second. Her nylon housecoat was on fire. She leaped to her feet like an impala catching the scent of an approaching lion. But Hannelore was glued to her seat, stunned. Linda's arms flailed in every direction as the flames licked her thighs.

It's strange how observers are sometimes slow to react in emergency situations. It took Hannelore all the willpower she could muster to pull herself away from the bewitching flames. She rushed to the sink, filled a dirty pan with water, and put out the fire. Van In was sure to laugh when she told him about it later. Hannelore realized she was having trouble keeping a straight face. Linda on the other hand started to whimper, gently at first.

"Does it hurt?" asked Hannelore, inspecting the damage. The bottom half of her housecoat was completely burned away. The charred nylon remains filled the room with a disgusting stench.

"I'll be OK," she said, still dazed.

Linda lifted her nightdress without the least embarrassment. She was wearing a minuscule G-string underneath, a tiny white triangle bulging between the folds of flab. One of her thighs had been badly burned. A three-by-six-inch ribbon of skin looked like a sloppily hung strip of wallpaper.

Hannelore refilled the pan and poured water over the wound. A puddle formed on the floor.

"Where's the bathroom?"

Hannelore remembered seeing a public safety film about burns. The best way to limit the damage was to hold the wound under running water.

Linda pointed upstairs.

The shower was full of unwashed laundry. Hannelore kicked it aside, pushed Linda in, and sprayed the burn with ice-cold water. Linda screamed like a banshee, but Hannelore paid no attention. She needed all her energy to keep her patient still. After ten minutes she was almost as soaked as Linda, who continued to scream "enough, enough" at the top of her lungs. She stopped when Hannelore turned off the tap. Both women were dripping wet, like a couple of dogs just in from the rain.

"Now I'm calling an ambulance," said Hannelore resolutely.

"No!" Linda shouted, on the verge of hysteria. "No ambulance . . . no hospital."

Hannelore was adamant. She had noticed the phone on the wall when she came in and ran downstairs. Linda hobbled after her.

"Please," she begged, "don't call an ambulance. Call my doctor instead. If he says I have to go to emergency, then I'll go."

Hannelore turned on her heels. *Quid pro quo,* she thought.

"If I can be sure you've told me everything, I'll—"

"Ask whatever you want," Linda ranted in desperation.

Hannelore considered the pros and cons. The burn didn't look too serious. Some ointment and a couple of painkillers and Linda would be fine. If the doctor had no problem with it, then no one could point the finger of negligence in her direction.

Mdina appeared on the horizon like a pink sandcastle. The rising sun colored the old city with the shades and tints of an impressionist painting. William Aerts ignored the idyllic spectacle and concentrated on steering his souped-up Toyota toward

Valletta. Brouwers had left the day before without completing his mission. Or was that a diversionary tactic? Aerts was familiar with the man's reputation. His presence on the island was incontrovertible evidence of Vandaele's determination to find him and deal with him.

Aerts had run though all the scenarios the night before in his head. It was only when he read a full report on the murder of Yves Provoost in *Het Laatste Nieuws*—the Flemish national daily always arrived on the island a couple of days late—that he made the rash decision to return to Belgium. In his mind it was the only way to save his skin. With Provoost dead he could now use Belgian law to protect himself. In certain circumstances, a defendant can appeal to the principle of exculpation. According to the Belgian penal statutes, a suspect can only be sent to prison if he fulfills certain conditions. He has to be in good mental health, for example. The rule is often used by lawyers as a handy way of keeping their clients out of jail. One of the less well-known grounds for exculpation is moral pressure. If the defense can demonstrate that their client committed a crime because they were morally forced to do so by a third party, the judge is obliged in principle to acquit him or at least give him a reduced sentence. Aerts figured he would get a couple of years max, and that was better than certain death at the hands of Vandaele's cronies. When he buried Dani, he was in Vandaele's debt to the tune of half a million. Without a postponement he would have been bankrupt in no time. Vandaele had proposed a friendly settlement if he agreed to bury the body. Under normal circumstances, a court would follow his line of argument and be less interested in the messenger than the one who sent him. And by exposing the scandal, the reason to take him out would be gone. With a bit of luck he'd be back on Malta the following spring.

13

Van In settled for a simple lunch: a cup of coffee and a couple of cigarettes. The cream cheese sandwiches Hannelore had prepared for him that morning were in the trash, still wrapped in aluminum foil. The coffee was watery, and the cigarettes made him cough. The future appeared grim. He was saddled with two homicides, evidence was scarce, and to make matters worse, Versavel had called in sick. Van In had reluctantly phoned the two remaining hospitals only to hear the same story: no one matching Herbert's profile had undergone a sex-change operation in the eighties. It didn't surprise him. Most men intent on that kind of metamorphosis back then were older than twenty-five. But as he had said before: no one was going to accuse them of carelessness.

And then there was Dirk Baert. The man's endless explanations and crime analyses had been messing with Van In's nerves the entire morning. But what bothered him most was De Kee's insistence that he not be present when Linda Aerts was questioned, and Carine Neels's unjustified absence.

Van In considered a couple of options. He could get drunk, or he could pay a visit to Carine and find out what she was up to. The clock in the cafeteria devoured the minutes at a snail's pace. It was only twelve thirty. Another four hours in the company of Baert was a challenge he wasn't willing to face. What if he started with a couple of Duvels, then paid a visit to Neels? The prospect cheered him, but Baert would screw it up. If he disappeared without reason, Baert would blab and he'd have to explain himself the next day to De Kee. The idea didn't impress him. He needed to be creative.

Van In punched in the number of the incident room. If he wasn't mistaken, Robert Bruynoghe was on duty. "Hello, Robert. Van In here. Could you do me a major favor?"

Officer Bruynoghe grinned when Van In explained his plans. It was common knowledge that Dirk Baert had few friends in the corps. "I'll take care of it, Commissioner."

"Thanks, Robert. I owe you one."

Bruynoghe called Room 204. "Hello, Chief Inspector Baert. Would you be kind enough to put me through to Commissioner Van In?"

Baert hated the formal language employed by some of the lower echelons. "The commissioner is at lunch. Can I be of assistance?" he asked, maintaining the formality.

"I've just had the state governor on the line. He wants to speak with the commissioner urgently."

Baert hung up without further questions and raced to the cafeteria to inform Van In.

Hannelore drove at a crawl down Steen Street and parked her Twingo on Market Square directly in front of one of the french-fries stands. The square had recently been redeveloped and was more or less traffic free. The connection between Steen Street and Wool Street was still accessible, but parking on the square was strictly forbidden.

A young policeman gestured that she should move along, a command she ostentatiously ignored.

A middle-aged French couple were studying the menu at the stand and chattering out loud.

"*Je n'y comprends rien du tout,*" said the woman indignantly, as if the Flemish words *frieten*, *mayonaise*, and *hotdog* were completely unrecognizable.

"A large fries with gravy and mayonnaise," said Hannelore, pushing the jabbering *grenouille* out of the way.

"*Ça ne va pas, non?*" the woman responded to Hannelore's rudeness.

Her husband was also about to say something unfriendly, but one glance at Hannelore made him think twice and he bit his lip.

"*Eh bien, Gerard?*" The wrinkled *Française* treated her husband to a withering glare.

"Hoi, madam. You deaf or what?" An enraged policeman lurched menacingly in Hannelore's direction.

"Can I help you?" asked the owner of the fries stand. Bald, thirtysomething, and with a nose like a meat cleaver, the man didn't want any trouble with the police.

"A large fries with . . ."

The rest of her sentence was swallowed up by the drone of a pneumatic hammer. It was one thirty, and a team of dutiful construction workers were getting back to work after a break.

"Can I see your ID card, madam?" the officer snorted in a broad Bruges accent. "You know you're not allowed to park here."

Hannelore threw back her head. "I park wherever I decide to park," she snapped.

The *Française* immediately sided with the officer of the law, nudging her husband and nodding approvingly.

The police officer was the spitting image of Clint Eastwood, complete with holster and Dirty Harry Magnum. For a moment he was at a loss for words. "So madam wants to be difficult," he said, his accent thinning.

"I want a large fries with gravy and mayonnaise," Hannelore growled as she turned back to the owner of the fries stand.

The poor man stared at her in despair.

"And throw on some gherkins while you're at it."

Hannelore smiled triumphantly and looked the young cop up and down. "I'm pregnant and I'm hungry."

Three Elixirs on an empty stomach were clearly taking their toll. Hannelore reeled and just managed to grab hold of the French tourist who had shuffled closer unnoticed.

"I suggest you explain yourself at the police station, madam. If you ask me, you're drunk as a skunk," said the officer, his accent thickening again.

"Me, drunk?"

Hannelore continued to hold on to the stranger for support, much to the annoyance of his faithful battle-ax.

The officer unclipped his radio mic and called the incident room.

"Problems, Delille?" said a voice in his other ear before Bruynoghe had the chance to respond.

Officer Delille recognized the voice instantly and didn't protest when Van In took the mic from his hand.

"Van In here. I'm onto it, Robert. Everything completely under control. Over and out."

"Commissioner, I didn't know—"

"Take it easy, Delille. You haven't done anything wrong. I know the lady. She lives with a loser of a husband who rattles her every day and drives her crazy."

Officer Delille nodded understandingly. At least he hadn't made a fool of himself.

"I want fries," Hannelore begged. A carousel was turning in her head with horses moving up and down.

"Monsieur," the tourist pleaded. Hannelore was still leaning heavily on his shoulder, and he was struggling to keep her upright. Van In stepped forward and took over, grabbing her under the arm and dragging her to the nearest bench. "Take care of the fries, Delille."

Hannelore sunk to the bench like a wax statue that had been standing too long in the sun. All the color had drained from her cheeks.

"Do you want me to call a doctor?"

Hannelore thought about Linda Aerts. A hospital was the last place she wanted to land. "First food, Pieter. A couple of bites and I'll be right as rain."

With her eyes half-shut, she peered over Van In's shoulder at a ghostly figure in blue holding out a portion of fries. She gobbled the warm snack in no time—gravy, mayonnaise, and all. When she was finished with the fries, Van In had Delille fetch a Coke, then nervously lit a cigarette.

"Feeling better?" he asked after a moment or two.

Hannelore licked a splotch of mayonnaise from her upper lip. "Much better," she said grinning.

Agent Delille urged a number of nosey tourists to move along. There was nothing for them to see.

Van In gave Hannelore the Coke. She smiled and emptied it in one go. The sugar pepped her up.

"That's the first and the last time I follow in your footsteps, Pieter Van In. Your way of doing things is backbreaking."

Hannelore told him the whole story.

"My fault as usual," said Van In resignedly. "You're lucky I happened to be in the neighborhood or you'd been sleeping it off in a cell."

"Doesn't every maiden deserve the assistance of a handsome knight?"

The influence of the Elixir clearly hadn't worn off. Van In looked around. A couple of Japanese tourists had settled on the bench beside them. Ten seconds later they had attracted the rest of the group, and Van In and Hannelore found themselves surrounded by a pack of chattering Asians. Luckily they had no idea what Hannelore was talking about.

"Are you still drunk?"

"Me, drunk? After three liqueurs? Are you crazy? I was nauseous, Pieter Van In, because I was hungry."

"Of course you were," said Van In.

"I was nauseous," she insisted.

"Mea culpa. Drunk or not, you're lucky I was in the neighborhood."

"That's what you think."

Hannelore rummaged in her handbag and produced her court ID card. "I've never heard of a deputy public prosecutor being arrested for a parking offense, have you?"

"Emancipation." Van In sighed. "You're not an inch better than the men."

"Really? What would you have done?"

"Nothing, sweetheart. All the cops know me personally. I don't need a card."

"Dirty pigs." She giggled.

Van In stuck out his tongue. The Japanese recognized the gesture and laughed at him in unison. Hannelore was having the time of her life.

Van In glared at the Japanese and stuck his tongue out at them too.

"I'd rather you told me what you achieved with your drunken capers."

Wilfried Buffel, a retired teacher, lived in a prewar house on Maria of Burgundy Avenue. A low wall and similar gate formed a symbolic division between his neatly maintained garden and the sidewalk.

Hannelore parked her Twingo on the grass verge beside the canal. The noise of a drainage sluice a couple hundred yards away sounded like a waterfall somewhere in the Ardennes. The murmur of water gave the drowsy row of houses an idyllic air.

"I'm asking myself how a retired teacher's going to help us with our inquiries," said Van In skeptically.

Hannelore shrugged her shoulders. Men just didn't understand a woman's intuition. "Let's just see if the man's at home first," she said crisply.

Buffel was reading a book by the window and saw Van In and Hannelore heading toward his front door. He himself was invisible behind the stained glass, as long as they didn't press their noses against it. Just to be sure, he slipped carefully into the corridor. A couple of smooth-talking imposters had tricked him out of fifty thousand francs the year before and left him suspicious of strangers.

Hannelore rang the bell. The elderly teacher had been waiting for it to ring, but it still made him jump.

"I have a feeling there's nobody home," he heard the man outside say.

"Patience, Pieter. The man is seventy-two. How fast would you react at that age?"

The woman had a pleasant voice.

"And you expect that old bugger to remember something about a student he taught thirty years ago?"

Buffel snorted indignantly. Who did that man think he was? He might have been having trouble with his legs, but his memory was just fine, thank you very much. He made a racket with the door from the living room to the corridor, waited for a couple of seconds, then opened the front door.

"Mr. Buffel?" asked the woman, with a glint in her eye.

"Yes, can I help you, Miss . . ."

"Hannelore Martens. I work for the public prosecutor's office. And this is Commissioner Van In of the Bruges police department. May we ask you a few questions?"

Buffel led them into the living room. He took his usual chair by the window. You never know what might happen. There was an earthenware tobacco jar on the windowsill. If he threw it through the window, his neighbors would hear the broken glass. That's what he hoped at least.

"We're interested in a former pupil and colleague of yours, Lodewijk Vandaele," said Hannelore coming straight to the point.

Buffel raised his hand to his head and ran his fingers through his thin gray hair. Why in God's name had he opened the door? Damn professional pride!

"Lodewijk Vandaele," Hannelore repeated patiently.

Van In fiddled with his nose. *This could take a while,* he thought, not exactly optimistic.

"It's all so long ago, miss."

"Come now, Mr. Buffel. Teachers tend to have excellent memories. My old teacher can remember exactly what kind of dress I was wearing for my first communion."

Her smile was so disarming that Buffel could no longer resist. He grabbed his pipe from a side table and filled it with tobacco from the jar on the windowsill. Van In stood and offered his lighter, comforted by the fact that the old bugger smoked. That gave him permission to do the same.

"I worked with Lodewijk Vandaele for close to ten years. He taught in the elementary school—fourth grade if I'm not mistaken. Lodewijk said farewell to the classroom after his father died. He took over the family business."

Buffel puffed at his meerschaum pipe. "He did quite well for himself after that."

"What was he like as a teacher?" asked Hannelore.

Buffel had been waiting for the question. Now he knew the reason for their visit. "I thought such matters had limitations, miss."

Both Van In and Hannelore stared at the elderly teacher in astonishment. "What matters, Mr. Buffel?"

The old man blew a thick cloud of smoke into the room. He didn't want his visitors to be able to look him in the eye. "Teachers crossed the boundaries of permissible affection often enough in those days."

Van In had heard a variety of definitions of pedophilia, but Buffel's euphemistic description almost made it sound safe for children.

"And was he convicted?" asked Hannelore, maintaining her cool.

Buffel sighed. The woman was too young to know what happened with scandals back then. "Lodewijk taught at a Catholic school, miss. The parish priest placated the parents, and the charges were dropped. That's how things were arranged in those days."

Van In nodded. When he was a youngster, every school had its own thigh fondler.

"Do you happen to remember the names of any of the objects of Vandaele's exaggerated affection?" Hannelore asked.

The old man sighed again.

"Provoost, Brys, and Aerts perhaps?"

Buffel returned his pipe to the side table, thereby putting a conscious end to his smoke screen. "I read in the paper about Provoost being killed," he said dispiritedly.

"Do you think Lodewijk Vandaele killed Provoost?" asked Hannelore.

The question seemed to frighten Buffel. "That's why you're here, isn't it?" he aked.

Van In stubbed out his cigarette. The old guy might have been onto something. He had read somewhere in a professional journal about the bond between pedophiles and their victims lasting a lifetime. There were cases of pedophiles in America who murdered their former students twenty years after the fact, and mostly for one or another banal reason. The primary condition was that the pedophile and his victim had remained friends. While there was no more sexual contact, the pedophile still tried to maintain a psychological hold on his students as adults. It left him with two sources of pleasure. If his student married, the pedophile would feel superior to the wife and consider her second-rate. In addition, he knew that if they had a couple of children, he would be best placed as a friend of the family to try his chances anew.

"Did Provoost have children?" Van In inquired.

Hannelore looked at Van In, nonplussed.

"A son and two daughters. Why? You don't think Vandaele killed Provoost so he could mess around with his children?"

Van In lit another cigarette. He was having a hard time understanding how Vandaele managed to overpower Provoost and tie him up. And what about the torture? Was Vandaele a sadist as well as a pedophile? "I think we're up a blind alley here, Hanne."

"Can I offer you some tea?" Buffel suggested unexpectedly.

"No, thank you," said Hannelore.

She didn't give Van In the time to suggest an alternative drink. She wanted to dig as deep as she could. Linda had sworn by all that was holy that Buffel was their man. "Were there other cases of . . . exaggerated affection, Mr. Buffel?"

The retired teacher shook his head. After all the fuss surrounding the Provoost case, Vandaele had moved to an alternative hunting ground. "Not at our school, miss."

Hannelore refused to be discouraged. "Something else perhaps?"

"What do you mean, miss?"

"Do you remember anything else about Provoost, Brys, and Aerts?"

"They weren't the easiest of children, miss."

"In what sense?"

Buffel hesitated. Like so many of his colleagues, he had been convinced in his early days that teaching was the finest career in the world. But reality had quickly proven the contrary. Children were nothing short of monsters who hated one another's guts. "I was a teacher for more than forty years," he said with caution, "long enough to have seen a thing or two. Children sometimes behave like wild animals, and there were moments that—"

"You would have happily smacked their heads against the wall," said Van In, completing the man's sentence. "Did you feel that way toward Provoost, Brys, and Aerts?"

A cold shiver ran down Buffel's spine as the incident returned to his memory. "They went too far once," he said, visibly shaken.

"It was the summer of 1966. During the vacation period, the children would come back to school twice a week for an afternoon of games. It was handy for the parents, and the school grounds were big enough to accommodate everyone. To tell the truth, it was more like a jungle in those days, where the boys could horse around to their hearts' content. The teachers took half-day turns supervising, and I happened to be on duty that afternoon. We weren't paid, of course."

"Those were the days," said Van In under his breath.

Buffel grabbed his pipe. His fingers trembled as he filled it. Van In offered him a light.

"Provoost, Brys, and Aerts were always around," said Buffel. "They formed a triumvirate, and I knew I had to keep a close eye on them because they were infamous for the rough games they liked to play. But everything seemed quiet that afternoon, nothing untoward. I was feeling a little listless. I should mention that my wife and I had treated ourselves to a couple of glasses of wine that afternoon with lunch. It was our fifteenth wedding anniversary."

Buffel was clearly having a hard time. His cheeks and jaw tightened, forcing the stem of his pipe upward at an awkward angle.

"Continue, Mr. Buffel," said Hannelore with an encouraging smile.

"Suddenly someone woke me—one of the new students." Buffel puffed furiously at his pipe. "What was his name again?"

"Don't worry about it, Mr. Buffel. I'm sure it'll come back to you later." Hannelore was on the edge of her seat.

"He and his brother had only been at the school a couple of weeks. 'Mr. Buffel, Mr. Buffel,' I heard the boy shout. 'They're . . .' Dirk . . . yes, that's a name I'll never forget." Buffel beamed. 'They're trying to kill Dirk.' I didn't have to think long to know who *they* were."

"Provoost, Brys, and Aerts," Van In observed redundantly.

Buffel nodded. The old man seemed to be reliving the scene. His eyes watered as he stared through the stained glass window.

Hannelore put her finger to her lips, signaling to Van In that he should keep quiet. His intervention had disrupted the man's concentration.

"Dirk and Dani Desmedt," said Buffel all of a sudden, his eyebrows knit. "They were twins. From Roeselare if I'm not mistaken. Their father had found a job in Zeebrugge, and they had moved to live in Bruges."

"You were talking about attempted murder, Mr. Buffel."

"I was indeed, miss. It still troubles me."

"Was it bad?"

Buffel took a deep breath.

"It was horrific, miss. They had stripped Dirk naked, tied him up, and stuffed his underpants in his mouth."

"They?"

"Provoost, Brys, and Aerts."

Buffel clearly and deliberately enunciated each name. Then he fell silent. Van In grinned knowingly at Hannelore. This time it wasn't his fault that the elderly teacher had lost his place.

"Please continue, Mr. Buffel."

The old man gulped and rested his pipe in the ashtray. "Provoost had fastened a clothespin to Dirk's nose, and every time the boy came close to suffocation, he would take it away. Then they started over again, until Dirk . . . my God . . . I've relived that nightmare time and again. If I'd only been completely sober that afternoon . . ."

Buffel sobbed bitterly. Hannelore fished a packet of Kleenex from her handbag, stood, and put a comforting arm around the poor man's shoulders. The elderly teacher surrendered to her embrace like a child being cuddled.

Van In lit another cigarette. The picture in front of him made him feel awkward, so he looked away. How was it possible that such a complicated case could be solved in such a predictable way? Provoost's killer had betrayed himself by repeating the ritual he had undergone as a child. Buffel's testimony was legitimate. None of the papers had reported on the circumstances of Provoost's killing. All they had to do now was find Dirk or Dani Desmedt and they had their killer.

Hannelore insisted on waiting until Buffel had recovered from the emotion. She made tea and only agreed to go when the elderly teacher had insisted three times that he was OK.

"So congratulate me," Hannelore jeered as they waited at the traffic light on Ezel Street. "And don't say the prosecutor's office never wrapped up an investigation."

"Thanks to my pioneering detective work," Van In quipped.

"If I'd had the chance to detain Linda Aerts for another twenty-four hours, I'd have finished the job myself."

"You and a couple of buckets of water, eh?"

"A couple of buckets?" Van In grinned. "You interrogated the woman under the shower."

The green light saved Van In from an elbow in the ribs. Hannelore hit the gas, and the Twingo took off like a startled mustang. "And now it's Herbert's turn," she said as she parked the Twingo illegally on Moer Street.

"Let me take care of that, young lady. One feather in your cap is enough for today."

Hannelore ignored his remark. She thought she'd done an excellent job. "I'm starving, Pieter."

"Again?"

"I'm eating for two, remember," she snorted.

"They exploded that theory twenty years ago, Hanne. Anyway, it's your turn to make dinner."

"Did you go to the store?" she asked.

Van In slammed the passenger door and looked up at the NO PARKING sign. He was witnessing a crime, but he shrugged his shoulders nonetheless. "There's some cheese spread in the pantry. What about some fries?"

Hannelore turned up her nose. She rarely did, but Van In always enjoyed it when she made a face. She looked like a schoolgirl sentenced to two hours of detention. "The Wittenkop has swordfish on the menu," she said with a hint of a question in her voice.

"No one's stopping you from taking me out," he said. "You can have the swordfish. I'm happy with steak Dijonnaise."

"Agreed, but the drinks are on you."

"No problem," Van In chirped.

He put his arm around her shoulder, and they walked hip to hip along Saint Jacob Street like a couple in love on their first visit to Bruges.

14

The steak Dijonnaise from the night before had been a pleasure. But as far as the booze was concerned—two bottles of white and three Duvels—it was payback time. The buzz of the alarm clock had activated a team of construction workers who were now working the inside if Van In's skull with sledgehammers. Hannelore pushed him out of bed and rolled over onto her other side.

In a fit of romance, Van In had promised her breakfast in bed, and she hadn't forgotten.

Van In staggered down the stairs like a lame dog. He popped a couple of soluble painkillers in a glass of water and two slices of bread in the toaster.

He took his meds in front of the mirror, looking like a joke in his pajama jacket with no trousers. The pounds flourished on both hips like mushrooms after a sultry downpour. It bothered him intensely, even with a hangover from hell and a head that was begging to be removed.

The toaster, like Van In himself, was a slow starter. It took an age for the toast to pop out of the thing. Van In checked the answering machine, more out of boredom than interest. The message light was flickering. Someone must have called when they were at dinner. "Hello, Commissioner Van In. Mrs. Neels speaking. Carine has disappeared, and I'm worried about her. Call me please. My number is 337173."

Click.

It took the best part of five seconds before Van In could weigh up the implications of the message. The toaster hadn't popped, and the smell of burned toast was beginning to fill the house.

Van In rewound the tape and listened a second time. He ran upstairs, shouting for help. Hannelore reacted immediately, not because of Van In but because she thought the house was on fire.

"Come quickly," Van In roared.

Hannelore fiddled the charred slices of bread from the toaster as Van In replayed the tape.

"Get dressed," she said. "I think we're in serious shit."

Five minutes later, Hannelore and Van In were in the Twingo, driving through the abandoned streets of Bruges in the direction of Daverlo Street.

"I ordered her not to go any further," said Van In sullenly.

"Operations like this shouldn't be improvised, Pieter Van In. I hope for your sake that nothing has happened to her."

"If she followed my instructions, she'll be fine," said Van In, sticking to his guns. "Maybe she hit the town with her boyfriend."

Hannelore glared at him. "You know as much about women as a vegan knows about hamburgers."

She took a sharp right at Gentpoort Bridge.

"House number one seventeen," said Van In.

William Aerts mingled with the people waiting in the airport departure hall. The chances of seeing a familiar face in such a swarm were pretty small, so he was all the more surprised to see Brouwers in the middle of an animated discussion with a buxom flight attendant at the Air Malta check-in desk. Something had to have gone wrong at Amand's place that made the old fox suspicious.

Aerts didn't panic, but he had to come up with a solution on the spot. He bought a newspaper and squatted on the floor next to a couple of backpackers, allowing him to keep a close eye on Brouwers without being seen. The girl at the check-in typed the information Brouwers had given her into the computer. Aerts saw her nod. His name had probably appeared on the screen at that moment.

The girl handed Brouwers a ticket five minutes later, confirming Aerts's suspicions. They were both booked onto the same flight. It made no sense to try to reschedule. Brouwers wouldn't leave until he was sure that his prey was already onboard. If he tried an alternative escape route, the chances were greater that the ex-cop would isolate him and take him out. Aerts figured he would be relatively safe on the plane and decided he would immediately hand himself over to the airport police after landing in Zaventem, something Brouwers probably wouldn't expect. He checked one of the clocks. Another thirty minutes before boarding and plenty of time for a practical joke.

Aerts got to his feet and calmly made his way to the nearest telephone kiosk. He called international information and asked for the number of the federal police at Zaventem Airport, near Brussels. He punched in the number, and after ten seconds, he was connected to Duty Officer Dupain. Aerts told the man that a fellow Belgian had approached him in Luqa Airport and asked him if he would be willing, for a fee, to take a package back to Belgium. The man had said that he had urgent business to attend to on the island and that he couldn't leave. Aerts had refused, of course, but he had found it strange that the same businessman had later bought a ticket after all. He provided Dupain with the flight number and a description of Brouwers.

Liliane Neels was waiting in the living room, her eyes red from crying. She reported between sobs what had happened.

"Carine said yesterday that she had something to do for her work and that she would probably be late. I asked her how late. Around midnight, she said. And when I asked her where she was going she said she was working *under the covers*."

Liliane started to sob uncontrollably. "She wouldn't even tell me what 'under the covers' meant."

Van In looked away.

"*Undercover* means that she had a special assignment," he heard Hannelore explain in a deadly serious tone. "Maybe she lost track of the time," she added. "Carine's a level-headed young woman. She can take care of herself."

"You're right." Liliane smiled through the tears. "She gets that from her father, God rest him."

Van In cursed the way he had tackled the case. Remorse nibbled at his soul. It was beginning to look as if he'd be responsible for the ruin of a young colleague, a girl. He was even sorry he'd put the fear of God into Linda Aerts. The woman had lived a miserable life, and he had only made it worse.

"Try not to worry, Mrs. Neels. Rest assured we'll do everything we can to find Carine. You have my word on it," said Van In.

"Thank you, Commissioner," said Liliane. "I hope you find her soon. Carine is all I have left."

Hannelore swallowed the lump in her throat.

A column of three police MPVs and three patrol cars headed along the main road to Gistel at a leisurely pace. Following Van In's orders, there were no sirens or rotating lights. The Twingo followed at the rear. In less than an hour, Hannelore had managed to convince the prosecutor and the examining magistrate to issue a warrant to search the buildings at Care House.

Onlookers watched in amazement as the silent caravan passed by. There was something unearthly about it without the usual sirens and swirling blue lights.

Carine slowly came around from the anesthetic. Her mouth was bone-dry. She tried to stand, but when that didn't work she leaned forward. Her arms were held back by a jangling chain. Panic is an irrational monster, and it always catches its victims unawares. Carine tugged hard at her fetters and tried in desperation to free herself.

The more the effects of the anesthetic subsided, the more conscious she became of what had happened the day before. After the test photo shoot, she had cycled home. Ilse had shown her the photos before she left, and they looked pretty good. Ilse had also told her she had contact with people in the magazine world and they paid good money for their models. "Under the table, of course," she said with a chuckle. "But you don't care about that, do you? With your financial problems, eh? You'll earn twenty thousand francs tonight. You can use it to pay off part of your debt, and even give yourself a bit of a treat," she added with a wink. "The charity does its best to help people in need. A young girl like you doesn't have to earn her money cleaning floors and toilets. Here at Care House, we're convinced that the easiest way to achieve your goal is the best way."

Carine had first planned to report back to Van In and tell him that there was nothing untoward going on at Care House. As far as she could tell, the charity was legitimate. But she was scared

Van In would be angry when he heard she'd disobeyed orders. So she decided to cycle back to Care House. The twenty thousand francs she'd been promised would come in handy. Carine had already regretted this decision a thousand times over.

The photographer who had kept a discreet distance the day before had grabbed her, chained her, and blindfolded her. Then the others arrived. Carine had screamed the first time, but it got easier, and after a while she felt nothing at all. All she remembered was the panting of pumping bodies and a squishing sound, like footsteps plodding through marshy soil. The men took her in silence. She stopped counting after the fourth. It seemed to take longer and longer for them to finish. Then they stopped all of a sudden, and she heard a door slam. Laughter outside the room got louder and louder until it sounded like an enraged hornets' nest. Her entire body shivered from the cold. It felt as if someone had rammed a block of ice between her legs. The cold dripped down her thighs. She trembled.

The door flew open again half an hour later. For Carine it seemed like an eternity had passed. When she recognized the smell of toilet cleaner, she started to sob. The man removed her fetters and forced her onto her hands and knees. The rapists lined up for seconds, and the nightmare started anew. Carine felt guilty for ignoring Commissioner Van In's advice. The man who smelled of toilet cleaner had also discovered her police ID and knew exactly who she was.

• • •

Ilse Vanquathem wasn't surprised when Van In rang the bell.

"Good day, Doctor," she said. "Come inside."

They searched Care House until late in the afternoon. Eighteen police officers turned the place upside down from the basement to the attic. A computer expert from forensics explored the charity's bookkeeping.

Ilse watched it all happen from a distance. When Van In questioned her, she refused to make a statement. When she was asked if she knew Neels, she said no.

The caravan of police vehicles departed like thieves in the night, the entire team seriously disheartened.

"Thank God we didn't use the sirens and the lights," said Hannelore. "If this escapade gets into the papers, we'll be the laughingstock of the whole country."

Van In dipped into his reserve pack of cigarettes. His throat was raw from smoking. "Someone must have informed them," he growled. "That bitch knew we were coming."

"Maybe the computer disks will come up with something."

Hannelore did her best to be positive. Van In couldn't be blamed for putting pressure on Muys, the dodgy tax auditor, but it had clearly been a mistake, and they were now paying the price.

Van In didn't react. He was aware of his blunder.

"I think we should tell Mrs. Neels," said Hannelore. "We don't want things to get any worse."

"Can I leave that up to you?" Van in asked, almost begging.

Hannelore hit the gas, and her tiny Twingo passed the caravan of police vehicles.

"Because you asked so nicely," she said with a sigh.

The federal police at the Zaventem airport did good business that evening. They intercepted an alleged drug dealer and arrested a man who was wanted by the Bruges police. Coincidence had put both men on the same flight. The potential dealer, Jos Brouwers, was released after an hour and a half for lack of evidence. William Aerts, on the other hand, was placed at the disposal of the prosecutor's office while they waited for the prosecutor to make a decision.

While Hannelore did her best to comfort Liliane Neels, Van In called the station. Carine's disappearance had put the Herbert investigation on the back burner. Van In had almost forgotten that he had ordered Baert that morning to track down the Desmedt brothers.

"Baert."

"Commissioner."

Baert scribbled geometric figures on the back of an expired duty roster. "Disappointing news, I'm afraid, Commissioner. The records office can find no trace of twins by the name of Desmedt."

"Listen here, Baert. I'm not in the mood for games. Buffel was unequivocal. The twins went to school in Bruges. Their parents moved here in the sixties. They have to have lived somewhere."

Baert's ballpoint hovered over the paper. "I contacted all the adjoining municipalities," he said, sure of himself. "Not one of the families named Desmedt, Desmed, or Desmet had twins who went to Buffel's school."

Lodewijk Vandaele pressed the red button on his remote. The newsreader's voice was abruptly cut off. A star-shaped flash shriveled into an invisible point on the TV screen. Silence filled the room. Vandaele was slumped in an armchair, his tired legs resting on a pouf made of red Moroccan leather. He was fed up hiding his condition from the outside world. Every sound that interrupted the rustle of the trees outside made him jump. Every fifteen seconds, he peered around the room, his eyes like a revolving lighthouse beam. A half bottle of VSOP hadn't succeeded in tempering his anxiety. He lit a Davidoff with an ordinary disposable lighter. He felt the energy drain from his bones. His rotten lungs rasped like weathered billows deep inside his chest.

"Why, for God's sake?" he asked himself under his breath.

The dying businessman thought about Provoost. His pupil was dead, and there was nothing he could do to change it. When the ulcer finally bursts, Brys will be lynched by public opinion. He himself had condemned Aerts to death.

Vandaele comforted himself with the memory of their young bodies, an image that had seen him through many a dark and difficult moment in the last thirty years.

The sound of the telephone ringing almost gave him a heart attack. The only thing he felt was pain. A good and peaceful death was set aside for the righteous alone. He longed for just such a death, but he knew it would not be granted to him.

Vandaele heaved himself with difficulty from his armchair. The Davidoff smoldered innocently in an overfull ashtray. The elderly man stumbled and banged his knee against the black grand piano, an unplayed instrument that took up most of the living room. The outsized piano was part of the facade behind which Vandaele had hidden himself for years on end. But there was no time left for music. It was much too late for that. There was nothing to be earned from art and culture, his father had always insisted. He wanted his son to succeed him as head of the family business. As a young idealist, Lodewijk Vandaele had defied his father and opted for a career in teaching. He wanted to break free and erase the blueprint others had drafted for him. Money was a seven-headed dragon that had to be opposed with might and main. Lodewijk saw himself as a modern Parsifal. He planned to devote himself to the education of the young, to helping them see that there was more to life than profit and a well-paid job. Young people needed room to develop, they needed cultural substance, and they needed a devoted teacher. But the outside world had never understood him. You weren't allowed to touch children, to hug and kiss them. It wasn't good for them, they said. But none of *his* students had ever been traumatized by such affection. Johan Brys had even made it into the government as a minister. Misunderstanding had turned Vandaele into the caricature he had now become. The idealist of the past had evolved into a bloodthirsty predator that had devoured his soul.

The telephone kept ringing. Instead of massaging his knee, Vandaele caressed the lid of his piano. The instrument represented everything he had dreamed of as a child. That was why he had waited until his father was a month in the grave before he bought it. No one had ever disturbed its snow-white keys, and no one ever would.

"Lodewijk Vandaele."

"Jos Brouwers."

Vandaele breathed a sigh of relief. "Mission accomplished I presume?" he inquired, his voice shaky.

A brief silence followed.

"Well?" Vandaele insisted.

It was the first time in his life that Brouwers had to admit failure. He fumbled for the appropriate words. "Aerts is an exceptionally slippery customer," he said bluntly. "I was right about him being on Malta . . ."

"So you let him get away."

"Someone must have tipped the bastard," Brouwers protested.

Vandaele was less angry than he pretended to be. William had always been docile, accommodating. The boy had given him hours of unforgettable pleasure. Vandaele was actually proud that his little darling had managed to outsmart the likes of Brouwers. "Don't worry, Jos. Perhaps I was a little premature in my judgment. William would never betray me. I'm certain of that."

Vandaele started to cough, choking on his own saliva. Brouwers pulled the phone from his ear and stared at it. The old man sounded as if he was on his last legs.

"I wouldn't be so sure, Mr. Vandaele. William Aerts turned himself in to the federal police at the airport. It wouldn't surprise me if he—"

"Your money's waiting for you, Jos. Assignment over."

Brouwers made some quick calculations. He didn't give a damn about the rest as long as the old bugger paid. "I'll be there in an hour," said Brouwers.

Buffel collected the key to the school archive from the parish priest in the company of Hannelore. The priest had no objection when the former teacher explained why he needed it. He was more interested in Hannelore's graceful charms.

"You may well be right," said Buffel as they turned into Ezel Street. "In those days we assumed that children would automatically be given the surname of their fathers at school. But with so many pregnancies out of wedlock, I suppose it's possible they used their mothers' names."

Hannelore supported the elderly teacher on her arm. Van In followed a couple of yards behind the strange couple. The joint venture between Hanne and Buffel was plainly platonic, and if it wasn't, he certainly didn't begrudge the old Lazarus his res-erection.

• • •

The elementary school where Yves Provoost, Johan Brys, and William Aerts had learned to read and write was in a dismal state. Wilfried Buffel hadn't been near the place for the better part of ten years, but he had no trouble finding his way to the tiny room in which the files on generations of children had been stored, left to survive the ravages of time.

"Ah-choo!"

Hannelore sneezed full-force as Buffel threaded his way through the dust-covered stacks. Van In tried to make himself useful by illuminating the piles of paper with his flashlight.

Buffel seemed to know what he was doing, as if he'd stopped maintaining the archives only the day before. Hannelore shifted piles of files at the elderly teacher's request.

"Take the flashlight," said Van In, swapping roles with Hannelore. "All this work isn't good for a woman in your condition. We don't want you overexerting yourself."

By the time Buffel shouted "1964," Van In had the feeling he'd shifted five tons of paper.

The teacher produced a pocketknife and cut the string holding the pile of papers together. "Desmedt, Dirk and Dani," he said after a second or two. "Father: Desmedt, Jozef; mother: Baert, Lutgart. Civil status: divorced."

Hannelore shivered as she popped the key into the front-door lock. Her thin jacket offered little protection from the creeping fall chill. While the deceptive noon temperatures created the illusion of a late summer, the evenings tended to be a disappointment. Hours in a dusty archive hadn't done her any good either.

"Shall I warm up some wine?" Van In suggested obligingly. Hannelore scuttled inside and curled up on the sofa. *Silence is also an answer,* Van In thought. He grabbed a plaid blanket and tucked her in.

"Dirk and Dani Baert," she said, her teeth chattering. "Now I understand why every turn we took was a blind alley. Baert knew we were looking for his brother."

Van In placed two glasses of piping-hot wine on the coffee table. "I'm beginning to think that Dani is Herbert and that our chief inspector Baert killed Provoost in revenge for what they did to his brother," he said dejectedly. "If this leaks to the press, it'll turn Bruges upside down and inside out."

"I can see the headlines . . ." she said.

Van In handed her a glass just as the phone rang. He cursed, put down his glass, and hurried into the kitchen.

"Hello."

"Sorry to disturb you so late, Commissioner, but . . ."

"Something wrong, Herman?"

Van In recognized the voice of the officer on duty. Herman Tant sounded nervous, and that wasn't his style.

"It's about a certain Aerts," he said, not giving too much away.

"What about him?"

Van In acted dumb. Tant didn't know what to say next. He

was beginning to feel sorry he had let himself be talked into calling the commissioner in the first place.

"Well?" said Van In impatiently.

"Aerts says he wants to speak to you and that it's urgent. I . . ."

Hannelore threw off the plaid blanket. Van In looked as if he'd just been granted a divine revelation.

"Are we talking about William Aerts?"

Hannelore shuffled closer.

"Yes," said Tant, relief evident in his voice. "The federal boys at the Zaventem airport arrested him a couple of hours ago. He refuses to speak to anyone but you. He says it's a matter of life or death."

Van In gestured that Hannelore should listen in.

"Tell them I'm onto it, Herman. Where is he right now?"

"In Brussels, Commissioner."

Van In knew what that meant. If he followed official channels, it would take a week before he got to speak to Aerts. He hung up and called De Kee. The chief commissioner wasn't at home. Van In listened patiently for the answering machine to say its piece. "For urgent matters call the police, it says."

Hannelore took the receiver. "Pour me another glass of wine," she said with a smile.

While Van In continued with the task at hand, Hannelore called Prosecutor Beekman. He had promised to help where necessary. Ten minutes later they received a response. Beekman ensured Hannelore that the federal police would transfer

William Aerts to Bruges under escort early the following morning.

"Satisfied?" she asked with a provocative grin.

Van In filled both glasses. "What would I do without you, Hanne? I'm deeply in your debt."

She smiled like the Mona Lisa and returned to the living room with her head held high. "There's a simple way to pay it off!" she shouted. "I left my wine in the kitchen. If you bring it to me, we're even."

Van In obeyed without question. He had often wondered how women managed to transform their men into submissive chimps. Now he knew. "Thanks, sweetheart. A cigarette for the queen of Sheba?"

Van In scurried back to the kitchen and grabbed a clean ashtray from the counter and a block of semi-matured cheese. He deserved a snack for all his efforts.

Jos Brouwers parked his Renault in front of his client's villa. Discretion was no longer important. He had failed, and that meant Vandaele would never employ him again. But the money would be waiting for him as the old man had promised. He was a man of his word.

The ex-cop turned up his collar and hurried across the lawn to the front door. The curtains were closed, but he could still see yellowish slivers of light through the gaps.

Brouwers rang the bell as a cutting wind whistled around his legs and whipped up the fallen leaves. He waited patiently for

Vandaele to open the door, but there seemed to be no movement inside, so he made his way to the window and drummed on the glass with the tips of his fingers. Still no sound, only that of the wind howling over the polder.

He cursed under his breath and returned to his car. He always kept a little box in the glove compartment with the tools he needed to pick locks.

Vandaele was sitting at the piano, his head slumped over the keyboard. A disgusting slime dripped from the keys. Brouwers retched when he spotted chunks of black tissue in the dark-red pool of blood. The old pedophile's face was contorted with pain. Vandaele was dead. He had vomited up his rotten lungs and choked in his own filth.

15

Chief Commissioner De Kee hung his spotless overcoat on the coat stand, brushed some imaginary dust from his shoulder, shook Van In's hand, and positioned himself by the window. The situation was precarious. Van In had called him half an hour earlier, and he had immediately jumped into his car.

"When can we expect him?" the chief commissioner asked.

"Eight thirty," said Van In.

De Kee turned to the window, his face riddled with concern. The Belgian judicial system had taken some serious blows in the past year. If Van In was right and Chief Inspector Baert was responsible for the death of Yves Provoost, his corps's image would have to absorb the damage. De Kee had always spoken about *my men*. As far as he was concerned, a blot on the escutcheon of the Bruges police was a personal slur. In that sense he was particularly aristocratic.

"And the other one?"

"Around nine," said Van In. "The federal police commander in Brussels promised he would have William Aerts on the road by eight a.m."

Van In lit a cigarette. It was *his* office, and he didn't have to ask his superior for permission.

"Is there some connection between the two?"

"They know each other from elementary school," said Van In.

"And you're certain that Dirk Desmedt and Dirk Baert are one and the same person?"

"The dates of birth match. If you ask me, Dirk Baert took his mother's name once he turned twenty-one."

De Kee started to pace up and down. He hoped Van In was wrong about the chief inspector.

"The details are in his file," said Van In, holding out a gray-green folder. "Dirk Baert went to school in Ezel Street, and he has a brother by the name of Dani."

De Kee waved his hand in disinterest. He would only be making a fool of himself if he were to insist on confirming the details.

Dirk Baert sensed something wasn't right when he walked into Room 204. De Kee's presence so early in the morning was about as exceptional as a visit by the crown prince to a swinger's club.

"Good morning," he said without looking up.

"Take a seat, Desmedt."

The sound of his old name hit Baert like a battering ram. "What do you mean, Chief Commissioner?"

"You know exactly what I mean, Desmedt. You're in deep shit, and the rest of the corps with you."

Baert took a seat. His legs felt like limp strings of spaghetti. De Kee had cut the umbilical cord with a single razor-sharp swipe. From now on he was on his own. "So I hated my father enough to change my name. You make it sound like I committed a crime."

Van In had expected a different reaction. It looked as if Baert wasn't going to be a pushover. "So you admit your real name is Dirk Desmedt?"

It was important to formulate questions during an interrogation that obliged the suspect to answer with "yes."

Baert nodded.

"Did you have a brother named Dani?"

Van In used the past tense on purpose.

"Yes," said Baert.

"And Dani is dead?"

"Dani disappeared. He left for the Netherlands twelve years ago, and I haven't heard a word from him since."

"Not a word?"

"Nothing."

"Commissioner Van In just wants to help you, Baert," De Kee interrupted. "If you tell him the truth, we can add a note to the report that you made a full confession of your own free will. That can make a hell of a difference in court."

"I don't understand what kind of confession you want from me, Chief Commissioner. But I can't deny that I'm familiar with the law," said Baert.

Van In and De Kee exchanged a meaningful glance.

"You've got three hours to think it over, Baert," said Van In as he punched in the number of the duty officer. "If you haven't made a decision by then, we'll be forced to hand the case over to the prosecutor's office."

The chief inspector bowed his head. *Why didn't they arrest him?* he thought in desperation.

"Hello, Herman. Van In here. Can you spare someone reliable for a couple of hours?"

Herman Tant checked the duty roster.

"Bart Vermeulen's around until one p.m."

"OK. Send him up."

Prosecutor Beekman, Hannelore's immediate superior, was one of a new crop of magistrates. In contrast to his predecessors, he hadn't been recruited from a pack of mediocre lawyers who had joined the party for lack of clients. He was forty-two but still looked relatively boyish when the light was right. That was because he had consciously chosen to drop the obligatory gray suits his colleagues insisted on wearing for the sake of decorum. Beekman wore a sports jacket most of the time and even left his tie at home on occasion.

"Make yourself at home, Hannelore," he said invitingly.

The prosecutor's office was airy and fresh, and lacked the

usual shelving weighed down by piles of musty dossiers. Beekman had even had the mandatory portrait of the king and queen reframed at his own expense in a more modern style.

"Officer Neels's disappearance worries me," he said.

Hannelore relaxed in a cozy sitting area by the window. The windowsill was full of cactuses. Beekman evidently liked spiky green. "Me too," said Hannelore. "But we turned the place over yesterday and found nothing. I'm afraid we're back at square one."

"And what does Van In think?"

"Pieter has enough on his plate with the other cases. He's convinced the interrogation of the two suspects is the only way to expose Vandaele's network. He's also pretty sure it will lead him to Carine Neels."

Beekman ran his finger over his right eyebrow. "Let me put my cards on the table, Hannelore," he said. "I got a call yesterday from the prosecutor-general asking me to slow down on the Herbert and Provoost killings."

Hannelore was aware that Beekman was sticking his neck out by sharing this information. Under normal circumstances, arrangements between a prosecutor and the prosecutor-general were not intended for the ears of young deputies like herself. "What does *slow down* mean?"

"The deep freeze," said Beekman flatly.

"You can't be serious, Jozef."

She always used his first name in private conversation.

"And I'm not finished."

Beekman ran his finger over his left eyebrow. "The request to brush the case under the carpet comes from none other than the minister of foreign affairs. He's afraid an investigation into a long-forgotten murder will be damaging for his party."

"The asshole," Hannelore thundered. "He was one of the boys who used the Love every other week."

"According to reports, other politicians were also involved," he said with caution.

"And now the bastards have to be spared."

If Hannelore hadn't looked up to Beekman as she did, she would have stormed out of his office in a rage. "Tell me, Jozef. What do you honestly think of that bunch of losers?"

"Technically speaking, the prosecutor-general is my immediate superior," he said with a hint of a grin.

Hannelore was happy she hadn't marched out in anger. "Technically," she sniggered. "That sounds promising." Beekman may have appeared unconventional, but he was still ambitious.

"Don't misunderstand me, Hannelore. I can't help you officially. On the contrary. I should be telling you off right now."

"I'm pregnant, Jozef. I could have you on child abuse if you're not careful."

Beekman couldn't stop himself from glancing at her belly. "You've been saying that for three months already. In our business we need evidence."

Hannelore was grateful for the compliment.

"There's little I can do officially, but off the record, you've got carte blanche. I don't give a shit who's involved in the case. Call me if you come up with something. I promise to turn West Flanders on its head if I have to."

"Even if the minister is involved?"

"If you have strong arguments, I won't hesitate."

"And if the prosecutor-general uses his veto?"

Beekman snorted disdainfully. "The magistrature isn't what it used to be, Hannelore. If you provide solid evidence, the prosecutor-general will change his tune soon enough."

"Pieter will be happy to hear it," said Hannelore with a smile. She shook Beekman's hand and hurried outside. It was time to get down to business.

Were the federal boys putting on a show or hinting that it was high time they renewed their fleet? That was the question Van In asked himself when a prewar armored truck drove through the gate into the Bruges police station's inner courtyard. William Aerts was accompanied into the station by two burly gendarmes in battle gear.

They only removed Aerts's cuffs after the necessary documents had been signed. Van In thanked his federal colleagues and steered Aerts to an interrogation room on the third floor. Rooms used for interrogation tend not to be the coziest of places, and this was no exception. It had a metal table, three chairs, and a mechanical typewriter. The compact Sony tape recorder and the thermos full of coffee added a modern touch.

"Take a seat, Mr. Aerts."

Aerts slumped onto one of the chairs, exhausted from a sleepless night on a hard police cell bed. Van In poured two cups of coffee and pressed the *record* button.

"So the prodigal son has returned," said Van In. "I hope our little conversation's worth the effort."

Aerts lifted his head, rubbed the stubble on his chin, and quickly took stock of the man in front of him. "Shall I start at the beginning, Commissioner?"

Van In nodded, rewound the tape, checked the quality of the recording, and pressed the *record* button again. He then leaned back and gestured that Aerts was free to begin.

The first part of the man's story had little relevance to the case. Aerts had purchased the Cleopatra from Vandaele and turned it into a luxury brothel. Important clients, however, were given special treatment in the Love. Everything was safe and discreet. Aerts worked on commission and only had to provide professional girls when the supply of volunteers dried up.

"So you were aware that Vandaele used Helping Our Own to recruit his victims."

Aerts sipped at his coffee and asked Van In if he could spare a cigarette. "I thought you'd figure it out," he said, grinning.

Van In took a cigarette and pushed the pack across the table.

"The richer the stingier, Commissioner. In the Love they fucked for free. Any young woman who had appealed to the charity for financial help was given a choice when it came to paying it back: cash or 'in kind.'"

"And they call that charity," Van In sneered.

"An inappropriate term indeed, Commissioner. Helping Our Own insisted their clients sign two documents. The first stated that they'd received a sum of money as a gift, and the second was an acknowledgement of debt for the same amount, an IOU if you like. Every transaction the charity entered into followed the same procedure. Old women, drunks, and respectable family men were expected to pay cash."

Van In now understood how the charity managed to balance its double-entry bookkeeping. The so-called gifts were in fact loans that were claimed back in neatly laundered cash. "And no one protested."

"Losers like to keep a low profile, Commissioner. Everyone who came knocking was carefully screened and vetted. Most of them were in temporary financial need and had nowhere else to go."

"For example?"

Aerts smiled at the commissioner's naïveté. Civil servants like Van In with fixed salaries had no idea what the insects living under the poverty line were willing to do to get access to the consumer society.

"People on benefits, men crushed by the burden of prohibitive maintenance costs, families with massive debts, students without scholarships, single women . . ." he said, shaking his head. "The fourth world doesn't only live in the slums, Commissioner. Hundreds of thousands of our fellow countrymen are on the edge of financial ruin, but they live apparently normal lives in ordinary houses in inconspicuous neighborhoods.

They earn just enough to pay the mortgage and feed themselves. And what they have left they spend on luxuries they really can't afford. Those are the kind of people the charity lends money to without charging interest: decent, honest, but poor citizens who mostly repay what they borrow."

"And the good-looking single women were given the chance to work off their debts."

"Correct, Commissioner."

"And a few of Vandaele's business associates took advantage."

"Correct again." Aerts grinned. "Vandaele's been around."

Van In had the impression that Aerts was being honest. "So if I'm understanding you, the charity collected money for good causes. The money was officially donated to people in need and unofficially recuperated in the form of interest-free loans."

"I have a good idea what your next question is going to be." Aerts smiled. "You want to know what happened with the laundered cash."

Van In knew where the money was going but feigned ignorance.

Aerts poured himself another coffee and helped himself to another cigarette. "Lodewijk Vandaele is an idealist. The chaotic, permissive society we now live in disgusts him. His goal is a society in which everyone knows his or her place and everything runs like clockwork."

"The Singapore model."

"Exactly, Commissioner. Singapore is a shining example. He wants to transform Flanders into a model state, and to do so, there was first a need to restore discipline. FLASYC had the potential to realize his dream."

"Isn't that a little hypocritical for a pedophile?"

Aerts shook his head. "You don't understand, Commissioner. Vandaele sees himself as a friend to children. He considers love between a child and an adult something pure and unspoiled."

"I'm sensing Vandaele has a couple of tiles loose," said Van In.

"We're on the same wavelength, Commissioner. Why else do you think I turned myself in?"

"I've been asking myself that very question."

"I was afraid of Jos Brouwers."

Aerts described the hired killer Vandaele had sent after him. "Vandaele was probably worried that I would say something about Dani's death."

"The transsexual," said Van In.

Aerts said nothing.

"Did you know her before?"

"No. Dani appeared one day at the Cleopatra looking for work. She claimed she needed money for surgery—breast augmentation."

Aerts made an ugly face, as if he'd just bitten into a chunk of rotten fish.

"That ugly, eh?"

"On the contrary, Commissioner."

"So you gave her a job."

"Yes."

"And was she good?"

"Was she good?" Aerts repeated the question. "You should know, Commissioner, that before a girl starts work at the Cleopatra, I . . ."

His voice cracked. There wasn't a movie director in the world who could have done a better job at portraying disgust with such depth.

"So you went to bed with him." Van In switched to the masculine pronoun on purpose.

Aerts was clearly struggling.

"And was the sex good?"

Words can sometimes hurt more than physical violence. In this instance Van In's words were like a branding iron on an open wound. Van In saw Aerts ball his fists, his knuckles turning white.

"There are two police officers outside the door, Mr. Aerts. If I were you, I'd try to calm down."

Van In had to admit he was enjoying the game. Nothing is more satisfying than exercising power over another human being. The euphoria it creates lies at the foundation of every totalitarian regime. But as a right-minded democrat, Van In considered it his duty to explore his own boundaries. Only those who have tasted the temptation of dictatorship can resist the lure of the extreme right. "You took the bait," said Van In, easing back a little.

Aerts stared into space. The stress of the last forty-eight

hours was beginning to take its toll. An inch and a half of ash hung precariously from the end of his cigarette. Van In offered him an ashtray and refilled the cups. "I took the bait," he said flatly.

Van In could imagine how Aerts was feeling at that moment. "Continue, Mr. Aerts. What happened next?"

"The following evening I had a visit from Provoost and Brys. They were both in the best of spirits, and they demanded the best girl I had on offer."

"And then you introduced them to Dani."

Aerts nodded.

"Knowing full well . . ."

"Provoost and Brys were arrogant snobs. They'd treated me like scum for years."

"And you saw your chance?"

Aerts gulped at his coffee and lit another cigarette. The confrontation with the past depressed him. Provoost and Brys had dominated his entire life. As a child he was expected to do their dirty work, and when they went to high school they never missed an opportunity to humiliate him. "Light another fart, William." "There's a fly in my soup. A hundred francs says William'll eat it!" Provoost and Brys bought him a beer for every trick he performed. When Aerts decided to go to college, they dropped him like a ton of bricks. Workers' kids were supposed to earn a living with the labor of their hands, they claimed. After a disaster of a first semester, Aerts went to Amsterdam and got involved in the drug trade. Four years later he returned to Bruges a wealthy man and began spending his fortune. It was time for other people to light their farts, eat flies, and trot half-naked across Market Square. That was when he met Linda and they decided to try their luck at the Cleopatra. Vandaele put him on the payroll and didn't spare the fanfare. Everything went pretty well until Provoost and Brys reappeared on the scene.

Van In offered him another cigarette.

"So you wanted revenge?"

"What would you have done, Commissioner?"

Van In smiled. There were bigger bastards walking around in Flanders than Aerts. "And you brought the gentlemen to the Love?"

"Indeed, Commissioner."

Van In now had a reasonable picture of the rest of the story. All the pieces were beginning to fall neatly into place.

"Less than an hour later Brys called me. He sounded nervous and stone-cold sober. He begged me to come to the Love right away. Something terrible had happened."

"They had killed Dani."

"Brys swore it was an accident. After an explosive threesome, Dani had confessed he was actually a man. Provoost went berserk, and there was a bit of a scuffle. Dani fell and hit her head on the corner of the bed. She died on the spot."

"I presume you know Dani's true identity?"

"True identity, Commissioner?"

"Does the name Desmedt ring a bell?"

If the surprise on his face was feigned, Aerts deserved an Oscar.

"Dani Desmedt?"

"Dani Desmedt from elementary school, Mr. Aerts. Remember the underpants and the clothespin?"

"That's impossible," said Aerts. "I would have—"

"Recognized him," said Van In with more than a hint of sarcasm. A moment of silence followed.

"Now . . . I . . . get it," Aerts stammered. "That's why Provoost was so angry. Dani couldn't have wished for a better way to even the score for the suffering they had put his twin brother through."

Aerts cleared his throat and brushed the cigarette ash from his trousers as if it was the past. "When I arrived ten minutes later, Provoost was in a panic. He had contacted Vandaele, who had insisted that I dump the body somewhere in the Ardennes near the German border."

"But you didn't, did you?"

"What d'you think? This was my chance to give the gentlemen a taste of their own medicine."

"So you buried Dani on the grounds of the Love."

"Would you have run the risk of transporting a corpse to the Ardennes for a hundred thousand francs?"

"You wanted more."

Van In fished the last cigarette from the pack. When he saw Aerts stare at it longingly, he called the incident room and had an officer dispatched to replenish supplies.

"I admit to blackmailing Provoost and Brys," said Aerts. "I was under financial pressure from Vandaele, and Dani was dead. Nothing could be done to change it."

"You needed money." Van In nodded understandingly. "Did Vandaele know that you were blackmailing Brys and Provoost?"

Aerts had seemed reasonably self-assured throughout the interrogation. Now his bottom lip started to tremble. "I don't know. He sent Brouwers after me, didn't he? I know Vandaele like the back of my hand. No one humiliates him without paying the price. And for betrayal there's only one price."

"Nemo me impune lacessit," Van In mumbled.

"What was that, Commissioner?"

Van In was thinking of Edgar Allan Poe's "The Cask of Amontillado." "You ran because they discovered the corpse on the grounds of the Love and Vandaele would know you'd failed to carry out his orders."

Aerts nodded.

"And by turning yourself in, you were hoping for a reduced sentence."

"I'm appealing to the courts, Commissioner. Mitigating circumstances . . ."

A young officer knocked at the door, came in without a word, and handed Van In a pack of Marlboros and a box of matches. Van In ripped it open, lit a cigarette, and slid the rest of the pack across the table to Aerts.

"Let me make a suggestion, Mr. Aerts. I'll supply a pen and plenty of paper. I want you to write it all down, the whole story.

Take your time. You know the chances of you leaving this building within the next twenty-four hours are relatively small. Then I'll let the investigating magistrate decide what to do with you."

"I know the law, Commissioner."

"I hope you do, Mr. Aerts."

Van In got to his feet and left the room.

Without Versavel, Room 204 felt like an icy crypt. Van In switched on the light and sat down at his desk.

Detective work is a combination of routine and procedures, an approach that rarely delivers. The big breakthrough in a case is almost always the result of an unforeseen circumstance, a spontaneous confession, an unexpected turn of events, or just pure luck. Aerts's confession was manna from heaven. Provoost had killed Dani, and Van In had everything he needed: a killer, a motive, and a witness. Aerts would claim "mitigating circumstances." A skilled lawyer would keep him out of jail without having to jump through too many hoops, and Van In didn't like it. He had the impression that Aerts was trying to save his own skin and had only revealed what would work to his advantage.

The disappearance of Carine Neels worried him more. He was almost certain that Vandaele's criminal network had swallowed her up. The improvised and hurried search at Care House had served only to set off underworld alarms and nothing more. And then there was Baert. In the last analysis, he was the only real murderer still alive, and police officers didn't get to claim mitigating circumstances.

Van In looked at his watch. It was almost twelve. Time to hear what Baert had to say.

Dirk Baert was sitting and barely reacted when Van In entered the room.

"So, Dirk," said Van In, "how are we?"

Baert looked up. Van In had never used his first name before.

"I know we haven't always been the best of friends, but I hope you don't think I'm doing this for fun."

Baert grinned sheepishly.

"I appreciate that, Commissioner."

Van In took a seat opposite Baert and heaved a deep sigh. "I know you did it, Dirk, and I understand why. Your brother once saved you from the claws of a couple of sadists, and when you read the autopsy report on Herbert last week, you knew immediately that Herbert was Dani."

Baert nodded. He had decided an hour earlier to confess everything. He actually felt proud of himself for once. Killing Provoost was an achievement—the only real achievement he had to boast about in his entire life. "I've been working for Vandaele for twenty years," he said. "I know what was going on in the Love."

Van In leaned back in his chair and listened. It took Baert more than three hours to tell his story.

Liliane Neels had no objection to Hannelore taking a look in Carine's room. The poor soul couldn't stop sniveling.

The bedroom was small, cozily furnished, neat, and tidy, almost the kind of thing you would expect to find in a handbook for interior designers. Hannelore opened the drawers in the hardwood lowboy one by one and rummaged carefully through the missing officer's lingerie. Liliane wasn't sure why there was a need to search her daughter's belongings, but she watched Hannelore's every move nonetheless. The fact that someone was interested in her daughter's fate was enough for her.

Hannelore had never searched someone's room before, so she had to rely on intuition. Delicate lingerie, pink linens, CDs with waltzes by Strauss and Beethoven symphonies, a sunset poster, a half-burned-out candle, and a crimson red sofa suggested Carine was a romantic soul.

"Did your daughter keep a diary?"

Liliane was surprised by the question. "A diary?" she repeated vacantly.

"Did you ever see her writing things down?"

Liliane wrinkled her forehead. "I remember her writing poems when she was sixteen, but a diary . . ."

"Did she use loose sheets of paper or a notebook?"

Liliane racked her brain. She wanted to help more than anything, but . . . "I don't remember," she said sniffling. "It's terrible, I know, but it seems like such a long time ago."

"Don't worry," said Hannelore.

A wooden bookshelf with a small TV cum video player on top graced one of the corners of the room. On the shelf underneath there was a row of videocassettes.

"She loved to watch movies," said Mrs. Neels, trying to be helpful.

Hannelore glanced at the titles: *Kramer vs. Kramer, Nell, Out of Africa, The French Lieutenant's Woman, The Sound of Music, Romeo and Juliette,* and *Zorba the Greek.* She noticed the word *Betamax* on the last video in the row. *No one uses Betamax these days,* she thought. *They took the system off the market years ago.*

Hannelore removed the cassette from the shelf. It felt heavier than an average videotape.

Liliane jumped to her feet. "Did you find something?" she asked optimistically.

Hannelore opened the box to find a cloth-bound notebook with the words *My Diary* on the front.

"Is that what you were looking for?" Liliane asked with an enthusiastic smile.

Just as Hannelore was about to open the notebook, her mobile started to ring. "Hannelore Martens."

It was Prosecutor Beekman.

"Vandaele is dead," he said. "His housekeeper found him this morning."

"Murdered?"

Liliane almost had a heart attack when she heard the word *murdered.*

"No, Vandaele was in the last stages of cancer. He vomited his lungs out."

Hannelore gestured to Liliane that there was no need to worry, but the woman started to sob nonetheless. "It's not about Carine," Hannelore said, covering the mouthpiece with her hand.

Van In kicked off his shoes, headed to the refrigerator, and grabbed a Duvel. Two confessions in one day had left him in a bit of a spin. Aerts's confession didn't bother him. The man had written it all down on paper, and there would be time enough to go over it later. Baert's confession was much more tragic.

Just as he was about to take a drink, he heard Hannelore's keys in the front door. He knocked back half the glass just to be on the safe side.

"Out together, home together," he said with an innocent smile.

Hannelore paid no attention to the Duvel. She seemed excited. "Carine went back to Care House for a test photo session after all, and she was planning another visit the night she disappeared."

She threw the diary on the table, and Van In read the passage to which she had referred.

"She says she's ready to do whatever it takes to successfully complete her assignment," Hannelore seethed. "If anything happens to that girl, I'm never going to forgive you, Pieter Van In. You filled her head with cowboy stories. I was in her room this afternoon. The child still believes in goodness and justice, romantic heroes, the whole nine yards. Life for her is a movie with a happy ending."

Van In let her blow off steam. The last entry in Carine's diary rang a bell in the back of his mind. "But one thing struck me about him: the man smelled of toilet cleaner," he read under his breath.

"What are you muttering about?"

"Benedict Vervoort." Van In laughed grimly. "The bastard stank of toilet cleaner."

"I'm calling Beekman," said Hannelore.

Johan Brys pulled a leather mask over his head and checked his instruments. Everything was neatly lined up. It wasn't the first time the minister had appeared in a snuff movie. Carine Neels was in the cellar, chained to the frame of an old-fashioned bed. She was naked. Benedict Vervoort attached his camera to a tripod, ready for a trial run. The container full of quicklime in the corner had to be kept out of the shot. He adjusted a couple of spots until he was happy with the lighting. The guests would be here in less than an hour, and he wanted to be sure everything was perfect.

Prosecutor Beekman listened carefully to Hannelore's report. "We can't screw it up twice," he said when she had finished. "And no one's going to blame us for strong-arming that kind of scum."

Hannelore nodded, and that was a sign for Van In to make his move. Within minutes, a trio of police MPVs was heading full-speed in the direction of Waardamme, sirens wailing. Van In and Hannelore followed in the Twingo.

"Does Baert know anything about this?"

Hannelore hit the gas on Baron Ruzette Avenue. Van In fastened his seat belt. "I don't think so. Baert only wanted revenge for his brother."

Hannelore slowed down at the bridge over the Bruges-Courtrai Canal. Her speedometer read *50 mph*. The Twingo protested when she ripped into the bend in the road.

Van In held his breath and tried to organize his thoughts. Dirk Baert's three-hour story needed more than just a word or two of explanation. "Dani needed money for a breast augmentation, and it was urgent. He asked his brother for advice, and he introduced him to the Cleopatra."

"In 1985?"

"Yes."

Hannelore overtook the MPVs, then slowed down.

"Baert's been on Vandaele's payroll for more than twenty years. He knew all about the Cleopatra," said Van In, lighting a cigarette.

"What d'you mean he was on Vandaele's payroll?"

"Baert worked as a spy. He kept Vandaele up-to-date on what was going on within the force, warned him if there were raids on the way, and helped incriminating police reports to disappear."

"How did he know the body was his brother?"

Hannelore took a cigarette without asking.

"Dani had had a lot of dental work done in the eighties, and it had cost him a small fortune. Baert started to suspect it when he read the autopsy. He also knew that Dani had broken his shin as a child and that he had worked for the gentlemen who ran the Love."

"So he decided to get rid of Provoost," she said incredulously.

"Not right away. Baert knew that Provoost was crazy about his brother, but he wanted to be sure."

Hannelore drove through the traffic light next to the church in Oostkamp. The MPVs provided the perfect cover.

"He decided to set him up and sent Melissa."

"Melissa?"

"His girlfriend," said Van In. "Baert met her at the Cleopatra. She had been one of Provoost's favorites before she and Baert moved in together. Melissa called Provoost on the evening of the murder, and the man was apparently up for a visit . . ."

"Now I get it. Melissa rings the bell, Provoost opens the door, and Baert cuffs him."

"Correct, according to Baert at least," said Van In.

"So Dani Baert was killed in 1985."

Van In shook his head.

"Baert claims the last time he saw his brother was in April 1986. Dani had just come back from the Netherlands after the breast augmentation. He wasn't happy with it and needed more money."

It took five minutes for word to get around and a lot less for the streets to fill. Commissioner Decloedt of the Waardamme police kept an eye on things as his Bruges colleagues forced open the front door of Vervoort's business. The procedure was illegal, but the prosecutor had assured them that he would take personal responsibility for the entire operation. The judiciary was ready to stick its neck out now and again.

The officers went about their business in an orderly fashion. Fifteen minutes later, Vervoort's office looked as if a tornado had struck it.

The invitees took their places on folding chairs lined up in the shadows. Carine listened to the commotion and cringed in terror. The light was powerful enough to penetrate her blindfold.

Vervoort opened the door, and Johan Brys appeared, pushing a cart in front of him. With the exception of his leather head mask, the minister was naked. An array of tools was laid out on the cart: knives, tongs, and bores . . . ready for use. A quiver of lust ran through the audience as the executioner entered the room.

Guido Versavel arrived at Vervoort's business looking tired and pale. Hannelore winked and pointed at the door to Vervoort's office. The sound of shattering glass and furniture being tossed around didn't bode well.

"Pieter went berserk when the search warrant yielded zilch," she said, concerned. "He's tearing the place apart."

Versavel had spent the last few days learning for himself what it was like to feel powerless. He opened the door to the office and stuck his head inside. The room had been wrecked, and the wrecker wasn't finished.

"Save the window for last?" asked Versavel with more than a hint of sarcasm.

Van In looked up. The rage in his eyes could have made a platoon of marines back off. He grabbed an office chair that had seen better days and pitched it through the window.

"Satisfied?"

Versavel opened the door wider and went in. "Hannelore called me," he said. "She's afraid you're going to hurt yourself."

"So what?"

Versavel edged closer, deftly navigating his way through the debris. "You're not doing Carine Neels any favors."

"Oh no?"

Van In smashed the heel of his shoe into a PC keyboard. Half the alphabet exploded in every direction.

"There's a huge mirror in the front office," said Versavel dryly.

Van In extracted his foot from the shattered keyboard. He stared at Versavel and ran his fingers through his sweat-drenched hair. "Can you conjure a white rabbit from a hat?"

"Maybe," said Versavel, unruffled.

"What d'you mean, maybe?"

Versavel fished a bundle of papers from his inside pocket. "Do you remember asking me to check out Catrysse's story?"

Van In lurched across the wreckage to stand in front of Versavel. His forehead looked like an apple after a winter in the attic.

"Catrysse lives in an abandoned farmhouse owned by Vandaele."

When Hannelore was sure that Van In's demolition work was over, she too went inside.

"Now you tell me," she heard Van In say.

Versavel apologized. "I was on sedatives, Pieter. It was only when Hannelore called me that I realized—"

"OK, OK," said Van In, clearly still irate. "Catrysse lives in a property owned by Vandaele and works as a gardener for the charity. What else do you have?"

"Catrysse's got a history with the police," said Versavel. "He was sentenced to two years in 1982 for raping a young girl, a neighbor's daughter."

"Jeez." Hannelore sighed.

"Baert must have known about that too," said Versavel, "but kept his mouth shut because Vandaele forced him to."

Van In didn't have to think much further. If Vandaele was protecting Catrysse, then he had to have a good reason. After Dani was killed, Vandaele closed down the Love. It only made sense that he moved his business elsewhere.

"Warn Beekman," said Hannelore. "I wonder what our gardener has been up to."

John Catrysse's job was to keep an eye on the driveway leading up to the farm. But now that all the guests had arrived, he decided to sneak down to the cellar and enjoy the spectacle from the shadows.

Carine Neels felt a scrawny male body glide over her. Someone removed her blindfold, and she blinked for a second or two in the glare of the spotlights. She froze at the sight of the leather head mask hovering six inches above her face.

Her heart skipped a beat and then another. She tried to scream, but when nothing came out, she closed her eyes. The man started to hump her wildly, but there was no penetration. It felt as if someone had propped a deflated balloon between her thighs.

Vervoort let the camera run. He knew it would take a while before Brys reached his climax.

Hannelore pushed the Twingo to its limits. The steering wheel shuddered uncontrollably in her hands as the speedometer needle went off the dial. Van In removed his gun from its holster and placed it on his lap. The MPVs followed at less than six hundred yards, their blue lights swirling, but without sirens.

Catrysse didn't notice the sound of tires tearing over the gravel on the driveway outside. The spectacle had him completely in its spell. It took the executioner all of ten minutes to ejaculate. *The thin guy always needed his time,* he thought, wondering who it was behind the leather mask.

Brys got to his feet, and Carine cautiously opened her eyes. For the first time, she caught sight of the cart and the instruments of torture. Her scream was harrowing, and the audience muttered approvingly.

Brys selected a pair of pincers. Vervoort zoomed in on Carine's left breast, shook his head, and signaled that Brys should wait. He took an ice cube and rubbed it over her breast until the nipple was erect. Brys nodded. He had gone through the scenario with Vervoort in advance. First he let the victim see the instrument of torture, as they did during the inquisition. Carine's screams were now beyond human. Vervoort filmed her twisted face. Brys placed the pincers on her ripe nipple and waited until Vervoort had framed the image to his satisfaction.

Van In threw open the cellar door, aimed his pistol at the man in the mask, and fired three shots. The first bullet penetrated Brys's right eye, the second shattered his shoulder, and the third made a neat hole in Vervoort's forehead as he stepped into the firing line.

Ten seconds later a first wave of police officers spread out over Catrysse's farm. A couple of audience members tried to escape in the confusion but were rounded up after a short chase.

Hannelore took off her jacket and attended to Carine. The girl was in shock and barely reacted to the chaos around her. She was going to need all the help she could get to recover from this, but she was strong, and a team of caregivers had already been assembled to receive her.

"Statistics would have given you one in a hundred thousand," said Versavel.

"Man does not live on statistics alone," said Van In philosophically. "I'd never have been able to forgive myself if we'd arrived five minutes too late."

While the police cuffed the audience members one by one,

Van In made his way upstairs much in need of fresh air. "What kind of world are we living in?" he asked himself when he was told the identities of the executioner and half the audience. De Jaegher, the incompetent police physician, was among them, as was Melchior Muys, the corrupt tax auditor. Van In looked up at the stars and hoped that there was a better life beyond them.

Hannelore placed the two steaming plates on the table. She hadn't made fries for the best part of three months, and she thought Van In might appreciate them. He had hardly eaten a thing for the last twenty-four hours.

"Guido."

Versavel had snuggled up next to the fireplace. After fifteen minutes his eyes had closed, and he was now enjoying the sleep of the righteous.

"Let him sleep," said Hannelore. "There's still some cheese left in the refrigerator if he wakes up hungry."

Van In wolfed down his fries in silence, treating himself to lavish amounts of mayonnaise.

"I wonder what the headlines will be," he said between bites.

"Policeman Shoots Minister of Foreign Affairs Dead," said Hannelore, tracing a line in the air with both hands. "Tomorrow you'll be the most famous man in Flanders."

Van In dipped his last fry into the greasy mound of mayonnaise on the side of his plate. "The bastard got what was coming to him. Let's see them try to brush the case under the carpet now."

He pushed his plate aside and lit a cigarette.

"From one cover-up to another," said Hannelore sarcastically. "What?"

Hannelore jabbed a fry with her fork. "If I understand things correctly, you're not planning to prosecute Baert."

Van In took a deep breath. "Dirk Baert's offense is a trifle compared to the dirty tricks the big boys were getting up to. Provoost and Brys got what they deserved. I see no reason to burden the state with an expensive court case. Justice has been done. No questions will be asked."

Hannelore gulped. He was right, in principle, but as deputy prosecutor it was her job to make sure that the law was enforced.

"Unless the public prosecutor insists on pursuing the case," said Van In.

"OK. I can't see Beekman raising any objections. But what do we do with Aerts?"

"Aerts confessed he was an accessory," said Van In. "I have his signed statement right here. With a bit of luck, they'll let him off."

He fished Aerts's statement from his inside pocket. "Our friend knows the law. He handed himself over more or less voluntarily, and he's asking for a reduced sentence. He claims he was forced to do what he did. And anyone who might have testified against him is dead, don't forget. No big deal. The real culprits have been tried and convicted."

Hannelore read Aerts's statement while Van In uncorked a bottle of Moselle and planted himself next to his snoring sergeant.

"Didn't you say Dani had a breast augmentation in 1986?" said Hannelore after a few minutes of reading.

Van In was struggling hard not to fall asleep. "Yes. Is that a problem?"

Hannelore reread the passage. "But Aerts claims here that the incident took place in October 1985."

"Jesus H. Christ," Van In cursed.

"What?"

"If that's right, then the little fucker screwed me over."

William Aerts watched the evening news in his cell. The entire country was up in arms after news broke that the minister of foreign affairs had been shot dead while making a snuff movie. Aerts realized the game was over. The courts would never let him go until every detail of his statement had been verified a hundred times.

Jos Brouwers arrived home to the sumptuous villa he had bought only a year before. The purchase was the realization of his final dream. The house was to be the ultimate status symbol, a visible climax to a successful career, and an ode to Gerda, who had taken care of him for so many years. In that order. But Gerda was never going to see the place again. She had packed her bags two weeks earlier, fed up, she said, of living a life in the shadows. There was no point in trying to catch up on lost time. She felt she had a right to her own life. The trip to the Caribbean had been a lie, something he'd made up for

Vandaele because he'd rather have dropped dead than admit she'd left him and his marriage was a failure. Brouwers pictured the couple on the coach in Malta, the man pouring a glass for his wife, both of them waving, both of them perfectly happy. Even Brooks was better off. At least he had the sensual Penelope when he needed her.

Brouwers poured himself a cognac and opened the safe. He selected an Israeli revolver from the arsenal he stored it in, a collector's item worth twenty-five thousand francs. Brouwers threw back the cognac, pressed the barrel of the revolver against the roof of his mouth, and pulled the trigger. His last thought was about the future owners of the villa. His brains would be splattered all over the wall and they would have to repaper the living room.

Van In shook Versavel and woke him up. "Work to be done, Guido."

Hannelore hung up the phone. She had first called Beekman and then the director of the prison. "We can question Aerts in fifteen minutes," she said enthusiastically.

William Aerts was accompanied to the visitors' room by three prison guards. He had suddenly acquired dangerous criminal status. Aerts abhorred the hollow sound of his own footsteps. He was about to face Van In, and the time of the interrogation hadn't been chosen at random. The commissioner knew that he'd lied. The entire movie replayed in his head as he walked through the corridors of the prison. Provoost had called him that evening. There had been an accident. Dani was dead. William had to get rid of the body, and Vandaele had agreed to pay him one hundred thousand francs for his services.

William dragged the corpse to his car and opened the trunk. When he was about to slam it shut again, he heard a groan. Dani was still alive. William made him an offer. If he kept his mouth shut and went back to the Netherlands, he would give him one hundred thousand. Everything went fine until Dani reappeared six months later and demanded more money for another operation. If William refused to pay, Dani threatened to put pressure on Provoost. In an attack of panic William grabbed hold of the transsexual and in the scuffle broke his neck. He buried the corpse on the grounds of the Love. He was now free to continue blackmailing Provoost and Brys.

Van In parked the Twingo in front of the prison. There was a clear sky above, with thousands of stars doing their best to dispel the darkness.

"By the way," said Hannelore when she got out of the car. "I forgot something in all the commotion."

Van In locked both doors. "Did you leave the iron on?" he asked with a grin.

Hannelore knew her husband. She liked his unique sense of humor and the way he reacted in exceptional circumstances. "No," she smiled. "The result of the amniocentesis was negative.

If everything goes according to plan, we'll have a healthy baby in a few months."

Van In took a last cigarette from the pack. The smoke made his eyes water. Or did he imagine it?

PIETER ASPE is the author of the Pieter Van In Mysteries. Aspe lives in Bruges, Belgium, and is one of the most popular contemporary writers in the Flemish language. His novels have sold over one million copies in Europe alone.

BRIAN DOYLE was born in Scotland in 1956 and is currently a professor at the University of Leuven in Belgium. In addition to teaching, he has translated a wide variety of books from Dutch and Flemish into English. In addition to the Pieter Van In Mysteries, his recent book projects include Jef Geeraerts's *The Public Prosecutor* (2009), Jacqueline van Maarsen's *Inheriting Anne Frank* (2010), Christiaan Weijts's *The Window Dresser* (2009), Tessa de Loo's *The Book of Doubt* (2011), Paul Glaser's *Dancing with the Enemy* (2013), and Bob Van Laerhoven's *Baudelaire's Revenge* (2014). He also translates poetry and literary nonfiction.

THE PIETER VAN IN MYSTERIES

FROM OPEN ROAD MEDIA

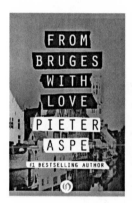
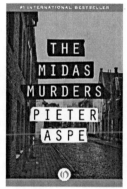
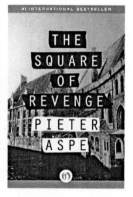

Available wherever ebooks are sold

OPEN ROAD
INTEGRATED MEDIA

CPSIA information can be obtained at www.ICGtesting.com
Printed in the USA
BVOW04s1234050615

403162BV00001B/1/P